W9-ADR-407

FROST

FROST

WENDY DELSOL

CANDLEWICK PRESS

Copyright © 2011 by Wendy Delsol

First edition 2011

Library of Congress Cataloging-in-Publication Data

Delsol, Wendy.
Frost / Wendy Delsol. —1st ed.
p.   cm.
Sequel to: Stork.
Summary: After her boyfriend Jack conjures up a record-breaking
snow storm, sixteen-year-old Kat Leblanc finds herself facing an unusual
rival in the form of an environmental researcher from Greenland who is
drawn to their small town of Norse Falls, Minnesota, by the storm.
ISBN 978-0-7636-5386-6
[1. Supernatural — Fiction. 2. Snow — Fiction.
3. Interpersonal relations — Fiction. 4. High schools — Fiction.
5. Schools — Fiction. 6. Arctic regions — Fiction.] I. Title.
PZ7.D3875Fr 2011
[Fic] — dc22   2010047656

11 12 13 14 15 16 BVG 10 9 8 7 6 5 4 3 2 1

Printed in Berryville, VA, U.S.A.

This book was typeset in Granjon.

Candlewick Press
99 Dover Street
Somerville, Massachusetts 02144

visit us at www.candlewick.com

For Bob
With love and gratitude

CHAPTER ONE

There was one thing, and one thing only, that could coax me into striped red tights, a fur vest, and an elf cap: Jack Snjosson. Make that Jack Snjosson in a Santa suit. Our high-school paper's for-charity lunchtime food drive offered an up-close-and-personal with the old fellow in exchange for a nonperishable. Jack, as the paper's editor in chief, was the unanimous choice for the red suit. Never the look-at-me type, he resisted, digging in deep the heels of his old work boots until he devised a scheme requiring company in his misery. My current ensemble was the result. As the paper's fashion editor, I found playing elf more than a little embarrassing, but at least I got first crack at Kris Kringle.

"Uh, Santa," I said, "aren't you going to ask me what I want for Christmas?" I scooched my striped limbs into the velvety folds of his lap.

"Tell me, what is it you want from old Saint Nick?"

"Santa"—I buried my face into his beard and whispered into his ear—"all I want for Christmas is . . ."

I couldn't help drawing out the moment. It was just too much fun and too surreal, even if my definition of *surreal* had all-new meaning since September. It was still hard to believe everything that had happened in just three short months. I really thought I was losing it when, shortly after the move from LA to Minnesota, I discovered that I was a Stork: a member of an ancient flock of soul deliverers. Things only got more complicated when I met Jack. Turned out he had a pretty nifty talent of his own. As a modern-day descendant of Jack Frost—uh-huh, *that* Jack Frost—he had the ability to control the weather. All the same, had you told me three months ago that I would ask Santa—and not even the real thing, instead my seventeen-year-old, bony-kneed, mahogany-haired, gem-eyed boyfriend—for what was possibly the only thing you couldn't get at the Beverly Hills Neiman Marcus, I'd have said you were cracked.

"A white Christmas," I said.

"And have you been good?" fake-Santa asked.

"Mostly."

He groaned. Because of his special ancestry, heat was

Jack's kryptonite. The heavy costume was uncomfortable to him; my proximity made it worse. Not to mention he wasn't really the PDA type and there was a line of at least twenty can-donating do-gooders—all girls—waiting their turn.

"Thanks, Santa," I said, kissing him briefly on the cheek and springing from his lap.

His face went candy-apple red. It was, as always, our combustible combination that tested his abilities. He made it through the rest of the lunch hour without incident, while I, his elfin helper, handed candy canes to both the naughty and the nice. When his lap was finally girl-free, he stretched, peeled off the press-on whiskers, and headed in my direction.

"Were you trying to kill me?" A much younger Jack seized me by the shoulders.

"What?" I asked, all innocence. "I was your helper." I shook my satchel of goodies as proof.

"You were no help at all."

"Ungrateful," I said.

"Unthinking."

"Unworthy," I countered.

"Unbelievable," he said, though his tone had softened considerably.

"Ahem." I looked up to see Penny standing behind us. "I just wanted to thank you guys for all your help. We collected ten boxes of food."

"That's great," I said.

"Are you two still gonna help us load the van after school?" Penny asked.

"We'll be there," I answered for both of us. In the three months since our fateful Homecoming adventures, Jack and I had become a unit. Nothing like almost getting sucked through a portal to another dimension by an evil soul-snatching Raven to fast-track a relationship.

I watched Penny walk away with a Prancer-like lope. She deserved the bounce in her step. She'd worked hard to promote and organize the food drive. I was glad it had been successful and was happy to have assisted by printing up flyers and plastering signs throughout the school.

Jack took advantage of my diverted attention and coiled a thick swath of my hair around his fist. "And what's this about wanting a white Christmas?"

"I do. Now that I've embraced living a stone's throw from the North Pole, I actually do."

"You? The California Girl? Not liking this mild winter?"

"It's wimpy," I said, laughing. It was true. Now that I lived in Minnesota, the recent start-of-winter warm temps and lack of snow seemed pathetic.

He arched his eyebrows. I loved the way it flared the blue of his eyes. "Wimpy, huh?"

CHAPTER TWO

The truck's radio crooned Bing Crosby's "White Christmas." The song worked on two levels: not only was it Christmas Eve, but the drive to Jack's family farm felt like going back in time. I always knew when we were close, because my watch began to spin counter-clockwise. The numerals even changed to Roman. At the road, stone pillars fronted the entrance with a carved wooden SNJOSSON FARMS sign strung between them. We pulled down a long gravel driveway. Apple trees dotted both sides of the narrow lane. They were barren, but I remembered them leafy and heavy with fruit. Even now, with their silvery bark set against the hard frosty ground, they were an impressive sight.

Jack parked in front of the house, and we got out. I filled my arms with wrapped packages, gifts for his family. I took a deep breath, lingering by the passenger side of the truck. I had been to his house many times and shared many meals with his parents. I had, however, never been for a holiday dinner. Reluctantly, my mom had agreed to a trade-off. I got to spend tonight at Jack's; in exchange, she got us both for Christmas dinner. A win-win, I'd thought, until, standing there, my nervous system lived up to its name.

Jack walked around to me and pulled my suddenly cement-bottomed feet toward the house. "Come on," he said.

I was mostly freaked about meeting Jack's grandmother, who was visiting for Christmas. The few things I knew about her hinted at an unusual woman. For starters, she had been the one to suspect and then advise Jack of my rightful membership in the Icelandic Stork Society. This, years before even I knew of my soul-delivery-service future. And she had recognized Jack's immunity to the cold as something extraordinary, even for one of the Veturfolk, the Winter People, a Norse race of arctic descent. Moreover, she had intuited our unique connection, the heightening of powers created by our predestined combination.

"We're here!" Jack called out.

"Finally." Jack's mom, Alda, met us in the small foyer,

wiping her hands on a dishcloth. She had Jack's sky-blue eyes and dark hair, though hers was streaked with gray.

We stamped our boots on the mat inside the front door. The house had old wooden floorboards throughout, even upstairs. They were scuffed and more warped than the Coen brothers, but I liked the colorful rag and braided rugs that cozied up each individual room and that no one was ever expected to remove their shoes. Besides, they kept the thermostat at, like, forty — below. Footwear, at its most basic design, was protection against the elements, one of which was cold. I'd come a long way from the girl who had once thought that shoes needed to match the outfit, not the season. You still wouldn't catch me sliding my polished toes into a pair of Birkenstocks, but I'd made serious progress. I was currently wearing the Timberland boots Jack had once broken in with a rock. With pink-and-brown argyle laces tied ankle-to-toe, they were both stylish and comfortable.

Jack's mom was joined by Jack's dad, Lars, a tall man with dull blond hair that thinned on top and was cropped neatly above his ears and through the sideburns. Alda hugged me and took the packages, while Lars, a man of few words, took my coat.

"Your *amma*'s waiting to meet Kat," Alda said to Jack.

I swallowed what felt like a golf ball — with an accompanying divot of turf.

Jack took my hand and led me through the kitchen and into the family room. His grandmother was seated on a chair near the Christmas tree with a needle and thread in one hand and a large bowl of popcorn on her lap. As Jack and I crossed the room, she set her things on the floor and stood to greet us. She was small and thin and wiry. Her eyes darted quickly to me, and though she wasn't one of the Storks, she was definitely cut of the same homespun cloth. I immediately brushed my hair off my face and straightened my shoulders.

"Amma," Jack said, "this is Kat."

"I'd have known her for one of Olaf's clan," she said, approaching me with a shuffle.

I extended my right hand. "Pleased to meet you."

She took my hand but didn't shake. Instead she ran her right index finger along my palm and then, curiously, into the groove separating my thumb from my fingers. Seemingly confused with what she found, or didn't find, there, she released me. "The power of three," she said with surprise. She scrunched her face into an impressive network of worry lines and stared at me hard and long. Then she turned and headed for the kitchen. "I think I'll make some tea."

When she was gone, Jack pressed his fingers to his forehead. "Sorry about that. She's a little unpredictable."

I was still holding my hand out in front of me, staring at it, as if any sense could be made of what had transpired. I'd heard of palm reading but didn't know the opposable thumb factored into the road map of one's life lines. "No worries." I shook it off. Hulda, our wise-woman leader of the Storks, had hacked a trail for me through what I would have once considered weird and wacky. "Does she drink the tea, or just read the leaves?"

"She may eat the leaves for all I know," Jack said. "And then the cup."

I relaxed. It was cool that we were able to show each other vulnerabilities, a synonym for *family* as far as I was concerned. Tomorrow was my turn. After Christmas morning apart at our respective home bases, we'd spend Christmas dinner with my pregnant mom, her boyfriend, Stanley, and my *afi,* my grandfather. And this without even my dad to factor in. He was still in California final-izing his plans to move to Norse Falls and open a wind turbine factory.

I sat back from the Snjossons' dining-room table, so stuffed even my ears were clogged. I had been wary of a fore-warned menu of mutton stew with rutabaga. Mutton, insofar as I could tell, just meant old lamb. And as much as I appreciated my meal having had a full life before end-ing up on my plate, old meat meant tough. As for the ruta-baga, anything that was classified as a tuber was not fit for consumption. The lamb, a term I definitely preferred to mutton, hadn't been half bad, after all. Jack's mom had used parsnips instead of rutabaga, a kinder and gentler member of the underground veggie world. And, though I routinely avoided words with the confusing Icelandic *d* that sounded more like a *th,* the *laufabrauð,* the leaf bread, with its intricate design was almost too pretty to eat and as complicated to say as it probably was to make.

"Gifts now," Jack's grandmother said, clapping her hands with authority. Her economy of words hinted at her being biologically related to Jack's dad, as would the matching bristled eyebrows.

We gathered around the tinseled tree.

Alda handed out rectangular packages wrapped in hunter-green paper and tied with raffia. "Kat first," she said.

I slid the soft-sided gift from under its ribbon, gently tearing the wrapping. Inside lay a hand-knit sweater of crimson red with a motif of snowflakes trimming its yoke.

"Thank you. It's beautiful," I said, holding it to my chest. "Did you make it?"

"I did," Alda said. "It's been so many years since Jack would wear one of my creations." I looked at Jack. His holiday attire consisted of a white button-down and Levi's, only a slight upgrade from his usual — faded T-shirts and Lee jeans. Despite temperatures tumbling daily, I'd yet to see him in a jacket. A Nordic sweater clinging to his ropy shoulders? I just couldn't picture it.

"I'm very flattered," I said. "It looks like a lot of work."

"It will keep the *Jolakottur* away," Jack's grand-mother said.

"I beg your pardon?" I asked, pushing my arms into the sleeves of the sweater.

"The *Jolakottur,* the Yule Cat," Alda replied. "An old character from Icelandic folklore. I'm surprised you haven't heard of it."

Families didn't get much more Icelandic than mine, so I was surprised, too. I could, of course, name all thirteen of the Yule Lads: Spoon Licker and Door Slammer tying as favorites, and Meat Hook had headlined as the bogey in a few of my childhood nightmares.

"The Yule Cat belongs to the child-eating ogress Grýla. At Christmas, everyone in the family must be gifted an article of clothing, or else the Yule Cat will attack," Jack's *amma* said, wagging her index finger.

"Attack?" I asked, poking my head through the neck and shrugging the sweater down over my torso. It was beginning to feel more like a warning than an old wives' tale.

"In the olden days," Alda said in a gentler tone than her mother-in-law, "people hurried to finish all autumn's wool work before the holiday season. Children were pressed into service with stories of a gigantic black cat that made a Christmas Day meal of anyone without a new piece of clothing."

Finally, a legend I could wrap my mind around. A vicious fashion-frenzied feline prowling the streets and tearing into the poorly attired.

The rest of the gifts were exchanged. I gave everyone, except Jack, a selection of California-themed items: Ghirardelli chocolates, La Brea Bakery granola, Napa Valley dipping oils, Palm Springs dates, Kern County pistachios, all of which my mom had thought of and assembled. In addition to the sweater, I received apple butter, an *All Apple All the Time* cookbook, and, from Jack's grandmother, a bag of rocks. Literally.

"They're moonstones," she said.

"They're very pretty." I shook a few from the small black velvet pouch onto my palm. They were of various colors from light browns to grays and engraved with symbols. I ran the tip of my finger atop one of the gold-painted engravings. It looked like a pitchfork.

"That one's *Mannaz,*" Jack's grandmother said. "The rune symbol for man. The runes are the Norse pre-Christian alphabet."

"Oh. I get it." I didn't. I already had an alphabet. It was working fine; I didn't think I needed another, not an ancient one, anyway. Besides, language seemed the kind of thing that moved forward or progressed, like science or medicine, or synthetic and blended textiles. "Thank you," I said. "They're very interesting."

It became painfully obvious that Jack and I hadn't exchanged our gifts. Alda raised her eyebrows. "Is that it for gifts?"

"I think I'm going to take Kat on a little sleigh ride," Jack said, standing up. "Is that OK? The horses could use the exercise."

"Sure," Alda said. "Don't be too long, though. You still have to drive Kat home."

"Watch out for the Yule Cat," Jack's grandmother said.

"I'm not worried," I said, accepting Jack's hand as he led me out of the room.

While bundling up, I was grateful for the new sweater; it was beautifully crafted, warm, and another layer in my connection to Jack's family. Bring on the Yule Cat, the child-eating ogress, and all thirteen Yule Lads — Meat Hook included — I mused to myself. I had complete confidence in my companion. The buddy system: now that was something I believed in.

CHAPTER THREE

Jack drove the sleigh down a path that headed to the back of the property, one that had been frequented by trucks and tractors during harvest season. A few scant inches of white powder covered the ground, but, by all accounts, the winter was off to a slow start, with snowfall well below average. The weak light of the winter sun was no match for the advancing dusk. There was less than an hour left in the day. I noticed that Jack had packed several very large battery-operated lanterns.

If passing through the road-front gate felt like time travel, dashing through the snow in an open sleigh felt like waking up on the front of a Hallmark card. I was sure that *Season's Greetings* was scrawled at our feet in calligraphy.

Finally, Jack pulled up along the edge of a small creek that gurgled with brackish water.

"Are you warm enough?"

I was bundled in both of the thick lap blankets that Lars had swung over the seat. "Yep."

He pulled me close to him. I tucked into the nook created by his outstretched arm. "Gifts now," he said, clapping his hands as his grandmother had.

I laughed. "I went first last time. Your turn." From inside my parka, I pulled a wrapped gift and placed it in Jack's hands.

He turned it over several times, shook it, knocked on it, and even sniffed it.

"It's a gift, not a melon," I said.

He took his time, lifting the tape gingerly, folding the paper back carefully. I finally reached over, dug my nails in, and ripped.

"There's always that way," he said.

Inside was a folded navy-blue LA Dodgers cap. He shook it out. "What's this?" he asked.

"A new hat."

With a puzzled look, he held it up to the fading light, turning it one way and then another. OK, so maybe the Dodgers were an acquired taste. "I already have a hat, a lucky one," he said teasingly.

The cap in question was, indeed, lucky, having once skittered and drawn me away from an out-of-control truck. Still, it wasn't the most stylish of things. "It's always nice to have options," I said.

"So, am I supposed to wear this thing?" He dropped it on his lap.

"Let me show you," I said, cramming it over his shaggy bangs.

"It makes a statement, I suppose," he said.

"The statement being: I'm with Kat Leblanc, California Girl, Dodgers fan."

"You think I need a reminder?" he said, lifting my chin with his forefinger. "You're not exactly the kind of girl one forgets."

"I'm sure you say that to all the girls you've saved from being dragged into another realm." Hard to believe I could be so flip about that horrible night and Wade's evil plan. I supposed making light of it was a way to deal. Jack had almost died. I shivered to think of it.

"Only the ones with whom I've survived drowning incidents and bear encounters."

It was comforting to know that he, too, could joke about our brushes with death, especially as neither one of us thought our ordeals were behind us. He kissed my eyelid. It fluttered as if about to take flight.

"But about the cap," he said.

"What about it?"

"Does it come in another color?"

"Dodger blue, buddy. No other color."

He adjusted its fit. It was a definite improvement over the mesh John Deere cap.

"Your turn," he said, pulling a small round-shaped package from under the sled's front seat.

Unlike Jack, I knew how to open a gift properly. Within moments the shredded paper lay at my feet and I held a beautiful snow globe on a squat black base. The domed scene depicted a dark-haired boy and a blond girl in a red coat skating on a tree-lined rink.

"How did you . . . ?" I asked with a catch in my voice. It was so eerily reminiscent of our fateful encounter: the winter day, five years ago, when Jack and I miraculously survived a skating accident. Even the red coat with white trim was accurate. "Did you have this made?"

Jack shook his head no. "I found it in a box of my grandmother's old Christmas decorations."

"But . . . it looks so much like . . ."

"Turn it over," he said.

I upended the glass. A stamp on the bottom read "*Gleðileg Jól* 1946."

"Merry Christmas 1946," I said.

"Yep."

Before even our parents were born, our likenesses were entrapped in a snow globe.

"Weird. Isn't it?" I asked.

"I don't ask anymore. I just accept."

He had the right attitude. Certain aspects of our lives

were almost too much to contemplate. I shook the globe. Snow fell, powdering the girl's hair and shoulders and dusting the pine trees. "I did ask for a white Christmas. It's perfect."

"That's just part one of your gift," he said, stretching out his arms.

A light snow began to fall.

"Hooray," I said, cupping flakes in my joined palms. "My white Christmas."

It began to snow a little harder.

I looked around, awestruck. "But how? Before, it only happened when you were mad, or jealous, or out of control in some way."

"I've been practicing," he said.

The flakes grew large and feathery. They clung to the horses' hides and tails, and my lap blanket was soon coated with a thick band of white.

"I can see that." I scooted in for a kiss, something we'd been practicing together. It struck me that, like the proverbial snowflake, no two kisses were ever the same. This one was all the more special, given the holiday setting. And it had a delicious contrast between the cold air and the heat we were generating. The tips of our noses were chilly, but our hot breath and lips were smoldering. I shrugged my hands out of my gloves and walked them under his shirt and up his ribs. For one of the Winter

People, his skin was always thermal. Nor would he ever have occasion to complain about my icy fingers. I sat on his lap. His groan, though not a complaint, was raw. Forget the Hallmark greeting card; we were now rifling through the pages of a Harlequin romance.

I pulled away and leaned my head back. The snow was falling like confetti now; giant crystalline flakes clung to my eyelashes and wet my face. I was startled to see Jack with a cap of white hair, as if the intensity of our kiss had prematurely aged him. Looking around at the cloaked landscape and night falling as fast as the snow, I knew it was time to bring things down a notch.

"Uh, Jack?"

"Yes."

"This seems like an awful lot of snow."

"Huh?"

"Maybe you should turn it off now."

"Crap!"

"What?"

"I'm trying."

"And?"

"It's not working."

I jumped off his lap. "Quit fooling around."

"I'm not." His voice was tight.

I could barely see my hand outstretched in front of my face. The wind howled like a wolf, hungry and irritable.

We'd jumped books to *Little House on the Prairie:* the blizzard scene where Pa had to tie a rope to his waist so as not to get lost between the house and the barn.

"We gotta go now," Jack said. "Before it gets worse."

"It's going to get worse?"

"It could," he said.

"How are we going to see our way back?"

Jack lightly switched the horses with the reins. "These girls know the way."

That didn't help. Our welfare was in the hands of a couple of nags: one called Moonbeam and the other called Bubbles. Neither name, if you asked me, inspired much confidence. I'd have preferred a Saint Bernard named Hero.

It was slow going. Even the horses shied their heads to the side with the winds whipping the snow every which way. Jack was quiet, which made me nervous. Every few minutes I could hear him muttering — cursing, technically — under his breath. And he was going to bust a lobe if he concentrated any harder on whatever it was he did to harness the weather.

My cell phone was at Jack's, in my purse, next to the front door, my "Stayin' Alive" ringtone probably not sounding so cute and retro anymore.

I could still see the outlines of trees on either side of the path, but barely. I wondered how the horses kept to the trail. As if sensing my concern, they came to an abrupt stop.

20

"Shit," Jack said with a lash of the reins. "Giddyap."
Nothing.

He tried again. Bubbles, or at least I think it was Bubbles, neighed in complaint. A headwind barreled into me. My face hurt from the cold, and I burrowed farther into my collar. Though I, better than anyone, knew of his resistance to cold, I still shuddered with sympathy for Jack.

"Hold the reins," Jack finally said. "I'm going to have to guide them."

He jumped down from the sled, carrying one lantern with him and leaving the other next to me on the seat.

The horses were in no mood and dug in their hooves obstinately. I could just make out Jack's form through the squalling snow at first coaxing, and then pulling, until he was finally engaged in an all-out tug-of-war with the animals. He may have had determination, but they had brute strength and were not about to be led into an abyss through which they had no guideposts, no point of reference, nothing but a wall of swirling white. And then it came to me. They needed a corner. Not literally, of course, as that could put us into a ditch or thicket of trees. They needed what my mother had always given me when we did jigsaw puzzles together: a small, manageable start, an achievable goal.

As cold as I was, I shrugged out of my white parka and then hastily took off my new red sweater. How, of all days, had both Jack and I managed to dress in white?

And dang, it was cold. My teeth chattered uncontrollably. They formed words of their own volition. They even got a little mouthy and crass. Good thing Jack was out of hearing range. They cursed us both: me for coming up with the stupid idea, and him for listening.

Coat back on and lantern and sweater in hand, I scrambled out of the sled. Fighting the driving snow, I made my way to where Jack struggled with the horses. I held the lantern and red sweater mere inches in front of one horse and then the other. I noticed they both lifted their heads slightly. Jack caught on and urged them forward toward the wagging sweater that, inch by inch, I pulled away from them. It was working. Evolution moved quicker, but at least it was progress, and who knows, maybe by the time we got back I'd have adapted for frostbite resistance, a mutation I supposed Jack already possessed. As things stood, I couldn't feel my toes or the tip of my nose. As if sensing our clearheadedness, even the snow and winds relaxed a little.

"It won't let up for long," Jack said. "But I think we can get back in the sleigh."

We settled back onto the wooden seat. I tucked a blanket around my frozen toes.

"Is it over?" I asked, lifting my mitted glove to catch flakes.

"Not even close," he said, switching Bubbles lightly. "We better hurry."

22

CHAPTER FOUR

When we finally pulled into the barn, Jack's parents rushed out with flashlights in hand.

"Thank God you're OK," Alda said.

"We're fine." Jack unhitched Moonbeam.

Lars stepped in and tended to Bubbles. "You had us worried," he said gruffly.

"Kat's mom called three times," Alda said.

"The storm just blew up so quickly." Jack's head dropped as he led Moonbeam into her stall. "We had a hard time with the team."

A howl of wind rattled the rafters of the old wooden structure. Jack's parents were aware of his special immunity to the cold, but they were not aware of his weather-wielding abilities. His grandmother had thought it best to keep quiet about it, even to his parents. "For their protection," had been her cryptic warning to Jack. And as much as I, too, kept my abilities from my parents, owing to a Stork oath, I, at least, had Hulda and my sister Storks for guidance and advice. Jack had no one except his grandmother and me. And neither of us was exactly a bucket of know-how. She had vague centuries-old legends of the special among the Veturfolk to offer. I had only a profound belief in our combined fates to comfort him.

"I've never seen anything like it," Alda said. "It looks like it's picking up again. We better get inside."

Eerily backlit by the fireplace, Jack's *amma* sat at the family room's picture window, entranced by the falling flakes. She had pulled up a straight-back chair and was munching from the popcorn bowl; a string of abandoned garland sat at her feet.

"Powers are out. Powers are out," she repeated.

"Yes, Mom," Lars said. "The phones are, too."

As much as I wanted to believe that she was talking about gas and electricity, she had said "powers"—plural. After the whole palm-reading thing, it had me wondering.

It took several minutes, but Lars was finally able to coax her away from the window. We set up in front of the fireplace, where it had been decided we'd sleep. We listened to the radio until well after midnight. With the exception of Jack, we huddled in blankets and crowded the fire. Jack's *amma* had the occasional outburst, but she soon settled. I hadn't been able to get hold of my mom, and I was worried. Though I knew she was with Stanley and Afi, her fireplace was gas with an electric starter. Also, I doubted she had a crank or battery-operated radio like the Snjossons'.

I watched Jack get up frequently, pace up and down the room, and stare out the window at the drifting snow, which continued to fall. By the sounds of their rhythmic breathing, I knew his family was asleep. Finally I got up, drew a blanket around me, and joined Jack at the window.

"What exactly happened tonight?" I asked.

"A big mistake."

"Was that all you?" I whispered.

He nodded his head reluctantly. "Once I got it started, I couldn't turn it off."

"I thought you'd been practicing."

"I thought I had, too. It's just . . . There's so many variables to consider. I practiced in the fall, when the preexisting air temperature wasn't as cold. I didn't factor in how quickly winter air masses would grab. I was always alone, too. You . . . I didn't factor in you." He was so gloomy it was material, gathering at his feet in a cloud of gray matter like Pig-Pen, Charlie Brown's sidekick. I wanted to absolve him of his self-reproach, remind him that it had been my idea. By the set of his shoulders, I knew that now was not the time.

On Christmas morning we woke to a ghostly white landscape. Snow lay in stiff peaks like a meringue topping. Tree trunks were buried, drifts crept up the side of the house and barns, and not a path or driveway was visible. The radio news made a big deal out of the fact that it was a snowstorm the likes of which hadn't been seen in almost two hundred years. Over thirty-eight inches of snow were recorded in Duluth, topping the charts and breaking all records since 1819, the date Fort Snelling was settled and weather events first measured. Our local snowfall was even higher, with estimates coming in at over forty inches. The phone and power lines were still down, and flights in and out of Duluth and International Falls were grounded. Motorists were stranded, as were rescue crews. Plows had to dig out plows. The governor had declared a state of emergency, with damages expected to exceed fifty million dollars.

But worse than all that—far, far worse—was the report of an accident. A car, carrying a family of three, had gone off a steep embankment, and a five-year-old boy had died. Hearing that was like a bullet to the chest.

After that news, Jack retreated to his room, skulking off without looking at me. I knew why. Though he'd been too kind to say it out loud, it was all my fault.

I went to the bathroom to cry in private. I collapsed onto the toilet, burying my face in my hands. I couldn't believe how arrogant and irresponsible I'd been. I had a gift: the ability to deliver souls. I'd found my match: another being of special abilities. And what had been my reaction to such fortune? I'd coaxed Jack into using his powers recklessly. There, in the Snjossons' half bath, wiping snot from my nose, I vowed somehow, some way, to make amends.

CHAPTER FIVE

On the morning of the twenty-sixth, once the roads were cleared, Jack drove me to Afi's. Luckily, my mom and Stanley had been there when the storm hit. With my grandfather's wood-burning fireplace and a big pile of wool blankets, they'd toughed it out much the same way we had.

It was a quiet drive. Since the storm, something had come between us. We continued to hold hands and share kisses, but our guilt was there: the crowd-making third.

We pulled up in front of the house and let ourselves in through the front door.

My mom met us in the foyer and pulled me into a hug. "What a relief. So many reports are coming in about the storm — stranded motorists, accidents, and that poor little boy."

Jack exhaled a ragged breath. I noticed he turned away from me. Who could blame him?

We moved into the kitchen, where Stanley joined us, taking my mom's hand in his. "Glad to see you kids are OK. What a night. One *we'll* never forget." He turned to my mom. "Have you told them yet?"

"Told us what?" My voice was tight. It had been a long two days.

Stanley held up my mom's left hand. Like me, she got rocks for Christmas. Only I'm sure hers didn't come in a bag.

"We're engaged," my mom said, wiggling the fingers of her left hand. The ring was a pear-shaped diamond.

I hugged and congratulated them both, as did Jack.

"We're thinking of a Valentine's wedding," my mom said. "Just family and a few friends."

I nodded and listened to their plans, but couldn't help feeling a hard smack of shame that we were talking weddings while another family was making funeral arrangements.

Afi rattled into the kitchen with a blanket around his shoulders and a mug in his hand. He didn't look so great.

"Are you OK, Afi?" I asked.

"Been better," he said. His eyes were glassy, and his

skin was bone-white and hung like a rumpled sheet around his eyes and over his cheekbones.

My mom took the mug from him. "More tea, Dad?"

He nodded a yes.

"What's wrong?" I asked.

"Old," he said.

"Older than the last time I saw you?"

Afi gave me a complete loop of his watery eyes. OK, so it wasn't the smartest question ever. We all were — technically — but my point was it had only been a couple days, yet he had aged years.

"We were cold at night, weren't we, Dad?" My mom clicked a fire to life under the kettle. "But at least the gas and electricity are on now. You'll sleep well tonight. Not everyone's so lucky. Plenty of areas are still without power. Our place and Stanley's, for instance."

Just as Stanley was about to comment, his cell phone rang. He stepped into the living room to take the call.

"What about the store?" I asked. "It should be open, shouldn't it?"

"It would have been closed yesterday, anyway," my mom said. "I suppose people might be disappointed this morning. They'll understand, though. The governor did declare a state of emergency."

"I'll open it up," I said. "People will need supplies."

"Aw, hon," my mom said. "They could drive into Walden. The plows have been out."

"I want to," I said.

Stanley appeared under the arched doorway. "I just had the most extraordinary call. From Greenland, of all places."

"Greenland?" my mom said.

"The Klarksberg Research Station. It's famous for its studies in global warming." Stanley paced back and forth, shaking his head like a wet dog, and holding his phone out like he next expected a call from the president or the pope. "The storm drew attention to the area. They found that research paper I wrote about our September microclimate of cold temperatures. That, and now this record snowfall, has them interested."

Uh-oh.

"They're sending someone here immediately to do fieldwork. They want me to collaborate."

"That's good news, right?" my mom asked.

Jack and I exchanged looks.

"Fantastic news," Stanley countered. "It's international recognition of my work and Walden's Climate Studies program."

"What exactly is it you study?" Jack asked Stanley.

"There are billions of tons of methane, the byproduct of decaying ancient arctic plant life, trapped below the permafrost. Based on the rate of climate change, I've created a model to predict the compound effect this methane will have on global warming."

As much as I knew Stanley was into his work, I still got the yawns every time he went all pocket-protector on us.

"It sounds fascinating," Jack said.

Huh?

"It is," Stanley said. "You know, there'll be plenty to do with the researcher coming so soon. And with everyone gone on break, I could use some help. If you wanted to come by the lab, you'd be more than welcome."

"I think I will," Jack said, nodding his head.

I gave him an are-you-kidding look, but he was too lost in thought to notice.

"I better get home," Jack said, snapping to. "There's still more snow to clear."

A few minutes later, watching from the front porch as his truck pulled away, I thought that I should have been at least a little cheered up. My mom and Stanley were over-the-rainbow happy. And Jack seemed genuinely gung ho about visiting Stanley's lab. So why did I feel like another cold front was moving in?

CHAPTER SIX

On New Year's Eve, as I Windexed and wiped display cases, Afi limped out of the back room. He was pale, with frosty white whiskers growing high on his gaunt cheeks.

"Good God, Kat, what do you have on?"

I stood and looked down. Afi never got my outfits. It was a running joke between us. This one, I supposed, was especially hard to comprehend.

"It's the grunge look." I posed for him, tapping the toe of my Doc Martens out to the side and displaying the full length of slash marks down the front of my baggy jeans. My chunky knit sweater with old leather buttons and its thumb holes at the base of the too-long sleeves hung mid-thigh.

"The what?"

"Grunge look."

"You look like that on purpose?"

"Yep."

Afi shook his head, but I suspected that it was more than fashion trends on his mind.

"Are you feeling OK, Afi? Why don't you go home?"

He looked around, as if unsure of his bearings. "You think I should?"

"Yes. Definitely."

He brought a blue-veined hand to his temple and rubbed. "I miss it, you know."

Uh-oh. He'd only been at the store for an hour, tops. Hardly enough time to work up a hankering for his couch. He'd been sick since the storm, and all he did the whole time was bellyache about being housebound. He wasn't making sense.

"Are you OK to walk?" I asked him.

"God, no," he said. "I'll have to fly."

I waited for him to explain. He said nothing. I tucked my chin in. I was the bird in the family, but you didn't hear me preparing for takeoff. Maybe Afi wasn't over the flu? Maybe he was sicker than we thought?

"Should I drive you?" I asked.

"Drive me? To Iceland? Don't be silly."

"Who said anything about Iceland?" I said.

"It's my home," he said, pulling his anorak from a hook by the door. "And you're right I should go."

Afi clomped to the door and was trudging down the snow-banked sidewalk before I could respond. I had no idea where he was headed.

I called my mom and gave her a heads-up on his strange behavior. She promised to check on him before going out for the evening.

As I scrambled to close up early, with New Year's plans for a party at Tina's boyfriend Matthew's house, my head started to itch.

Shoot. A scalp rash was the archaic means by which we Storks communicated a nine p.m., same-day meeting. As always, I exhaled a huff of steam at our prehistoric ways. Even courier pigeon would be more technologically advanced and would at least keep with our bird theme.

I punched Jack's number into my cell phone. We hadn't seen each other since the day after Christmas, when he dropped me at Afi's house. In the space of five days, he and Stanley had become the new couple — as two-ply as Charmin Ultra — poring over Stanley's research notes, running around the county collecting data, and preparing for the researcher's arrival. And I was still running my own personal shopgirl marathon.

"Hey. It's me," I said.

"What's up, buttercup?" It was a corny line, and he overused it, but it made my insides melt. It did. I heard the slosh.

"A little wrench in the evening."

"Uh-oh."

"Stork duty."

"But you'll be done by what? Nine-o-two?"

It was true that our Stork meetings — though always long, drawn-out affairs whose rules and regulations probably predated the Roman Republic — accounted for mere minutes of real time, but it was a little rattling that the guy knew me well enough to punch a hole in my busy-delivering-souls alibi.

"Except that Hulda always keeps me after." Now I sounded like a whining schoolgirl. "I think I should meet you at Matthew's."

"OK. See you there, then."

I hung up, sensing my stomach gurgle. There was an awkwardness between Jack and me. We talked daily by phone and both had legitimate distractions; still, there was a muck-filled puddle in the road we were both politely stepping around.

The only good news of the day was that the normally wicked boiling and bubbling and prickling of my scalp wasn't nearly as bad as in the past. *About time.*

Though I had another itch, and that was to shake things up a bit.

CHAPTER SEVEN

Our flock was in urgent need of a new meeting place. Now that Starbucks had bought Hulda's store and was "opening soon," our usual gathering spot—Hulda's dungeon—was about to get more foot traffic than was good for an ages-old clandestine organization. We'd already discussed the issue at three meetings with the unanimous-but-one consensus that—*drumroll*—the topic should be discussed further—*cymbals crash*. I was, for the record, the but-one. If you asked me, we should assign a couple of location scouts: they'd go out with maps and cameras, return with suggestions, and the group would put it to a vote. Problem was, no one asked me. Hulda had tabled the discussion with her customary, "We wait for a sign."

I swore, one of these days, I was going to walk in with a big picket *sign* that said: DECIDE SOMETHING.

I tugged the knit cap with braided ear tails over my scabied scalp that, thankfully, looked worse than it felt. Though construction crews had been transforming Hulda's old Fabric and Notions Shop for weeks, my key still mystically fit in the lock, even though it was an entirely different door. I walked through the dark shop, a jumble of carpenters' tools and painters' equipment, all neatly stored for the night. The door that had once been marked OFFICE, though I had only once ever seen it in that incarnation, was now a coed restroom. I super-hated coed bathrooms. For starters, I had a fear of being walked in on, and secondly, I had an even stronger fear that men didn't wash, construction crews in particular.

I turned the handle to the door with my shirtsleeve and found, naturally, the same dark hallway, naked bulb, and winding stairs. OK. Things like this about the Storks still made my spine curl.

I settled into my Robin's seat, the much-coveted second chair, an honor I'd never asked for and over which Grimilla, aka Grim, still bore one big galumph of a grudge. Well, that and the fact that Penny — Grim's granddaughter and sole heir — had become a little more rebellious since meeting me. I looked across to Grim as she heaved herself into her Peacock's chair. Her gray-blue eyes chopped me with one quick, dismissive glance. *Nice to see you, too.*

Hulda walked into the room, followed by Dorit, or a shell of the Stork once known as Dorit, anyway. Dorit had been conspicuously absent from recent meetings. Her hair hung lank, her normally pudgy face appeared lined, and she had the slow, heavy-footed shamble of a convict. I even looked at her feet for shackles, but her hobble was self-imposed. I'd never seen anyone so beat-down. Granted, she had to be one steaming kettle of regret. She'd foolishly, over the course of many years, confided top-secret information to her grandson Wade. Enough, even, for him to murder out of jealousy his own sister, a future Stork; to fall in with soul-snatching Ravens; and to summon the centuries-closed Bifrost Bridge—his fatal mistake.

Hulda motioned for us all to stand. Dorit took her place behind her chair, but I noticed she did not pull it away from the table, as most of us had.

"Before roll is called," Hulda said, "our first order of business will be to read the verdict of the World Tribunal as pertains to our suspended Stork, Dorit."

You'd think, as second chair, I'd have known that Dorit's case was being reviewed by the World Tribunal, or that we even had a World Tribunal. Once again, communication was not the group's strongest suit. I also noted the omission of the word *sister* before "Stork" or *Fru* (the Icelandic for Mrs.) before "Dorit."

Hulda unfurled a scroll of brown paper that looked

old enough to be the Cro-Magnon Carta, or whatever form of law prehistoric man governed with. I looked over her shoulder, half expecting it to be written in hieroglyphs. "Dorit Giselda Arnulfsdottir."

The room went quiet as a Verizon dead zone.

"You have been accused" — continued Hulda — "of disclosing Stork secrets to a Raven, an act which resulted in the death of Hannah Ivarsson."

Dorit sniffled at the mention of her granddaughter and removed a cloth hankie from her sleeve.

"As well as injury to Jack Snjosson and to Katla Gudrun Leblanc, a sister Stork."

Note to self: Keep mouth shut, even to Jack. Gossip can go bad — very, very bad.

Hulda rolled to a new section of paper. Dorit's sniffles became sobs. "The tribunal's decision is an . . ."

A collective intake of air sounded like the start-up of a small engine.

"Immediate and lifelong termination of Stork affiliation and privileges."

Dorit crumpled to her knees. We all gasped. I, too, was caught up in the emotion of the moment. Though it wasn't a death sentence, her reaction and the responding clucks and squawks were funereal. The Storks whose chairs were on either side of Dorit helped her to her feet, or attempted to, anyway. Once composed, she resisted any offer of assistance with angry flaps of her arms. She

40

gathered a ragbag purse from her feet, yanked the cloche hat from her head, and slapped it on the table.

"You have made a mistake you will come to regret, Hulda," Dorit said with an accusatory wag of her thick index finger. She clutched the bag to her chest and stormed out of the room, causing the candles to flicker and all the Storks to chatter like loose dentures. I heard words like "insolent" and "an insult to Fru Hulda" volleyed back and forth. Not only had Dorit threatened our esteemed leader, she had, perhaps even more shockingly, addressed her as simply Hulda.

Upon Dorit's dramatic exit, Hulda braced the table as if exhausted. She turned to one of the quietest of members. "Fru Svana, if you would be so kind as to see to Dorit's chair."

Svana, our Swan, pulled the chair away from the table and then turned it backward, facing out. I remembered that this was the way my chair had been the first night I stumbled into a meeting.

"Fru Hulda," I said, "may I ask a question?"

"Yes, child. Ask."

I noticed I was "child," whereas the omission of a tiny article in front of Fru Hulda's name had set the room atwitter. *Whatever.*

"How will we replace Fru Dorit?"

"This discussion is not on the agenda," Grim interrupted.

Hulda sighed and then turned to me. "Katla, you remain after meeting. Yes?"

"Yes. Of course." Lucky for Jack, I wasn't able to discuss Stork business, otherwise he'd have earned an IOU for an ItoldU.

"Fru Hulda," Grim said. "Perhaps after the meeting you will remind our fledgling member of protocol."

Dang, Grim was harsh. I shot her a look. And though I suspected Penny would bear the consequence of my glare, and was sure my messages to her would never again be delivered, I couldn't help it. And besides, I was second chair. And it wasn't like there was a manual to follow. If there was, it was probably carved into some ancient stone in the north of Iceland. Furthermore, I'd been demoted from child to fledgling.

The rest of the meeting was a snore. We accomplished nothing. Not one thing. The agenda, besides giving Dorit the boot, called for the discussion of a new meeting place. We discussed it all right, but decided—as usual—*nada.*

After the Storks had filed out, all—except Grim—wishing one another "Happy New Year," I remained in my chair next to Hulda.

She tapped my wrist. "So, you wish to know how new Storks come to be."

"Yes."

"But do you not remember your own arrival?"

"Of course I do, but it had seemed unusual." Unusual

was an understatement. That night while working at Afi's store, my scalp had felt like it was going to crawl off my head. I'd looked across the street to see Hulda's shop open for the first time in months. To hide my head pox, I'd borrowed my poor dead *amma*'s beret and hustled over for bargains on velvets and satins. When the beret accidentally fell off, Hulda took one look at my blistered scalp and spooked me into following her down to a dungeon full of old soul-delivering birds, literally, where I was pronounced a member — the youngest ever, at that. So what, I asked myself, were the chances of this being standard recruitment practice?

"You found us," Hulda said. "This was a sign. Now, as we did then, we wait for a sign."

Holy cow. If I remember correctly, it had been a three-year wait to find me. It just seemed there had to be a better way. "I wonder" — I said, thinking out loud — "if it wouldn't do our group good to be a little more proactive in certain things."

Hulda gave me a wide-eyed look. In a grave tone, she said, "We have, for centuries, followed a strict protocol. We rely on signs and dreams and omens to guide us in the selection of new Storks, just as we rely on signs and dreams to identify souls and vessels. These ways are not for us to change."

Wasn't it Hulda who once said "The bamboo that bends in the wind is stronger than the oak that resists"? I could tell, though, that I was already skating on thin ice. And as someone who once fell through a not-so-frozen lake and nearly died, I preferred terra firma.

"And Fru Hulda, are you worried about the way Dorit left us? She threatened you."

"It is not Dorit I fear. Though she has disappointed and endangered us all, she has a good heart. She is shocked and her pride is wounded, but she has learned her lesson. Our secrets are safe with her."

It wasn't a bank I'd be depositing in, but I hoped Hulda was right.

"It was, rather, Wade's actions that night," Hulda said, "that most frightened me. The portals—the *Álaga Blettur*—the power places, if the seals were weakened when recently opened, if a wedge . . ." Hulda waved hands in front of her face, as if parting a curtain. "Listen to me. Such an old worrywart. Go. Be young. Enjoy this night."

I wasn't in the mood to contemplate wedges unless they were of the heeled variety. I wished her a Happy New Year and hightailed my feathers out of there. It was close to nine-thirty. Plenty of party time remained.

44

CHAPTER EIGHT

I drove to the New Year's party straight from the Stork meeting. Surprised by the number of cars, I parked on the street a few houses down from Matthew's. I had thought it was supposed to be a small group. As I walked down the sidewalk, I spied a lone figure huddled against a beat-up truck.

"Jack? Are you waiting for me?"

"Yes."

"It's freezing out here." Even I couldn't quite grasp his absolute immunity to the cold.

"How was your meeting?"

I tucked my arms under his and clasped my hands behind his back. "You know I can't talk about it." As much as it was a small comfort to have at least one person outside council who knew about this crazy responsibility of mine, the secrecy surrounding our Stork duties was often overwhelming.

"Fine." He rested his chin on my head. "How about telling me if you're in the mood for a party."

"I'm in the mood to be with you. Anywhere."

"Good answer." He took my hand and led me toward Matthew's house.

The party was in the basement, more aptly described as the entertainment level. There was a pool table, Ping-Pong table, long granite-topped bar, and huge U-shaped sectional front-and-center to a theater-worthy plasma HDTV. And there were kids everywhere. Way more than I expected.

Jack stopped to chat with Matthew. I spotted Penny and Tina sitting at the bar with Cokes in front of them.

"Happy New Year, girls," I said, giving them both hugs. I pulled up a stool on the other side of Penny. "Big crowd."

They exchanged looks.

"What's wrong?" I asked.

Penny motioned with a dip of her head toward the TV area, where a big group, guys mainly, were watching a football game. They were loud and already rowdy. I noticed Pedro among them.

"Most of them weren't invited," Penny said.

"Matthew's a nervous wreck," Tina cut in. "He promised his parents he'd keep it small and that there wouldn't be any drinking. If they come home early, he's dead."

I looked again at the group. I noticed they were mostly football players from our school and that many of them were drinking beer.

"Can't Pedro talk to them?" I asked. "About the beers, anyway."

"Pedro's the one who brought them all," Penny said with a roll of her eyes. "Without even checking with Matthew. Plus, he's had a Coors in his hand since he got here."

"Oh," I said. "Is Matthew going to ask them to leave?"

"No," Tina said. "Not yet, anyway. Only if they get out of control. But it's just ruining the entire night for him. He's all stressed out."

Jack joined us at the bar. I raised my eyes warningly as he presumably summed up the mood of my two friends. "Do you want me to talk to Pedro?" he asked Penny.

"Good luck getting his attention," she said. "He's ignored me all night."

Overhearing Jack and Penny's conversation, Matthew stepped behind the bar. "Forget it," he said to Jack. "I just don't want any trouble. As long as they stay cool and take their empties with them."

More kids arrived, gathering at the bar. Matthew and a buddy of his handed out sodas from the fridge. Jack and I got talked into a game of pool. We lost, but didn't let it stop us from challenging Tina and Matthew to a game.

Around eleven, the Ping-Pong table was folded up, some *Top 40*s cranked through the cable-music channels, and a small dance floor got going.

Jack and I took seats at the bar. Matthew asked if we wanted anything, and I asked for a Coke. I spun my stool to watch the dancers when I heard Matthew behind me say, "What the hell?"

"What's wrong?" Jack asked.

I turned back around.

"There was a bottle of vodka here earlier; it's gone." He held up an empty bottle of Jack Daniels. "And this was full."

The three of us looked at the dancers, as if expecting to see a bottle being passed around brazenly, or a big back-pocket bulge on one of the linebackers stomping to the music.

The song changed to a slow one, and couples, one of which was Pedro and Penny, paired off.

"I can't believe this," Matthew said.

Tina joined Matthew behind the bar, swinging her hips to the music and trying to tempt him into a dance. He wouldn't budge; he wasn't going to leave the rest of his parents' liquor unattended. Tina, Jack, and I kept

Matthew company in his vigil. He was concocting schemes to refill the bottle, at least temporarily: iced tea, watered-down coffee, and even flat root beer were thrown around as possibilities.

A few minutes before midnight, Jack slipped his hand into mine and pulled me away from the bar and out the sliding-glass door to a patio.

"Do you mind?" he asked, leading us to a garden bench. "I don't want to share you at midnight."

"When you put it that way," I said, huddling into the warmth of his offered arm.

"Can't think of a better way to welcome a new year."

"Any resolutions?" I asked.

"Actually, there is one."

I was certain this was a clever segue into a remark about us, something that would lead perfectly into a New Year's kiss. "What is it?" I asked.

"To devote myself to Stanley's climate-change studies."

"You're not serious?" Devote? It was an odd word choice.

"It's interesting and important," he said. "And of all people, I should know the science behind weather. Maybe it's the key to understanding this *thing* I have."

He said "thing" as if his abilities were a curse, not a gift.

"I guess that's good," I said, though probably without

too much conviction. "To learn how to best control or use your abilities."

"I don't want to control my abilities," Jack said. "I'm more interested in getting rid of them."

"Get rid of them?"

"They're dangerous. You know that better than anyone."

I was speechless. The little boy's death had me just as shaken as him. And the whole thing was more my fault than his. Still, I hadn't seen denying or abandoning our gifts as the answer.

From the house burst out a raucous chorus: "Ten, nine, eight . . ."

"But Jack . . ."

"Five, four, three . . ."

"No buts," he said.

"Happy New Year!"

Before I could argue further, Jack swept me into a kiss. A subject-changing, resolve-melting, backbone-buckling smooch.

We were interrupted by loud voices that sounded more angry than celebratory. We rushed into the house just in time to see one of the football players duck as a barstool whizzed past his head and slammed into the wall with a deafening thud and splintering of wood. Two guys charged each other, only to be pulled apart by Pedro and three others. Within minutes, the commotion had settled, and the two guys had been kicked out, but the damage had already been done.

Matthew held the broken leg of a stool in one hand as he rubbed a deep dent in the wall with the other. Penny stood glaring at Pedro with her hands on her hips.

"What?" Pedro asked. "I didn't do anything. I was clear across the room."

"The hell you didn't," Penny said, brushing past him.

CHAPTER NINE

Afi decided to open the store for a few hours the morning of New Year's Day, and I was heading over to help out. He had received a new shipment of groceries delayed by the storm and figured the locals, many snowbound over the holidays, would appreciate a chance to stock up.

"Good morning and happy New Year." A bespectacled woman looked up from one of the back aisles, where she was shelving cans of baked beans like she worked here or something.

"Can I help you?" I asked.

Afi came padding out of the back room. "Have you two met?"

The woman stood. "I was just about to introduce myself." She held out her hand. "Ofelia Dagmundsdottir. And you must be Kat."

I cocked my head to the side and shook her hand warily. "Dagmundsdottir" meant only one thing: Icelandic. No real surprise there. But what was she doing stacking cans? I gave her a quick once-over. Fifty-something, I'd guess. Light brown hair with gray leaching in at the roots pulled into a loose back knot. Blockish figure. Soft brown eyes.

"Ofelia responded to my help-wanted sign," Afi said.

"What sign?" I asked.

"The one I was just about to put up when she walked in."

"What an odd thing," Ofelia said. "I came in, had a good feeling about the place, asked if he needed help, and next thing I knew I was hired."

"To work when?" I asked, not enjoying being so out of the loop.

"When you can't and I don't want to," Afi said.

"When will that be?" I asked.

"A lot," Afi said, heading back to the storeroom.

"He says he's been a little under the weather," Ofelia said. "I'm new in town, so even if it's just temporary — I'm grateful."

I scrunched my mouth to the side. Starbucks was hiring; that was common knowledge. Jaelle, my good friend, had about another week waitressing at the Kountry Kettle, so that was another available position. Not to mention my dad's factory was about to open; not that I could see her assembling wind turbines, but, still, hundreds had stood in line on a cold December day to interview with Dad's fore-man. We were practically a boomtown, so why would she want to work here? Besides, I knew what Afi paid.

"Where are you from?" I asked.

"North Dakota."

"What brings you here?"

"Paulina, the owner of the used bookstore, she's my sister."

"She doesn't need any help?"

"I'm already staying with her. Besides, she doesn't, but it sounds like your grandfather does."

"Experience?" I knew I was out of line and being difficult, but Afi had to be about the sweetest, most trust-ing guy — ever.

She looked at me with a kind, but curious, expres-sion. "Yes."

Afi came out of the back room with a crate of eggs. "Your mother called a few minutes ago," he said to me. "She's been at my place cleaning and cooking, and now she's gone and planned a party. Your dad arrives later, and she said you could call that boy of yours."

"Let me get that for you." Ofelia took the eggs from Afi and headed for the wall of glass-fronted coolers.

I followed her and watched, leaning against the wall

54

as she stacked the eggs onto the shelf with the short end of the carton facing out, just how Afi liked them. Lucky guess? Afi was meticulous about the sell-by date being face-out. "Answer their questions before they think 'em" was his justification.

"Barbara's Boutique in Devils Lake," Ofelia said, startling me.

"I beg your pardon?"

"References. Should you need them." Ofelia closed the cooler door. "Barbara's Boutique was my last place of employment. I'll leave their number with your grandfather."

"Oh. Good. Yes. I'm sure he would have asked, anyway," I said.

While Ofelia carried the empty crate to the storeroom, I scratched *Devils Lake* onto a notepad.

Later that day, we watched football. I could barely concentrate, waiting impatiently for my dad's call. Finally, a little past six, I snapped my phone shut. "That was Dad," I announced to the group. "He'll be here in a few minutes." I was so excited I bounced up and down, causing the floorboards in Afi's living room to groan.

Jack rubbed my arm. "Do you want to meet him outside?"

"Can that California boy even drive in the snow?" Afi asked.

"He can surf, ski, snowboard, and water-ski. He can drive a jet ski, a snowmobile, and a Harley," my mom said. "I think he'll be fine in a rental car on a plowed road."

"Sounds like quite a guy," Stanley said. "I'm looking forward to finally meeting him." The crazy thing about Stanley was that he was, in all likelihood, telling the truth. He seemingly felt no ill will, nor begrudged any of us our past with my dad—my mom included. Either he was the most clueless guy in the world, or the nicest. Today, given my all-around good mood, I allowed the latter.

Headlights, coasting toward Jack and me at our post in front of Afi's, pierced the quiet street. I hadn't seen my dad since Thanksgiving and was hopping up and down more from anticipation than cold. I could see that Jack found my excitement amusing.

As soon as my dad's foot hit the driveway, I rushed him. He was ready for me and hoisted me in a hair-lifting, good old-fashioned merry-go-round of a twirl. Jack had to jump to get out of the way of my swinging legs.

"Finally," I said as he set me down.

"I told you," he said with a wink and a rub of my head. "I wasn't coming till I had a home base for my Starbucks card."

My dad was a serious, needed-rehab coffee addict, and not just any ol' cup of joe—Starbucks double-shot soy latte.

"You'll be glad to know they open tomorrow," I said. "There'll be all kinds of free stuff, but I'm sure they'll be glad to take your money, too."

Jack and my dad shook hands and wished each other a happy New Year. Seeing the two of them all buddy-buddy made me confident that "happy" was indeed in the cards for the next twelve months.

We joined my mom, Stanley, and Afi in the living room. Stanley jumped up and, after being formally introduced to my dad, insisted on giving him the comfy armchair while he dragged a stiff ladder-back out of the dining room for himself. My dad entertained the group with stories of his Christmas morning surfing and Christmas dinner of fish tacos and Coronas on some deck in Malibu.

Stanley's phone rang, and he excused himself while my dad launched into the rest of the story about midnight Fatburgers with no less than two guys in Santa suits.

"Busy day at the airport," Stanley said as he returned to his seat. "That was the researcher from Greenland, who also arrived today and is already checked into the hotel. And if we thought we were busy before . . ." This last part, I noticed, he directed at Jack.

"You can count on me," Jack said.

For my dad's benefit, my mom explained Stanley's coup in getting such global acclaim for his studies. I'm sure my dad would have acted more interested if he hadn't been so tired from a day of travel or had known of Jack's recent involvement with the project. Or if Stanley, under my mom's proud gaze, hadn't puffed like a best-in-show pug.

We ate dinner and watched more football. After the game, my dad gave me my Christmas gift, which he insisted wasn't late, just hand-delivered. As I was clawing the paper from one totally awesome iPhone, it hit me — hit my head, anyway.

No way. I checked my watch; it was eight-forty. Never before had the cap hit so late or so hard. We always had several hours' warning before a council meeting; moreover, we had just met yesterday.

"I forgot the charger," my dad said. "I'll drop that off soon as I get a chance."

I popped up off the couch, hugged my dad, thanked him big-time, clutched my new Internet-providing, GPS-capable phone to my chest, and raked my right hand deep into my scalp.

As I sat back down on the couch next to Jack, he gave me a look. I rolled my eyes at him and whispered, "I need an excuse."

Jack got up and returned a few minutes later with the pot of decaf. He earned points with my mom for refilling both her and Afi's cups and with me when his cell phone — the modern device he'd only recently caved in to — buzzed not thirty seconds later.

"Where are you?" Jack said into the phone. He

listened for a moment. "Not a problem. I've got cables." He snapped his phone shut and said to the group, "A buddy of mine has a dead battery. I'm gonna give him a hand. It shouldn't take long."

"I'll come with you." I had my coat and hat on, Jack had his keys in hand, and we were out the door before anyone could question us or comment in any way.

For all I knew, they were in there shaking their heads at the goofiness of puppy love. I didn't care. All I wanted was to get my butt to council before my head launched like a rocket.

"Again?" Jack asked. "Didn't you guys meet yesterday?"

"It's weird. Something's up." That was already probably too much shared information. Anyway, Jack had enough to worry about without me dumping Stork business on him.

I reached under my earflapped, fur-lined cap and scratched. I wondered if our much-debated change of location was the reason for the unexpected meeting. After all, Starbucks opened tomorrow, and what would a shop full of cappuccino-sipping customers think of a gaggle of women who all piled into a single-stall restroom?

I had Jack park down the street. The last thing I needed was Grim accusing me of disclosing our whereabouts to my boyfriend, one known descendant of the ice-at-their-core Winter People, as Hulda had once described them. I could just hear the way Grim would pop the *k* ominously as she spat the word *Veturfolk*.

I turned my key in the lock and, though I bustled through quickly, was pleasantly surprised to see the shop so clean, well-stocked, and fully operational. My mood changed quickly as I descended the stairs, already hearing a commotion below.

Once inside our meeting room, I surveyed a scene of chaos. The place had been trashed: all the chairs were scattered, many broken; our candles and bowls of medicinal herbs were smashed on the flagstone floor; and someone had spray-painted in a large, streaky black scrawl across the wall, BEWARE!

"What has happened here?" Fru Svana asked in a frightened voice.

"My book!" Fru Birta cried. "My book. It's missing."

I bent down to examine the broken pieces of my seat, when I noticed a dark shape next to Hulda's chair.

"Hulda!" I said, rushing to her side.

Within seconds, old Grim had muscled her way to Hulda's other side. Like no paramedic I'd ever seen, Grim held a hand on Hulda's forehead and spoke in what I could only describe as tongues. The way she hissed and sputtered, it sure as heck sounded like she had more than one.

Hulda stirred and groaned, but her face was gray, her entire body trembled, and she looked older than time itself. Suddenly, and with her eyes popping open, she croaked, "Enemy in our midst," in a raspy voice. After which, she collapsed in Grim's arms.

Above the ensuing pandemonium, Grim tended to Hulda with the same vigor and urgency she had that fateful night when it had been Jack lying unconscious. She then barked a single command: "Cortege!" Instantly, three Storks stepped forward and fell to their knees alongside Grim. Before I could react, the trio—obviously much stronger than they looked—had carried Hulda out of the room. Grim looked at me. "Her affliction is very alarming. Something I've never seen. And beyond my skills," she said with a droop of her shoulders.

All-out panic was starting to take hold. Reports of missing or damaged items were shouted from one Stork to another, as were conjectures. "It had to have been Dorit," one particularly hawkish voice called out. "She threatened Hulda, after all," another agreed.

I could see that Grim was visibly shaken. Whatever had gotten to Hulda—it was serious. And though I myself was foaming with fear, I knew we needed direction.

"Let's assemble what we can of the chairs," I said over the hubbub. This would give the group a diversion and me a few minutes to think.

An inventory revealed that Dorit's seat was missing; no surprise there. My chair had its two front legs snapped off. Several others were also unusable.

"We'll stand," I said. "I'll keep it brief. Fru Grimilla, where have they taken Fru Hulda?"

"She has, of course, been taken to the Healers," Grim said. Her "of course" implied my lack of basic knowledge, a shortcoming of which I needed no reminder.

"And how will we be updated on her condition?"

"The cortege will bring back a report," Grim replied impatiently.

So. I was on my own then. "With Starbucks opening and now this"—I gestured to the BEWARE! graffitied on the wall—"I think we should immediately assign a new meeting place. I propose my *afi*'s shop." Remembering their hand-signal voting procedure, I continued, "Raise one finger if you agree—two if you oppose."

Everyone, except Grim, wagged a single digit at me.

"Norse Falls General Store it is," I said. Afi's shop was local, familiar, and had a back door. I'd have to rearrange a few things in the storage room, but at least it was a place of business and thus unremarkable as a gathering point. And it closed at nine, so in a perfect world I could send Afi home early, lock the front door, open the back—and convene our secret order of soul deliverers. I knew that perfect worlds didn't exist, but it didn't deter me.

"And we should schedule another meeting date," I said, "when we can all be updated on Hulda's condition. And report any suspicious activity."

A rumbly sound came from Grim. "We do not pre-schedule meetings."

"Forgive me, Fru Grimilla," I said, walking toward Hulda's Owl chair, the first chair, "but as second chair, I make decisions in Fru Hulda's absence."

Grim took one quick inhale, but said nothing.

I stepped onto the raised platform of Hulda's seat. "And has the group ever been vandalized before?"

Grim's throat activity had a gargly, pre-spit quality. "Of course not."

"Then I think the rules are changing," I said, seating myself on Hulda's chair. Mine was broken, after all. "We meet, therefore, four days from now, usual time. There will be no cap." This point gave me particular pleasure. Sure could do without that ridiculous means of communication.

"I don't know what to do about the chairs," I said, looking around.

"The chairs," Grim said, "can take care of themselves."

Right, and so can I. "Thank you, Fru Grimilla, as always, for your gentle guidance."

We locked eyes.

"Meeting adjourned," I said loudly and with a clap of my hands, knowing full well that Hulda always closed with a slight bow to her head and a soft "Peace be." The clap at least made it seem like I was in command. In truth, I didn't know what I was doing. Grim passed behind me with a loud huff. I didn't have her fooled, either.

CHAPTER TEN

"Kat. I could use some help in here," my mom called from the kitchen.

I had just gotten home from our first day back at school and was hoping to just chill for a while. Besides a backpack full of assignments, worries over Hulda tugged at my shoulders. I found my mom surrounded by pots and pans and two open cookbooks. She was squirting anchovy paste from a tube into a metal bowl.

"Stanley and the visiting researcher will be here in an hour," she said, brushing bangs from her face.

Judging by the state of the kitchen, an hour wasn't going to cut it. "What are you making?" I asked. "Besides a mess."

"Dressing for the Caesar salad right now. But I've got a bouillabaisse on the stove and all the ingredients for a crab dip appetizer ready to go."

"Uh, Mom," I said, leaning over the bowl and sniffing at the inky black squirt of anchovy. "What if our guest doesn't like fish?"

My mom stopped, the wire whisk suspended midair. "It's all fish, isn't it?"

"Pretty much."

She rested the whisk on the counter and brought her hand to her tummy. "I've been having the oddest cravings. Yesterday I ate a sardine sandwich. And when I chose the menu earlier today, it had sounded delicious."

"To a porpoise, maybe."

"And what about Jack?" my mom asked.

"What about him?"

"Does he eat fish?" She set back to work mixing the dressing. "He showed up at the lab after school, so Stanley's bringing him along."

The evening was sounding better already.

"I guess he'll have to. What's for dessert?" I asked.

She lifted a brownie mix from the counter. "Funny you should ask."

I didn't think it was.

An hour later, we had the kitchen tidied, the crab dip and crackers set out, and my brownies cooling. Neither of us, however, had time to change. I was barefoot with rolled-up jeans and a black-and-white-striped long-sleeved T. That morning the prison-themed garb had seemed a good way to sum up my back-to-school mood. My mom wore old black stretchy pants over which a faded green sweater was stretched across her expanding midsection. It wasn't her best look, but I knew she still wasn't feeling too great and wasn't really up to shopping for maternity wear or scaling our pile of laundry — what I liked to call Mount Ever-there. I made a mental note to run a load before bed that night.

I heard the doorbell and then Stanley's familiar "Yoo-hoo. Anybody home?"

My mom smiled and wiped her hands on a dishcloth, and we both headed for the front door. A few steps into the foyer and I stopped, gobsmacked. *Researcher? My foot.* What stood in front of me was the most stunning, statuesque runway-type I'd ever seen in person, and I'd once spotted Claudia Schiffer at LAX. She was peeling from her rod-straight shoulders a full-length coat of pure-white fur. Her black leather boots shone like obsidian, her white woolen skirt hugged curvy hips, and her long ebony hair cascaded down her back in a plummet of silky ribbons. She was a mile taller than Stanley, and in those skyscraper heels even looked down on Jack.

My mom and I both stood as rigid as plaster casts. Like me, she had obviously expected the researcher from Greenland to be male and backwoodsy, but there was something else about the woman that had my jaw clamped so tight my molars hurt. In our stupor, we forced Stanley to take her coat and bag.

"Lilja, Kat, allow me to introduce Professor Brigid Fonnkona," Stanley said, enunciating the hard *g* in Brigid.

"Pleased to meet you," my mom said, shaking Brigid's hand. She was making a much quicker recovery. I was still staring openly. "Won't you come in?" My mom directed our guest toward the family room with a sweep of her arm.

I took the luxurious fur from Stanley. Jack hung back with me.

"Wow," I whispered. "She's gorgeous."

He shrugged his shoulders. "I hadn't noticed."

If I'd had a gold star to stick on his forehead, I would have. He'd just have to make do with the happy face I flashed him. My attention turned to the bulky coat I was holding. Not that I was some kind of expert furrier, but this pure-white pelt was definitely real and of an animal that required a heavy-duty self-heating system. Was it legal to sell—or wear, for that matter—polar bear coats? And no way was this thing bought at Saks. No label, no tags of any kind, expertly hand-sewn, and lined with a material that even I couldn't place. I hung it in the hall closet—seriously doubting that the wire hanger was up to the task—and followed Jack into the family room, where my mom was pouring glasses of white wine. Brigid smiled at Jack and patted the open spot next to her like he was some kind of tail-thumping pooch. He sat down, and she crossed one long leg over the other, sliding her body an inch or two in his direction. Stanley was seated in one of the leather chairs across from them. I sat on the floor at one end of the coffee table, helping myself to a cracker full of crab dip and keeping a sharp eye on the newcomer.

"You are old enough to drink aren't you?" my mom tittered nervously.

"Of course," Brigid said, accepting the offered glass.

Funny my mom should ask that. In the hallway, I'd been certain she was about the age of my mom and Stanley. Now, next to Jack on the couch, she seemed much younger. Only a few years older than us. And her striking features were hard to classify. Exotic for sure, but I couldn't decide if she was Asian, or Hispanic, or Middle Eastern, or even Pacific Islander.

"Should we call you Professor Fonnkona?" my mom asked, taking a seat on the arm of Stanley's club chair.

My mom was a professor, too, but I'd never heard her use the title with her peers before.

"Please. Call me Brigid."

Her accent was difficult to pinpoint as well; it definitely had a guttural Scandinavian or Germanic crispness to it.

At the front door, I heard two knocks, a pause, and

then three more quick raps. There was only one person I knew who had a signature knock.

"That's Dad," I said, bounding from my spot on the floor.

I found him peeking his head around the front door. "It's just me. I brought your phone charger."

My mom joined us in the small hallway. "Oh. Greg. It's you," she said, looking at the cord in my hand.

My dad must have heard voices from the family room. "Did I interrupt something?"

"He can come in, can't he, Mom? Maybe stay for dinner?" She didn't move — stuck to the spot I'd put her on.

Luckily, Stanley joined us in the foyer. "Greg. Nice to see you again." They shook hands. "Come on in. Meet our guest."

My mom shot me a glare before we joined the group in the family room.

My dad was already seated in the other club chair and leaning forward to accept the glass of wine being delivered by Stanley.

"Greenland, huh?" my dad said. "Are you actually from there?"

"My studies have taken me all over the world," Brigid replied.

Not necessarily an answer to the question.

"Exactly what is it you two are studying?" my dad asked.

He was being polite. Anytime my mom tried to explain mathematical theorems to him, he said, in a fairly good robot voice, "Does not compute."

"Variations to the global-warming phenomenon," Brigid said. "This area's micro-climate of cooling trends is intriguing. If we can explain this anomaly, seek to re-create its properties, we can apply these findings to other regions whose ecosystems are in danger."

What the—? My dad was inching forward in his chair and gobbling up every word Brigid said. This from the guy who claimed PBS stood for the Prattle, Babble, and Sedation channel.

"Fascinating," my dad said. And I could tell he meant it.

I looked around the room. Was it me? Or was everyone hanging on her every word? Jack, who would not get another happy face from me anytime soon, was just as transfixed as the rest of them. I knew it wasn't purely her discourse that had them all—weirdly, even my mom—so riveted. Brigid's eyes were wide, long-lashed, and had a decidedly feline upturn to them; her lips were very full and garnet-red; and her teeth were a brilliant white. It was so not fair that she was intelligent, too.

"Have you eaten?" Stanley asked my dad.

"No, as a matter of fact. And something smells good."

"I'll set another place," my mom said with a small sigh of resignation.

I watched as my dad escorted Brigid into the dining

70

room, pulled her chair out for her, and seated himself at her right elbow. She was the toast of the table, regaling us with stories of her travels. She'd been everywhere, places even my smart mom had never heard of. It all left me feeling vaguely uncomfortable, though I couldn't precisely state why. Maybe it was because she was the kind of star who didn't just dwarf those who surrounded her — she sucked 'em into some kind of dazzled orbit. It was also possible that the princess in me wasn't used to sharing my dad's attention and affection. Whatever the reason, the evening was not going well. I was the party pooper at the table, the turd in the tub.

"Kat, why don't you help me with dessert?" my mom said.

"I'll help clear," Jack said, pushing back his chair and gathering plates. He had either been trained well, or was seriously angling for brownie points with my mom. I had to inwardly chuckle; he might not get a badge to sew on his good-deeds sash, but brownies were on the menu.

My mom started a pot of decaf while I got out dessert plates, forks, and a spatula.

Jack returned with a second round of dirty plates; an empty-handed Brigid followed him.

"Anything else?" Jack asked.

"See if you can find the mint-chip ice cream," I said. "It's my dad's favorite."

Jack bent down to the pull-out freezer drawer and

began rummaging through our wide assortment of CPK pizzas, Stouffer's mac and cheese, and, my personal favorite, Amy's black bean burritos. Lately, with my mom feeling worn down with her pregnancy, dinner meant something zapped.

"Can I do something?" Brigid asked.

With the coffee burbling, my mom leaned back against the counter. "No. No. You're the guest."

"I don't mind," Brigid said, fiddling with a long, jagged crystal pendant.

"What an unusual necklace," my mom said.

I hadn't noticed it, or the cleavage it nestled into. My attention was now drawn to both. The stone was clear as glass and chiseled into a stalactite-like formation of long, pointy rock.

"Is that a real diamond?" I asked, the words escaping my mouth.

My mom gave me a look, but, honestly, she was the one to mention it.

"This trinket?" Brigid zippered it back and forth along its silver chain. "A family piece."

Which didn't really answer the question — only made me more curious — about her family, for starters.

"It's beautiful" my mom said. "And looks one-of-a-kind, and very old. Is it an antique?" It was, I knew, a more subtle dig for information than my previous "Is it real?"

Brigid brought her hands behind her neck and

expertly unclasped the chain. She held it out for us to see. "It was mined not far from where I grew up."

Again, not necessarily an answer to the question.

"Got it," Jack said, pulling his head from the freezer. He stood, holding a carton of ice cream. As he thrust it out to show me, his hand somehow collided with the pendant Brigid was still holding up. Things happened so fast my eyes, and certainly my brain, had a hard time working it all out. Brigid dropped the necklace. It shattered. Both she and Jack dove to the floor in reaction. And then Jack cried out, "Ouch!" and shook his left thumb, which now had a pinprick of blood at its tip.

"You've been cut," Brigid said, shuddering as if one drop of blood was a gruesome sight.

Still crouched on his knees, Jack rubbed the blood away with his thumb.

"It's just a tiny jab," he said, scrambling to a stand. "But, boy, that sucker hurt."

"Your necklace," I said, realizing the extent of the damage.

Brigid picked up the chain and swung it back and forth. Only a short jagged piece of crystal remained; the other two inches of the stone were glassy shards. "It was an accident," she said. "Do not worry too much about it. It was old, had some sentimental value, but I promise you, it wasn't valuable."

Whether it was watching the pendulum-like motion

of the remaining shard or empathizing with Jack, who continued to cradle his thumb, I wasn't sure, but my stomach took a rough-seas roll.

My dad, having heard the commotion, joined us in the kitchen. "Is something wrong?"

"Nothing a broom can't fix," Brigid said, accepting my dad's assistance standing up.

From a drawer, I found a Band-Aid for Jack, and then swept up the bits of Brigid's stone or crystal or diamond or whatever the heck the glittery fragments were. The ice cream hadn't even been mint chocolate chip, but rocky road. It took me all of three seconds to locate the correct carton myself. Apparently Jack, like my dad, didn't have what my mom called the "finding gene." Her theory was that it required two X chromosomes, as did table manners.

I plated the brownies while my mom scooped the ice cream. Jack sat at the island, suddenly quiet and brooding over his sore finger. I remembered that my mom also listed tolerance to pain as a girls-only genetic trait. My mom carried the coffee service into the dining room; my dad followed with a tray of brownies *à la mode;* Brigid went with them, casting a glance back at Jack as she left. I settled onto the stool next to him. His sulk was unusual, but I assumed the incident had him feeling guilty.

"It's really a shame about that necklace," I said. "So weird the way it shattered like that. How's your cut?"

"It's no big deal," Jack said.

"It wasn't your fault."

"I said it's no big deal." He got up from his stool, leaving his dessert untouched, and followed the others into the family room.

My head jerked back; it was the first time Jack had ever snapped at me. I sat staring at my dessert. Did Jack feel that guilty about the necklace? Despite Brigid's denial, it had to be valuable. Did he worry that he'd ruined his chances of continuing as Stanley's helper? Was the cut deeper than it looked? Or was I making something out of nothing? Laughter erupted from the family room, Jack's throaty chuckle rising above the others; I got up to join them. Whatever the incident had been, it had clearly blown over. So why was I in no mood to laugh?

CHAPTER ELEVEN

"Can you believe she was on the second helicopter that flew over one of the uncontacted tribes of the rain forest?" Two days after the dinner party and Jack was *still* talking about Brigid. "She knows all about their customs."

I leaned back on the bleachers and stretched my legs, briefly admiring my bubblegum-pink knee socks paired with the kelly-green Converse high-tops. Below, Mr. Addomy, the P.E. instructor, demonstrated how to wield a lacrosse stick.

"I thought her area of study was the polar regions," I said.

Mr. Addomy asked for a volunteer to pitch him a few balls. I sat on my hands.

"That's her concentration, sure, but she's interested in any corner of the biosphere that is experiencing a sudden and potentially catastrophic mutation to its ecosystem. Deforestation of the tropics is disturbing everything from plant diversity to animal habitats to weather patterns."

"Snjosson," Mr. Addomy called over the rows of bleachers, "Why don't you show us all that flick of the wrist I was just demonstrating?"

Busted. Normally I'd feel sorry for him. Even a bit guilty for being the other head in an unauthorized tête-à-tête. I was, however, so sick and tired of hearing about Brigid that I welcomed the interruption. Jack hangdogged his way down to Mr. Addomy, who tossed him a few easy balls. Frustrated and clearly embarrassed, Jack gave it several brow-scrunching attempts, but he never quite managed the "flick of the wrist" Mr. Addomy made look so easy. Jack, I could tell, wasn't used to coming up short. With an iron clamp to his jaw, he handed the stick back.

After that, the gym was divided, boys on one side and girls on the other, for our first crack at lacrosse. And I'd thought it was some nice upper-crust lawn game, like croquet or badminton. More like hockey on steroids — for the criminally insane.

Upon exiting the locker room, I found Jack leaning against the wall and practicing the "flick" with an imaginary stick. Irritation chiseled his cheekbones. *Man,* the guy really didn't like to fail. About as much as I didn't like rough sports.

"You're limping," Jack said, pushing off the wall.

"Enjoyment of that game should be one of the criteria the FBI uses to profile serial killers."

"That bad, huh?"

"Terry Andriks is deeply disturbed."

Jack laughed and took my book bag from me. "Let me lighten your load."

As ever, his mere presence did. By the time we reached the lunchtime school-newspaper meeting, I was considerably better.

I took a seat at my usual desk between Jack and Penny in the circle.

"Why don't we take the first half of the lunch to work independently on our stories?" Jack said to the group before sitting down.

Work independently meant we'd yak about anything and everything. It happened at least once a week. Sure, we were putting out a school paper, but that didn't necessarily mean we were all hard-boiled reporter types. On the contrary, plenty of us — myself included — viewed being liberated from the whole lunch scene as equal to, if not greater than, exercising our freedom of speech.

Penny and I discussed the upcoming production of *The Snow Queen.* On Friday, there would be rehearsals for the following week's auditions. We were deep into our design-class project for costumes and sets. It was due by the end of January, and the winning teams would be announced the first week of February.

"I really think we should try out for the production," Penny said. "At least for small parts. It'll give us a better feel for what they're looking for set-wise. Plus, it'll be fun."

A turn of events I hadn't seen coming. "I'm not really an actor," I said.

"You don't have to go out for a speaking part. There's a chorus."

"I'm not much of a singer, either."

"I think they judge more on dancing, anyway," Penny said.

I wasn't about to fess up, but I'd spent enough of my childhood at Madame Bleu's Dance Academy to know the difference between a *grand plié* and a ball change.

"Just think about it," Penny said.

The last time Penny had pulled that line on me, I'd ended up as the fashion editor of the school paper — not five minutes later.

I pointed a recently filed fingernail at her nose. "Don't sign me up. I haven't said yes yet."

She raised her hands in a gesture of innocence. I knew better. I looked over to Jack, having expected him to offer some sort of comment on the prospect of me dancing, or worse, singing. His nose was buried in a book. I leaned over and read the cover: *Ice Sheet Data and the Melting of Greenland* by Brigid Fonnkona. *Big surprise.*

I looked at my watch. "Bell's gonna ring soon."

Jack jumped to attention. "Sorry, guys. The time got away from me today." He flipped open a notebook. "Did everyone get some work done?" He was met by a sea of blank stares. He continued to fiddle with the notebook on his desk. "Don't forget stories are due on Monday."

Everyone began gathering their things.

"Listen, Penny," Jack said, resting an elbow on my desk. "Is there any chance you could write my column for this issue?"

"I'll do it," Pedro said, walking up.

I had been a little surprised when, at the start of the meeting, Pedro had sat across the room from Penny. Whatever had happened between them at Matthew's party wasn't over yet.

"He asked me," Penny said quickly. "And I'd be happy to."

Pedro scratched at his cheek. "Whatever. Just offering." He turned and left.

"Why can't you do it?" I asked Jack.

The bell rang.

"Kinda caught up with something for Brigid — and

Stanley," Jack added quickly. He stood and picked up his books.

I followed him out of the room wondering who I was more likely to get a song and dance out of these days: Penny or Jack.

CHAPTER TWELVE

Unbelievable. At 8:59, Afi's back room had been a jumble of boxes and crates wedged on wobbly shelving units or piled high on the floor. At 9:01 it was transformed into our Stork crib, complete with heavy oval table, the somehow-mended bird chairs, and lit—by whom?—candled sconces. I would never, ever get used to some of the more fantastical aspects of this soul-delivery business. I pinched myself as a reality check. It hurt.

I sat in my Robin's chair this time. Grim was the last to arrive. Her dragging feet were an obvious sign of her continued opposition to a prescheduled meeting.

"Fru Birta," I began. "Is our book still missing?"

"Yes."

"Then no need to call roll. It's obvious, anyway, that we're all here—besides Fru Hulda, of course."

I saw Grim stiffen, bristling at this change to our meeting's program. What'd she expect Fru Birta to do without the book, though? Whittle attendance into the table? Ink it onto her lined palm?

Two spaces down from me, I eyed Dorit's old chair, turned away from the table as mine had been that fateful first night. Also catching my attention were its carvings. They were, again—as mine had once been—birds of all kinds, no longer Dorit's puffers.

A commotion at the door lifted my eyes. There stood Ofelia with a curious look on her face and an armful of papers.

Shoot. A security breach. What was she doing back? I'd sent her home an hour ago. I was about to quickly invent some sort of explanation for this crazy meeting and usher her out, when she pulled a soft brown derby from atop her stack of papers, placed it on her head, and walked briskly to stand behind Dorit's old chair.

"Fru Ofelia Dagmundsdottir submitting transfer papers," she said, placing a small pile of crumpled sheets onto the table.

What the—? Transfer papers? It made no sense on several levels, the obvious one being that it sure didn't look like her head was bugging her. And documents for a swarm of old gals who used hand signals, not ballots, to decide the fate of hovering souls? And transferring from where? She told me she was from North Dakota.

Ofelia looked to Hulda's empty seat. "Your first chair. It's vacant?"

Grim rose from her own chair and walked to where Ofelia stood. "Fru Hulda, our Owl, is not well." She lifted Ofelia's papers from the tabletop. "Katla, as second chair, would you like to check these, or should I?"

And what exactly would I be checking for? Spelling and punctuation errors? Watermarks against the light?

"If you'd be so kind, Fru Grimilla?" I said.

Grim rifled through the pages quickly. I watched Ofelia as she stood patiently behind Dorit's place. She would be, besides me, the youngest member of this group. Even Grim, well into her sixties, was spry for this lot. I also remarked that her sister, Paulina, owner of the used bookstore, was not among our ranks, though she seemed slightly older than Ofelia. Interesting. As was so much about the Storks.

Grim straightened the papers against the table and handed them to me. "Everything appears to be in order. Until our book is returned, we cannot formally enter Fru Ofelia. Until that time, Katla, you may welcome her to our group."

Luckily I remembered how Hulda had welcomed me. "*Velkominn, vinur.* Welcome friend."

"*Velkominn, vinur,*" the Storks chorused in reply.

Ofelia turned her chair, which now bore the chiseled images of turkeys, to face the table and seated herself. So Ofelia would be our Turkey. It at least explained that little wattle under her chin.

All eyes turned to me. I had, after all, called the meeting. "Fru Maria," I said to one of the cortege members. "Would you be so kind as to update us on Fru Hulda's condition?"

"I believe it would be best if I updated the group," Grim interrupted.

When and how did Grim come by this "update"?

Grim sat up straight and placed her clasped hands on the table. "Fru Hulda is extremely sick, but in a safe place. She is unresponsive — in a coma of unknown origin. Praise be that she is being cared for, but the situation is very, very troubling. It can only be assumed that Hulda was attacked."

The room erupted in gasps and squawks and cries of alarm.

"What can we do?" Birta asked.

"I fear for all of our safety," Svana said.

I needed to calm everyone down and bring some sort of order to the meeting. "Sisters, let's discuss this rationally."

"Would it not be helpful," Ofelia interrupted, "to begin by repeating Fru Hulda's last words that fateful night?"

Hmmm. I didn't remember saying that Hulda had

spoken, nor was Ofelia present the night of the attack. Besides, to term them "last words" was definitely *not cool*.

"Before she fell ill, Fru Hulda said, 'Enemy in our midst.' This only days after one of our former sisters had her Stork affiliation terminated and had warned us all that we'd 'be sorry,'" Grim said.

Sure. *Now* Grim wants to be helpful.

"What about Dorit?" I asked, trying to remain in charge. "Does anyone know anything about her state of mind?" I asked.

The room was so quiet I could hear the flare of the candlewicks.

Finally, Fru Svana spoke up: "The family has moved without a word to anyone."

That couldn't be a good sign. Granted, there couldn't be many happy memories for them here, but the timing was suspicious.

"Fru Svana, you were friendly with Dorit, weren't you?"

Svana looked around nervously. "Before the events of . . . September."

"But of everyone, she trusted you most," I said.

"Yes."

"Fru Svana, would you feel comfortable trying to locate them? It seems to me that we should know where she is."

Svana squirmed in her seat. "I could try."

"Thank you. And to all my sister Storks," I said,

looking around the room, "I want to ask for your help during this difficult period. I am new to the council and the second chair, and I never asked for any of this." Grim cleared her throat with a loud honk. "But I'll do my best to serve during Fru Hulda's absence. Fru Grimilla, I trust if there is some change in Fru Hulda's condition that you will call a meeting."

"I will."

"And if anyone feels in danger or threatened or encounters something unusual that they will call a meeting?"

A roomful of heads nodded and said, "We will." Even Ofelia joined in.

"Have we reported our missing book to anyone at the World Council?" I turned to Grim as I asked this.

Grim's chin jutted forward as she spoke. "Fru Birta could accomplish such a task."

There was the smallest of nods from Grim directed to Birta.

"I would be honored," Fru Birta said.

"And of course, business as usual, should a soul seek guidance," I said.

More nods and affirmations.

"Then meeting adjourned." Hulda's customary *peace be* just wouldn't spill from my lips. I was determined to do things my way. Besides, I didn't think we were at peace—far from it, in fact.

CHAPTER THIRTEEN

Friday arrived without too much drama preceding it. Penny and Pedro made up. He'd apologized to Matthew, and a whole group of the football players had pooled money to pay for a new bar stool and repairs to the wall. Jack continued to head over to Walden as soon as school let out, while I relieved a still-weakened Afi from his post behind the register or, alternately, found Ofelia in his place.

After school, Penny stopped at my locker. "Don't forget rehearsals start today."

Phooey. I had. Plus the fact that I'd even agreed to give it a chance. Penny's successful angle had been that these were just optional rehearsals so kids had a chance to learn the songs and dance steps before actual tryouts.

I'd held my tongue, but honestly—practice to audition? Wasn't that kind of like begin to get going? Still, I supposed it was cool that everyone got a fair shake.

"So I'll see you in the auditorium," Penny said, walking away.

Jack popped his head around my open locker. "What for?" he asked.

Ugh. We'd barely spoken in the past two days, so I hadn't shared the fact that Penny had sucked me into another of her extracurriculars.

"Penny and I are attending the practice auditions for *The Snow Queen.* You know, for our project." I left it ambiguous enough that our participation could be nothing more than note taking and stage measurement.

"Sounds like fun," he said distractedly. So distractedly, in fact, that I suspected any reply of mine—shaving our heads or becoming circus acrobats—would have received the same reply.

"So you never called last night," I said.

"Sorry. I stayed late because . . . guess what?"

"What?"

"I got offered an internship. I'll earn math and science credits for the work I'm doing. Plus, I'll get out of school two hours early every day so I can log more lab hours at Walden."

I could tell that Jack expected me to act happy, so I plastered a smile on my face in a big good-for-you facade, but there was something I didn't like about Jack getting sucked into Stanley's research project.

"I'll get to work on Brigid's field studies."

Bingo.

"And it's not just high-school credit. If I attend Walden in the fall, I'll get three units of university credit as well."

"But you're just a high-school student. Aren't there college kids who should have priority?"

"Just a high-school student?" I could hear the hurt in his voice.

"I didn't mean it as an insult, it's just that . . ."

"What?"

"It's so sudden and all-consuming."

"Brigid is only here for a short time. I have to take advantage."

Something about the phrase "take advantage" made me recoil. I wondered just who was taking advantage of whom, but judging by the squint in Jack's eyes, I didn't dare air the remark. "Congratulations," I said. "Really. I mean it. And I'm sorry if I didn't sound supportive before."

"Thanks," he said. "Gotta run." He hurried off so quickly that I wondered if my apology had truly been accepted. I didn't have much time to dwell; I was cutting it close for auditions already.

There were about thirty kids hanging around in the auditorium when I got there. I'd expected a bigger turnout. I thought back to when my school in LA had done a production of *Oklahoma*. A friend of mine had been in the chorus, and I attended a sold-out opening day with so many cast and crew on the stage at curtain call I had honestly wondered if we were approaching the real Oklahoma's census numbers.

Penny waved me over, and I skirted around the small crowd. I noticed Monique, our prom queen and Wade's former girlfriend, was one of the hopefuls. No longer a victim of Wade's mind control, she was almost tolerable. Almost. She still had a whiff of entitlement about her. Due to the story Hulda had concocted to explain Wade's demise, Monique was now the former girlfriend of a hero — a dead one, all the more noble. Or so she thought. At least she now acknowledged others, though her inner circle remained small. Matthew was there, too, with a couple of his fellow band members. Not a huge surprise. The guy loved music.

As we waited, gathering around the back of the auditorium, I heard a voice behind me. "Kat, Penny, I'm so glad you girls are trying out," Ms. Bryant, our design teacher, said with a warm smile. "As a first-time assistant director, I'm glad to see some familiar faces." Ms. Bryant was, hands down, my favorite teacher, ever. She was friendly, smart, funny, attractive, and could accessorize like nobody's business.

"I had a hard time talking Kat into it," Penny said

with a beatific daze in her eyes. We were all a little in awe of Ms. Bryant.

"I'm glad you did," Ms. Bryant said, rubbing Penny's arm. "As always, your enthusiasm is infectious." She walked up the steps to the stage with a flash of toned leg peeking out from under the dark mocha of her side-slitted skirt.

What Penny had said was true, but, still, a little help up from the bus she threw me under would be nice.

"This is going to be a great production," Penny said, nudging me in the side. "Are you in now?" she asked.

I brushed tire marks from the side of my face. "Possibly."

"Let's get everyone onstage," said Mr. Higginbottom, the speech and drama teacher and the production's director.

I led Penny to a spot way in the back, well-positioned for hiding and keeping an eye on the rest of the talent pool.

An hour into the tryout, I had to admit it didn't suck. I'd always loved to dance. Mr. Higginbottom had an over-the-top enthusiasm for all things Broadway. That, paired with surprisingly graceful moves from his burly-chested, triangular frame, had me giggling and having way too much fun to deserve the sweat glistening my forehead. But that was just the dancing; the singing portion was next.

We were sorted into three parallel lines and handed

lyrics to the opening number: something entitled "Village Life." I expressed a sigh of disappointment at the opening words of the song:

Another day of happy lives we villagers embrace,
Lucky are we one and all to live in such a place.

Penny shot me a look — one I deserved. No way would the *Blade Runner* commando theme I had envisioned for the sets and costumes work.

And dang if the little ditty wasn't kind of catchy. During the first two run-throughs, Mr. Higginbottom and Ms. Bryant sat in the audience and listened to us as a group. On our third time, Mr. Higginbottom walked between the rows.

"Very nice, Peturson," he said to Penny. "Breathe, Leblanc, breathe," was directed at me.

"No offense," Penny said once we were finished and retrieving our bags and coats from the auditorium seats, "but you're chirping out the words. I don't think you open your mouth wide enough."

Chirping? If only she knew.

"Tell you what," Penny continued, "if you help me with the dance moves, I'll help you with a few vocal basics."

"Am I really that bad?"

"Not bad. Just a little tweety."

93

Great. Another bird reference. "All right. Let's team-tackle this thing."

My throat was dry, my legs were achy, and I still had a gob of homework to do—nonetheless, focusing on something other than my worries had been a good diversion. The Christmas blizzard still weighed on me heavily and continued to be a taboo topic between Jack and me. Pile onto that my fears for Hulda, and no wonder I welcomed the distraction.

CHAPTER FOURTEEN

I worked at the store Saturday morning. Penny and I sang and danced that afternoon till we got the giggles and snorts so bad that I accused her of enlarged adenoids and she claimed I peeped. We were both right, which only made us laugh more. I spent my Saturday night at the movies with Penny and Tina and our noses in a big tub of buttery popcorn, which was cool, but still it wasn't like that heady rush I got just sharing air with Jack. We had last checked in with each other around noon. He was at the lab and expected to be there for a while. "Don't count on me" was his advice for the evening's plans.

Sunday morning, I got my first look at my dad's new digs in Walden.

"I like it," I said, trailing my hand across the sleek gray kitchen countertop.

"It's temporary," he said, "but at least it's recently remodeled."

As a college town with more in the way of shops and restaurants, Walden was a better fit for my dad than Norse Falls.

"So where are we having brunch?" I asked.

"Wherever you and Brigid want to go."

"Brigid?"

"I invited her. She'll be here any minute."

"Why didn't you ask me?"

"Ask you what?"

"If I wanted her to join us."

"Why wouldn't you?"

"What are you guys — like dating?"

"Hon, you're overreacting. It's just breakfast."

Uh-huh. And once upon a time my parents had sat me down *just to chat.*

The doorbell rang. My dad ran for it like a birthday boy for a tower of gifts. *Just breakfast — my foot.*

Brigid walked in looking even more fetching than she had six days ago. She wore welded-on jeans, heeled boots, and a short fur: brown and spotted this time and still incredibly real-looking. Wouldn't environmental types be into the whole PC gamut: Save the Whales, Go Vegan, PETA Forever?

"Sorry I'm late," she said, handing her coat to my dad like he was some kind of manservant. "We worked into the wee hours last night." She turned to me. "How's Jack feeling this morning?"

Something about her having last contact had me breathing through my nose and had my right foot itching to do a bull-like scrape at the ground. "Fine," I replied, knowing it would take more than hard work to get the better of him.

"Who's hungry?" my dad asked. "And where should we go?"

"I hear the Pantree is very good," Brigid said.

"Green Eggs is better," I chimed in.

We stared each other down.

"I'm getting the C.A.T. in the Hat omelet," I said, folding my menu.

"It's not really cat, is it?" my dad said with a grimace.

"Cheddar, avocado, and tomato," I replied.

"Sounds delicious," Brigid said.

I glanced down quickly at her coat, wondering *Which one?*

The restaurant was packed, and the waitress took her time getting to us. I don't like bad service any more than the next guy, or gal, or giant Greenlander, but I felt a little sorry for the frazzled girl. Brigid, obviously, did not. She clapped her hands like some sort of boarding-school tyrant and called out, "Waitress!"

The harried server appeared, and we ordered. While waiting for our meals, we managed to speak, but talk about nothing. Our food was delivered. I noticed, swallowing a smile, that Brigid was served last, her plate dumped down with a clatter.

"*Bon appétit,*" my dad said, shaking a big glug of ketchup onto his scrambled eggs.

Brigid scrunched her nose and turned away, her shoulders betraying her disgust with a small tremor. "Ketchup on eggs?"

"Absolutely," my dad said. "Why? You got something against ketchup?"

"It's just so very . . ."

"So very what?" my dad asked.

"Red . . ."

I looked up at her over my forkful of omelet.

". . . looks awful against yellow," she continued.

Weird, but I got a strange vibe and couldn't help feeling that last bit was an afterthought.

I asked my dad to pass the ketchup. I'd have asked for the mustard, too, had there been any.

"So how did you and Penny do yesterday? Ready for those tryouts?"

I wished I hadn't told him, and not because he said it with a little bit of a mocking tone.

"What tryouts?" Brigid asked.

That was why.

"Kat and her friend Penny are auditioning for the school musical."

"How wonderful," Brigid said, stumbling over the *w* and giving it a pronounced *v* quality. "Which musical?"

Vot do you care?, I wanted to say. I didn't. I played nice. *"The Snow Queen."*

"As a musical?"

Lord forgive me, but I almost laughed out loud. *Moosical.* It was funny—in my current mood it was, anyway.

"I don't know where they got the script or the score," I said. "I'm pretty sure it hasn't made it to Broadway yet."

"Sounds very interesting. I have stage experience, you know."

"Really?" my dad said. "Where?"

"All over," Brigid said. "London, Stockholm, Copenhagen."

Just my luck. Brunch with the singing scientist. I scooped a big forkful of omelet into my mouth. At least I had Jack to look forward to later.

Sunday afternoon; finally, time with Jack. A study date. Not exactly my idea of rip-roaring fun, but it was at least something I knew he'd agree to.

I placed a glass of milk on the table in front of him and draped my arms over his shoulders. "Whatcha workin' on?"

Besides the scratch of his pencil, the house was as quiet as a morgue. My mom, who'd spent all yesterday and all morning in bed with back pain, was finally up and out shopping with Stanley for baby things.

Jack pointed to a chart with ascending red peaks. "Shrubs and forests encroaching on the once-barren tundra."

"And that's bad because . . . ?"

"Because it means more heat is absorbed by the vegetation."

"You're really into this stuff, aren't you?"

He reached up, looping his arms behind my neck. "I am. And I'm sorry to be so distracted lately. It's just . . ." He pushed his chair back and turned to face me, holding my hands in his. "I think it's important, for me — more than anyone — to understand climate change and its effect."

"But if your resolution is to —"

"I would. I'd get rid of it in an instant, but until then . . ." He pulled me onto his lap. "I feel somehow that this is important — for us."

Us. One of my favorite words. I slipped my hands around his waist, cuddling into him. "I miss you."

"Nothing to miss. I'm right here," he whispered into my ear.

100

True. In a way. Still, something about his preoccupation with the research project was a pebble in my shoe.

He pulled his head back. "I may as well tell you now."

Uh-oh. "What?"

"I'm stepping down as editor of the paper."

"You're what?" I asked, jumping off his lap.

"It's more hours than I'm willing to spend right now. I'll stay on the staff. I'm even thinking of my own little weather-study column, but editor in chief—it's just too time-consuming. We've all been told to clear our calendars for the next few months."

"Months? Isn't Stanley asking a bit much?"

"Actually, that came from Brigid."

The pebble got bigger.

"She's just a visitor. She can't tell you what to do."

"She's not telling me what to do. I'm asking her what I can do," Jack said, his eyes shining with the kind of glaze that dripped off donuts. "And her temporary status is exactly why it's so important. I need to make the most out of my time with her. She's smart, has been everywhere, and has tons of connections. This is a huge opportunity for me. Plus, she's exciting."

He almost had me, right up until exciting, anyway. Not a good word choice, as far as I was concerned.

"Exciting?"

"Well, yeah. It's really exciting."

"But, before, you said, 'She's exciting.'"

"No, I didn't."

"Yes, you did."

"I think I know what I said. Besides, what's the difference?"

"Night and day. North and south—poles, if that helps?"

"Jeez, Kat, you're putting words in my mouth. I'm excited about the work; that's all."

I wasn't putting words in his mouth; I knew it.

"Fine, let's just drop it and—" I was interrupted by the sound of voices.

My mom and Stanley came into the kitchen. He had his arm around her waist. At first I thought it was just his normal chivalric code of honor, but then I noticed she was eggshell white.

"Are you OK?" I asked.

"Just overdid it a little today," my mom said.

"Maybe you should call your doctor," I said. She really did look ghostly.

I followed behind as Stanley helped my mom into the family room and eased her onto the couch. "Trust me—that was my suggestion an hour ago," he said. "I almost did it myself."

"I have an appointment first thing in the morning," my mom said. "If anything changes before then, I'll call. I really just think I'm tired." She fluffed a pillow behind her and turned to me. "Don't take it personally, but you weren't any easier on me than this one," she said, patting her small melonlike bulge. She even wore the color of a ripe honeydew. It amused me that my pregnant mom still unwittingly favored chartreuse: the aura color Fru Birta saw haloing potential vessels.

The thing I'd take "personally" is a big fat double-wide of blame if anything happened to my mom or the baby during this pregnancy — the pregnancy I'd "personally" brokered for both of them. As if I needed more to worry about.

Back in the kitchen, I found Jack jamming notebooks into his backpack.

"Are you going already?" I asked.

"Sounds like your mom could do with some peace and quiet."

True, but it wasn't like our page turning and pencil tapping would be much of a bother.

"Besides," he said, "last night was such a late one, I'm kind of out of it."

I walked him to the door and said as nice a good-bye as I could muster, but it was my turn to feel out of it.

CHAPTER FIFTEEN

Even without Jack's heads-up from the day before, I'd have known something was stewing the moment Mr. Parks stepped into the room for our lunchtime session. To say he had a hands-off style of managing us was one big whomp of an understatement.

"If I could have everyone's attention."

He got it, all right.

Mr. Parks sat on top of a desk with his feet propped up on the attached seat. "Given a recent opportunity to earn university credit, Jack has decided to step down as editor in chief."

Murmurs of surprise whistled through the room.

"We're not losing him," Mr. Parks said with a fanning of his palms-down hands. "He just won't be in charge anymore."

"Who will?" Pedro asked.

"I imagine—" Mr. Parks began.

"I'd like to apply," Pedro interrupted.

"What?" Penny said, jumping up from her seat. "I'm the assistant editor."

"But I'm a senior," Pedro said. "The editor in chief has always been a senior."

Mr. Parks scratched his stubbly chin, obviously not pleased to miss his lunch or be embroiled in a tug-of-war. "Tell you what," he said. "You two write me up your first Letter from the Editor, and I'll decide based on merit." Mr. Parks slid off the desk. "Sound fair to everyone?"

Penny and Pedro exchanged looks, and both shrugged. The room got library-quiet. Jack stuck his nose back into the stack of articles he had in front of him. I didn't know where to look or what to say; I got busy on idyllic set designs for *The Snow Queen.* Though idyllic was hardly the way I'd have described the scene before me.

After the bell, Penny followed me to my locker.

"Can you believe that?" she asked.

"Crazy," I said.

"Is it just me, or has the guy changed lately?"

I honestly didn't know which "guy" she was talking about.

"Why would he burn me like that?" she asked.

The fact that she took the burn personally tipped the scales toward Pedro.

"And he can forget about me lending him my chem notes for the test tomorrow."

Phew. Definitely Pedro. Penny looked at me as if expecting a reply. I'd only known him a few months, so I didn't have many back issues to reference. Besides, the only safe place in a boy-girl spat was Switzerland: clean air, mountaintop views, and neutral.

"Is that test tomorrow?"

"I'm home," I called, hanging my coat on a hook.

No answer.

I walked through to the kitchen. "Mom?" She wasn't there or in the family room.

Stanley appeared on the steps. "She's upstairs."

"What did the doctor say?"

Stanley leaned his forearms against the kitchen island. "Her blood pressure is up. Her potassium counts are dangerously low. The doctor recommends bed rest for the time being."

"Bed rest?"

"Just for a while."

"Is she awake?" I asked.

"She's awake. I warn you, though. She's working on a to-do list . . . for both of us."

If Stanley could joke about my mom's neat-freakin' ways, it couldn't be all bad — nevertheless, I trudged up the staircase with a bad feeling.

"You're home," my mom said, popping a pretzel Goldfish into her mouth with one hand while jotting notes with the other.

"Bad news, huh?" My mom was not the lounge-around type.

"Nothing we can't handle," she said, ripping a page from a notebook.

"We" had a long list of chores, the first of which was to make her a tuna melt.

CHAPTER SIXTEEN

Three days later, clutching another of my mom's lists, I stood in front of the Walden Inn, a small boutique hotel with banquet facilities. It had a charming curb appeal: snowdrifts nestled against the red brick, leaded-glass bay windows, and a green canopy over the entryway. From the icy sidewalk and the gloom of a wintry dusk, the building seemed a beacon of warmth.

The clerk at the front desk smiled and directed me through glass doors to the sales and catering office. Past the empty reception desk, I could see a woman with her back to me working on a computer.

"Excuse me," I said.

She turned. "Is there something I can help you with?"

"Are you Julia? The catering director, by any chance?"

"That's me."

"I'm Kat Leblanc. You've been helping my mom, Lilja, with her wedding plans."

"Yes. Of course. The Olafsdottir/MacLary wedding."

"My mom's pregnant and on bed rest for a while. She asked me to come by and pick up some samples you have for her."

How tawdry it must sound — wedding plans for my knocked-up-but-ready-for-round-two mother.

"Your mom and I spoke earlier. Come on back." Her smile was so genuine I knew instantly she wasn't the kind to judge.

She led me to her desk. It was an L-shaped cubby with a visitor's chair pushed up against one of the wings of the cubicle.

"Sit down," she said, removing a stack of index folders from the padded seat.

She fiddled her mouse into position and then double-clicked on a file. As I waited for her to pull up my mom's file, my eyes roamed over her desk. A photo of a toothy young boy was front and center. He looked vaguely familiar. She turned and found my eyes upon the image. She lifted the frame and held it to her chest.

"My son, Jacob."

"It's funny, but I feel like I've seen him . . ."

"In the paper probably." Her eyes blinked in rapid succession. "He's the boy who died during the blizzard."

I sat there, my entire body Gorilla-Glued in place. *How could—? Of all people?*

"You don't have to feel awkward," she said. "I want people to ask me about him. To remember him. Even to know him posthumously—as crazy as that sounds."

I didn't think anything was crazy anymore. "He looks happy."

Julia laughed out loud. "The day this picture was taken, he'd been in such a foul mood. I loved him dearly, but he did have a stubborn streak. For a half hour I'd bribed him with toys and candy, but nothing would get him to smile. Finally, I employed the oldest trick in the book. I looked at him and said, 'Whatever you do, Jacob, do *not* smile for the camera.' That little bugger lifted his chin with the biggest, cheesiest grin ever." Julia pulled the photo back and looked at it, nodding her head softly. "I just loved that little contrary side to him."

"What kind of things did he like?" I asked, sensing her pleasure in remembering him.

"Trains. He was just crazy about Thomas the Tank Engine. Ever heard of it?"

"I think so."

She returned the photo back to its position of honor. "Well, he could have told you every one of the engines' names and something about their personality. Thomas was his favorite, but he also got a kick out of S. C. Ruffey, the troublemaker."

"That's really sweet," I said.

"He was," she said without the slightest hint of resentment.

I was moved by her love for Jacob, which was so tangible I could practically see it coil like smoke between us.

A paper rolled off the printer, jogging me from that image.

"Here we go," she said, lifting it from the fold-down tray. She placed it on top of a cardboard box. "This should give your mom a few options: napkin samples, menus, place cards, and some photos of table arrangements that have worked." She held the box out to me. "I hope your mom feels better. Have her call me with any questions."

A few moments later, I found myself, once again, staring up at the radiant building now set against an even darker backdrop. I had very good vibes about the place—even better vibes about Julia. I left with a fizz of hope in my chest and an idea. It was the best I had felt in a long time.

CHAPTER SEVENTEEN

By the time *The Snow Queen* auditions took place, the number of interested students had grown to around forty. The cast required thirty. Twenty-five percent of the kids currently standing in the wings of the stage wouldn't make it. Now that I'd invested practice time into the auditions, I was hoping to make the cut.

"Group three's up," Mr. Higginbottom called out.

I hightailed it onto stage with the four other dancers in my audition group: one of Matthew's band buddies and three sophomore girls. The first dance move was a spin to a slide right followed by two high claps, a spin to a slide left followed by two low claps, three heel-toes to the right and a twisting shimmy to the floor. I hoped that was it, anyway. It's what Penny and I had practiced, and once I got into it, I didn't know what anyone around me was doing.

Penny did well. She wasn't a natural like Monique—who really did know how to pop her trunk—still, Penny didn't stumble or falter in any way. Matthew was the one who surprised me. For someone so tall and with such a slump-shouldered gait, the boy had something. He wasn't necessarily smooth, but somehow the moving parts—the way they snapped and jerked—were mesmerizing.

It took a long time for all eight groups to complete the four dance sequences. Before we moved on to the voice auditions, Ms. Bryant informed us of a fifteen-minute break.

Penny and I sat against a side wall of the auditorium gulping from water bottles.

"Good work," I said, wiping my mouth with my sleeve.

"You were awesome," Penny said. "Monique tapped her toe impatiently every time you were onstage."

"Singing's next," I said with a shake of my head. "This could get ugly."

Voices near the back of the large hall caught my attention. An angled shaft of light illuminated the arrival of an unexpected visitor: Brigid.

What the hell? I couldn't get away from the woman. I

must have made some small squawk. I know my mouth flopped open like a hinged lid.

"Who is that?" Penny asked.

Before I could even reply, Mr. Higginbottom announced over the microphone, "If everyone will take a seat." The house lights came on.

"I'll explain later," I mumbled to Penny, sliding my back up the wall and pushing off with my right foot. We took the two closest seats and I watched as Brigid sauntered down the center aisle of the space. Her short, black, fur-trimmed leather coat showed off her impossibly long legs and tight jeans. Penny's question of "Who is that?" echoed through the room.

When Brigid reached the front row—where Mr. Higginbottom and Ms. Bryant had set up a small workstation complete with table, file boxes, and scattered papers—Mr. Higginbottom awaited her with a glad hand and a big smile on his face. They chatted for a moment, and then he leaned down to the judges' table microphone.

"I have some very exciting news." The guy was panting more than speaking. "Doctor Brigid Fonnkona, a renowned scientist and celebrated vocalist, will participate as a guest judge for audition vocals. We are very, very honored to have her."

Hmmm. A double-very. The guy was squealing like a schoolgirl. I squeezed my eyes closed and cursed the fates.

114

Brigid was directed to the open third seat at the table. Funny I hadn't noticed the vacant chair earlier.

Mr. Higginbottom took the middle seat, next to Brigid. "Doctor Fonnkona, would you like to tell the group a little about yourself?"

"Please, everyone, call me Brigid." It was clear she was no rookie with a microphone. Despite her accent, she both enunciated and projected every word. "I am indeed a scientist here on a research project, but, before that, I spent a few years on tour in Europe with several productions, most notably *Cats.*"

Why was I not surprised? There was something decidedly feline about her. But wasn't that musical ancient? Her age still had me baffled. That first meeting I'd pegged her as fortyish. Though next to Jack she'd seemed like she belonged in high school. Now here, she seemed as thirty-something as Ms. Bryant. *Makeup? The right light? Botox?*

"I hope I can be of some assistance, and good luck to you all," Brigid finished.

"Everyone backstage. Listen for your number to be called," Mr. Higginbottom said to the screech of feedback.

If I hadn't been nervous enough, I now had Brigid's inscrutable face among the judges. *Perfect.*

I stood in the wings with Penny and Matthew watching kids called by some crazy random numerical system. What good were numbers out of order? Currently up was number twenty-three. The way it worked was we each trudged out to a lone microphone in the center of the stage. Once there, to the accompaniment of Mrs. Winkle, the front office secretary, we performed two song snippets: the first stanza of "Killing Me Softly," — Mr. Higginbottom's proclaimed favorite — and the first stanza of the "Happy Village" song from our own production. And this was just to try out for the chorus. If you were going out for a lead, you had to stay for a third portion of the auditions: speaking lines and a full song from the musical. Thankfully, I had spared myself that humiliation, as I was not going out for a lead. Penny, on the other hand, was, and bounced nervously at my side.

"Number seventeen," Mr. Higginbottom called out.

Monique danced to the awaiting microphone, actually danced with fluttery hand movements and a kicky little skip. Born to perform. Mrs. Winkle began the short lead in to the "Killing" song — and that's what Monique did, killed it. Nailed it. Whatever you want to call it. Though the Snow Queen's "Winter Palace" song wouldn't be performed until later, during the third round of the auditions process, if this were any indication, she was head of the pack for the icy lead. I noticed Brigid had nodded approvingly at the conclusion of Monique's solo.

"Next up, number five," Mr. Higginbottom said.

"Wish me luck," Penny said.

I squeezed her hand. "Good luck. But you don't need it."

And she didn't. She did great. Her voice didn't have the maturity of Monique's, but it was clear and pure.

I was the one without luck as the kids were called onstage one by one. I kept checking the number twelve pinned to the front of me. I was the very last of the choral auditions. Because I wasn't nervous enough. I walked out on shaky legs. I could hear them quiver like a bowstring. *Excellent.* Who needs piano accompaniment when your own legs can play banjo?

"Whenever you're ready," Mr. Higginbottom said.

I got through the first song segment all right, nothing great, but at least I didn't spaz out or anything. Then I made the mistake of looking at Brigid. Something lurched in my throat; I tried to mask it with a small coughing fit.

"Are you OK?" Ms. Bryant asked. "Do you need water?"

"I'm fine," I said without conviction.

My voice cracked on the second song. Big-time. The kind of fissures a geologist would chart and measure. It helped a little to focus on Ms. Bryant. She smiled and nodded as I rushed through the last few lines. I was back in the wings next to Penny before I knew it.

"I blew it," I said to her.

"The first one was good," Penny said.

Which only confirmed that the second one sucked.

Mr. Higginbottom thanked those of us who weren't trying out for leads and announced another short break.

Penny and I walked together toward the seats where we had left our things.

"I could stay and watch the solo auditions if you want," I said.

"Are you kidding?" Penny said. "Get out while you can. We're going to be here for a while."

I wrapped a scarf around my neck. "You sure you don't mind?" I lifted my book bag, demonstrating its bulk and heft with a small groan. "I do have two tests tomorrow."

"Not to mention a drawing assignment." Ms. Bryant approached us with arms crossed in mock sternness. It didn't work. The upturned corners of her mouth gave her away.

"It's in here," I said.

"Nice job on the tryouts, girls," she said.

"Penny did great," I started, "but I—"

"For the chorus, you'll probably be all right," Brigid interrupted, coming from behind so suddenly I jumped out of my skin. It felt prickly upon return.

Probably? It was hardly an endorsement.

She turned to Ms. Bryant. "I wanted to introduce

myself personally — we didn't have a chance before things started." Brigid extended the long fingers of her right hand, her nails polished in an opalescent swirl of pastels. "Brigid Fonnkona."

"Sage Bryant," Ms. Bryant said, holding out hers.

Their hands clasped briefly and then released.

"Oh." Ms. Bryant's left hand fluttered to her throat. The color drained momentarily from her face before she recovered, tapping a finger to her lips. "I wonder if I saw you in the London production of *Cats*? It was years ago . . ."

Light glinted off the sheen of Brigid's gloss as she broke into a coy smile. "I may deny it if your memory stretches too far back."

"I couldn't even be sure it was *Cats* I saw in London. It might have been *Phantom*. Or *Lion King*. I've seen so many shows in my travels. But I'm rambling. If you'll excuse me, I have to get something from my room before we start back up."

Brigid turned to Penny. "You show much promise. Are you going for a lead?"

"Yes," Penny said, pinking with the attention.

"Good. Very good," Brigid said, walking off.

"That's Brigid," Penny said.

"Yes," I groaned.

"Jack's Brigid?"

119

I didn't like the sound of that. Not one bit. Not even from Penny, who I knew meant nothing by it. "She's hardly Jack's."

"I didn't mean *that*. It's more that . . . You described her . . . but I didn't believe . . . I mean, she's . . ."

It wasn't like Penny to gum up like that, not with me, anyway. But she didn't like to come right out and trash people, either.

"Amazing," Penny finished.

It was my turn to be dumbstruck. All I could think was, *Et tu, Brute?* Instead, I swallowed that and about three other wisecracks and wished Penny one last good luck. I exited the back-of-the-house doors, barreling into Jack.

"What are you doing?" I dropped my book bag onto the floor of the auditorium lobby and gave him a small shove to the chest. "You scared me to death."

"Sorry. I wanted to surprise you."

"You did."

He picked up my bag with one hand and took my hand with the other. "You did good."

"You were watching?" I groaned.

"Through a crack in the door. I didn't want to make you nervous."

"I blew the singing."

"But you nailed the dancing."

"How long have you had your nose in that crack?"

"A while."

Excellent. Because humiliation's better when shared.

"What's up with Brigid judging?" I asked.

"Can you believe she's a stage star, too?"

"Not really."

"Talk about multitalented."

I'd rather not talk about her, period. And I'd rather you didn't, either.

"And willing to mentor others," he continued.

I sighed, letting him finish his little fanboy outburst.

"I mean, what doesn't she do?" he asked.

That very same question had my tongue curled tight. There were other puzzlers I swished back and forth, too. Who had time for all the studies and travels Brigid boasted of — plus a stage career? And there was another niggling uncertainty that wondered who Jack had come here to see.

He took me by the hand into the charcoal of falling darkness. Detecting my shiver, he pulled me close. I turned back toward the building briefly, sending Penny warm thoughts.

CHAPTER EIGHTEEN

Friday after school, Penny and I stood in front of a large corkboard propped up in the auditorium lobby.

"You made Gerda, the little girl." I clutched Penny's arm and jumped up and down in celebration with her. "That's the second-biggest role."

"And you got the ice fairy dance solo," Penny squealed.

A role I hadn't known existed, never mind auditioned for, but now that I saw my name singled out— I was excited. Monique, no surprise, was the lead: the Snow Queen. Matthew, in an unexpected turn of events, was cast as Kay, the lead male, or boy, in this case.

"This is going to be so much fun," Penny said.

"And work," I said, stretching my mouth with a grimace. "How will you handle this, plus homework, plus editor in chief?"

Penny clasped a hand to her mouth. "Shoot. Mr. Parks is interviewing us."

"When?"

"Now," she said, running off with the briefest of waves.

I took two steps toward the exit when it hit me — the cap. Dang. I was not in the mood for scabies or a meeting. I set my book bag on the ground and began rummaging through it for an emergency head cover. As I stood back up —

"Boo." Jack grabbed my waist from behind.

I swung at him with the fur-lined trapper hat — hard. "Are you stalking me?"

"Absolutely."

"I thought you'd be at Walden."

"Stanley gave us the night off."

I wondered who the "us" was, but didn't ask. "About time."

"Mostly because we're working tomorrow."

I shrugged the hat over my head and exhaled my dissatisfaction.

"At least I can go to the game tonight," he continued.

The varsity basketball game. Darn it. I reached a hand up into my scalp and scratched, one long, dramatic rake.

"Super Stork flies again?" Jack asked.

I nodded.

"Game's at seven. Your meeting isn't until nine, right?"

I shot him a brow-stretcher of a look. "I am not sitting in the bleachers with this thing." I pointed at my head.

"But I finally have a night off."

"And I don't."

"Can't we ever just have a normal night?"

Honestly. He, of all people, wanted to have *that* conversation? "I'm going to Afi's to hide for a while."

"You want some company?"

"Love some."

Walking down Main hand in hand, it occurred to me that it didn't matter where Jack and I were—a basketball game or behind Afi's cash register—I was happy just being with him. We passed by the bookstore; Paulina, Ofelia's sister, came to the door.

"I have that book you were looking for, Kat."

I pulled Jack into the warmth of the store. The floor-to-ceiling books had a slightly musty smell to them, but Paulina, as a counterattack, sold soaps and candles. Today I detected a lemon verbena aroma holding at bay something Twain or possibly Poe. I scratched under my hat. As promised, the condition was finally becoming more tolerable—but, still, a ridiculous way to communicate.

"Here it is," Paulina said, handing me a spine-cracked copy of *The Snow Queen* from a shelf in the kids' section.

"A little young for you, isn't it?" Jack asked.

I'd already read the story off the Internet, but somehow my designs were coming up flat. I was hoping the picture book would inspire me.

"I guess I'm a kid at heart," I said, running my hand along a display of beautiful children's books. My palm came to a halt atop a blue train with a smiling face— *Thomas the Tank Engine.* I lifted it and quickly flipped through the pages. The scenes were of a quaint countryside, a busy train yard, and a round-eyed happy engine named Thomas.

On impulse, I placed it on top of my other book and headed for the register.

"I kinda get the first one, but what's up with the trains?" Jack asked.

"It's for a friend," I said, confusing even me.

"No one I need to be jealous of?"

"What? You think I'm two-timing you with a younger man?"

His eyes narrowed.

"And buying my boy toy gifts in your presence?" I continued.

Jack looked away. He seemed genuinely uncomfortable with the conversation. Seriously though "boy toy" was funny. Lighten up already.

Paulina rang up my purchases.

"I'm enjoying getting to know your sister," I said as I pulled money from my wallet.

"She likes the work," Paulina said.

I raked at a bothersome patch near the nape of my neck. "It's been a big help while Afi's recovering. We were lucky she showed up the very day Afi had decided to hire someone." I stowed the two books in my satchel and pulled it over my head in an across-the-shoulder fashion.

"Craziest thing," Paulina said. "I'd just spoken to her a few days before, and she was talking about changes she wanted to make to her garden. Next thing I knew, she was on my doorstep with all her earthly possessions claiming she'd been called home. Called by whom, I'd like to know. It wasn't me; and there's only me." Paulina shook her head. "She always was a free spirit."

Back out into the cold and bleak afternoon chill, I kept my hands buried deep into my pockets and my head down, fighting more than just a headwind. Words like "earthly" and "spirit" gave me the willies.

Only Afi was at the register when we stamped our snowy boots at the front mat.

"Can you work?" he asked me after I'd untwisted the scarf from my cold cheeks.

"Yeah. Sure. Why don't you go?" I said, carefully omitting use of the word "home" this time.

"I think I will," Afi said. "There's a can of fish chowder and a bottle of beer calling me."

Again with the "calling" reference.

Afi started toward the coatrack and then stopped,

scratching his whiskers. "Of course, the only place to get real chowder is Café Riis."

"Where's that?" Jack asked. I knew better.

"Holmavik, of course," Afi said.

Jack looked at me, confused.

"In Iceland," I mouthed.

Afi shrugged his coat over his spare shoulders and left, muttering something about Viking beer.

"Are you going to take your hat off?" Jack asked.

"No."

He took a swipe at my head, but I was too fast for him. "I want to see it."

"No way." I clamped a hand on my hat.

Jack's cell phone rang, distracting him. I listened to his brief replies: "Hello. Good. Now? I can be there in a half hour."

"Who was that?" I asked.

"Stanley. There's a big announcement he's giving to his staff. He wants me to be there."

"He didn't say what it's about?" I asked.

"No. Some big surprise."

Jack was out the door so quickly I didn't have a chance to ask him about plans for later — or who else would be present at the meeting.

CHAPTER NINETEEN

With a half hour to go until meeting time, I sat at the register removing portions of my scalp with the fingernails of one hand, while flipping through *The Snow Queen* picture book. The first few pages were a prologue, something long and boring. Prologues, if you asked me, were like base coats of nail polish, not worth the time or effort. The book's illustrations, on the other hand, were beautiful: glittery and silk-spun and all kinds of inspiring. I looked up and got spook-bumps to find Ofelia an arm's length away. I'd heard nothing, seen nothing.

"You startled me."

"I'm early," was all she offered by way of reply.

I noticed the soft brown hat was tucked under her arm; her scalp had no angry lesions; and she appeared torment-free, calm even. So why did her presence now, as on that very first day in Afi's store, fluster me?

"How do you do it?" I asked.

"Do what?"

"Avoid the cap."

"Ah." She turned the Thomas book to face her. "My previous council were renegades in this respect."

"Renegades?" The word itself had a nice zip to it. "In what way?"

She placed her palm flat on the book, covering the little engine's body. "What emotion, above all, do you suppose a renegade or maverick — or however you want to term those who effect change — overcomes?"

I was taken aback.

"What is it that grips you the moment the cap appears?" Ofelia asked.

"Pain," I blurted out.

"But is the pain manageable at first?"

"At first, yes. But, by now, I know what's coming." Realization dawned. "Wait, I change my answer to fear," I said in a choky voice.

"Precisely." She removed her hand from the book. "Such a sweet story."

I blinked. She made it seem like she'd absorbed it as we were speaking.

"Do you know the book?"

"I do now."

I got the willies, one stop past goose bumps on the scare train. And I wasn't a wait-and-see kinda gal.

"Ofelia, do you have some kind of psychic ability?"

"Ah. You recognize a kindred spirit."

Kindred? Spirit? We were now pulling into the heebie-jeebies station. And I didn't even want to think about a final destination. What was it with her?

"Are you talking about me?" I asked.

"Of course." Her finger ran the length of the Thomas book's spine, yet it was my own that felt a cold digit trail from nape to waist. "This book is a medium of sorts, right?"

A medium? Hardly. More like a small, as in a small voice that was telling me to run fast and far.

"Kat, your humor is just one of your many gifts."

Kind of a compliment, sure, except that the only funny bits had been in my head. And the last time someone — Hulda, to be precise — had talked to me of gifts, I'd ended up at a portal to another realm.

"You must trust yourself and your instincts," Ofelia continued. "Your youth is significant. Now, more than ever, Fru Hulda would encourage you to explore your gifts."

"Do you know Fru Hulda?"

"No. Shame. Had I arrived just one day earlier."

The timing of Ofelia's arrival — the same day as Hulda's collapse — had me wondering. And how much of a *shame* was it for her to have the unchaperoned ear of the novice interim leader? "Then how do you know what she would want?"

"I may not *know* Fru Hulda, but I know *of* Fru Hulda. Of her open mind. Of her open heart. I feel it is why I was called home."

Sure, she said all the right things, had big Bambi peeps, but there was still something that bugged me. And I even knew she could sense my distrust, but there wasn't anything I could do about that, or about her, for the time being.

The arrival of Grim and then the others put an end to our meeting of the minds. Our Stork powwow got under way a few minutes later.

We began with an update on Hulda, except there really wasn't anything to report. She was still in a faraway "safe place," and there'd been no change to her condition. Our next topic was also a bust; Fru Svana had been unable to discover anything about Dorit's whereabouts.

I moved on to the evening's business. Ofelia, with a soul to deliver, had prompted the meeting.

"I have been contacted by an essence," Ofelia began as was customary. "A girl: vivacious and intelligent. For one so smart, I divine either a thirty-year-old doctor or a thirty-five-year-old teacher as the vessel."

"You divine!" Grim snapped.

"Yes."

"We do not claim to divine," Grim said. "We merely

recommend, based upon those candidates by whom we are contacted through dreams or physical manifestations. To divine is to pretend some sort of influence upon the nomination of vessels."

Ofelia held her hand up in defense. "My apologies, Fru Grimilla. It is simply a misunderstanding of verbiage. My old council tossed about the word divine with quite a different meaning than what you describe."

"It is not a term accepted here," Grim said.

We managed to get through the rest of the meeting without Ofelia committing any more acts of heresy. I couldn't help but be a little relieved that there was finally another rogue Stork to take the heat off me. But exactly why had Ofelia called her previous council renegades? And what was up with her sixth sense? And exactly what had she meant by divine? And why did she rile me so?

By the time our meeting was done, despite the whole time-bending thing, I caught only the last minute of the basketball game. Even though the scoreboard showed us ahead by ten points, I could tell that something was wrong.

"What's up?" I asked, plopping down between Jack and Penny on the bleachers.

Penny narrowed her lids into mere slits, gazing onto the court. I watched as Pedro stole the ball and drove it back for a layup. Pedro, for a little guy, was one tough point guard.

"Did something happen?" I asked, concerned by the boil in Penny's coloring. Even her hair seemed redder.

Tina dumped an arm over Penny's shoulder. "Pedro got editor in chief."

"No way," I said.

"No shit," Penny replied.

Jack pretended to watch the game, but I could tell by the way he bit his lip, he was listening.

"What did Mr. Parks say?" I asked.

"I don't want to talk about it," Penny said. The buzzer sounded, signaling an end to more than the game.

Outdoors and out of the chaos of the mass exodus, Jack and I lingered a few paces behind Penny, Tina, and Matthew. "Did you know about Mr. Parks's decision?"

"Yes," Jack said.

"What?"

"That doesn't mean I had anything to do with it."

"It's bogus. She has more experience."

"But he's a senior. It's his last chance."

"Are you on his side?"

"Since when did an opinion constitute a side?"

"So you are on his side."

"It wasn't an election. There are no sides. Mr. Parks made his decision. Can we just change the subject?"

"Fine," I said. Except it wasn't. We were both irritated.

We walked in silence, the mood just as frosty as the night air.

Jack finally broke the stalemate. "I have news from Stanley's meeting."

With my Stork meeting and Penny's sulk, I'd forgotten that Stanley had called a project meeting. "What is it?"

"I'm going to Greenland."

"You're what?"

"You heard me right." He was suddenly animated, chipper even. "A two-week field study in April. One week will be during Spring Break. The other I'll have to get excused for. Brigid has invited a small team of us to observe the gathering of the quarterly ice-sheet measurements. It's a really big honor. She picked me over some of the graduate students."

I'll bet she did.

"It's gonna be awesome," Jack continued.

"Greenland?"

"And way, way, up there. We're talking Arctic, baby."

Forget chipper. The guy was downright gleeful. And only my snowman would consider the frozen roof of the world as a Spring Break destination. "Congratulations, I guess. You sound really excited."

"Gonna be epic," Jack said.

Who was this guy? And what had he done with Jack? And moreover, *epic* was how Homer's vacation could be described—if he didn't just go ahead and call it the *Odyssey*.

134

We joined our friends at one of the Kountry Kettle's back tables. It didn't feel the same without Jaelle as our waitress, but it was nice to know she was happy working as my dad's office manager. Shortly after we had placed our orders, the basketball team came bursting through the door, celebrations already begun. Coat still on, Pedro came and stood in front of our table.

"How's everyone doing?"

"Good," everyone but Penny replied. She sat staring at the tabletop.

"Not talking to me?" Pedro asked her.

"We can talk," Penny said.

"How about outside?" Pedro replied.

Penny drew her coat over shoulders and followed Pedro out the door. About ten minutes later, she returned, while he joined the team at a table up front.

"Well, that's done," Penny said with a slight catch in her voice.

"What's done?" I asked.

"We broke up."

"You what?"

"For the record, he broke up with me. Said I was being a bitch about the editor thing. That if I couldn't be happy for him, we weren't meant to be." Penny, who had managed to keep it together until then, burst into tears.

Tina and I spent the next half hour in the bathroom with Penny, returning to cold food and the eyes-down faces of Jack and Matthew. When I dropped Penny off that night, she told me not to worry about her. She'd been seeing a jerky side to Pedro since New Year's. As much as I wanted to think that the split was mutual, for the best, I couldn't help notice the droop in Penny's shoulders as she trudged up her front steps.

CHAPTER TWENTY

Monday evening, I stood in front of the Walden Inn clutching the box of sample wedding odds and ends. It had become clear, over these last two weeks of January, that my mom was not going to bounce through this pregnancy, never mind down the aisle on Valentine's Day. Bed rest, I came to learn, meant that someone else had to do the meals, dishes, laundry, and shopping. Stanley tried to pitch in, but he was so overworked with his research that it looked like he was the one suffering from preeclampsia. The big surprise was my dad helping out when and where he could, driving my mom to some of her doctor's appointments, and even occasionally shoveling out our driveway so I could get to school, work, or run my mom's bullet-pointed errands. The woman was nothing if not calculating—a true mathematician. On top of all this, I had rehearsals three nights a week. The physical demands of the dancing were a welcome diversion to everything else that was going on, but still I felt a little guilty for having a life. At least my mom's odd combination of Pollyanna Does Polynomials resulted in her absolute confidence that she and the baby would be fine. She, therefore, insisted that the rest of us carry on and be go-getters to her stay-putter.

I gave a half-cocked salute to the overly friendly front-desk clerk, who smiled and waved like we were long-losts. I wasn't in the best of moods, as a crush of obligations was balanced on my head like some primitive earthen water jug—we're talking both heavy and slosh-prone. Design projects for *The Snow Queen* production had been turned in that day, and all weekend, Penny and I had drawn until our fingers cramped—gnarled for life a real possibility. I felt good about the costumes, but the set designs had me nervous. Particularly as even glass-so-full-gonna-spill Penny had deemed them "not our best work." Because of the design project, editor in chief Pedro had extended the deadline for my column and Penny's article until tomorrow, but that only meant I had a night of writing ahead of me. The breakup between Penny and Pedro was still raw and made our lunchtime journalism club more awkward than Diversity Day at Dunder Mifflin.

138

Lately, it seemed everyone and everything in my life was cause for worry. Health concerns for my mom and Hulda. Afi so homesick for Iceland that he was symptomatic: fatigued, achy, red-eyed, and sniffly, which only meant that the mysterious Ofelia was a full-time rather than part-time lurker. And Brigid was still slinking around, writhing her way into every corner of my life and charming the Diesels off my dad, the too-short Haggars off Stanley, and the Levi's off Jack. Jack: another raw edge. We were both so busy that, lately, our relationship had been boiled down to text messages. I was really beginning to hate that smiley-face icon.

With all this bearing down on me, I pushed through the doors to the catering office. Julia smiled up at me.

"Kat," she said, "your mom e-mailed me you were on your way. It's such a shame they've had to postpone. How's she doing?"

"OK." I set the box on her desk. "Bored, more than anything else."

"And a summer wedding will be beautiful. We can have the ceremony in the gardens."

"That sounds pretty." I was reminded of how the essence of my half sister had been revealed to me via a dream sequence as a shy, red-haired lover of nature. She would like an outdoor ceremony.

"And it's something for everyone to look forward

to during these next few months," Julia said with unreserved cheer.

I felt instantly shamed. Julia had — because of me — recently buried her only child, yet I was the one Eeyoring over every aspect of life while she reminded me how lovely the Hundred Acre Wood would be come summer. Gads, did I never learn?

"I'll try to remember that," I said.

"And we'll make it very special. Twinkle lights and fireflies outshined only by the bride."

"Fireflies. Jacob would have liked that." I had no idea where the comment came from. Even I thought it was random. "What little boy wouldn't, right?" I asked, trying to cover for my blunder.

Julia put her hand to her throat. "He just loved them. That's probably why I even thought of them. He was fascinated by them. Called them sparkler bugs."

"How cute."

Julia's face flushed pink. At first I thought I'd embarrassed her or made her sad, but then I somehow knew she was happy to remember him, to share bits of who he was with me, with anyone.

"So if Thomas the Tank Engine had needed the help of fireflies to get him out of a dark tunnel . . ." I said with a small lift to my shoulders.

"Oh. Now. Jacob would have thought such a story had been written just for him."

I pulled my gloves from my pocket. "Thanks again for all your help. We'll keep in touch."

"Please do," Julia said.

And I intended to. I finally had a plan, even.

That night—after making pasta for my mom and me, writing my column, and running a load of towels—I took out *Thomas*. A part of me had felt silly just buying the book, never mind paging through it, but to read it out loud? The other part, one I was trying to develop, felt determined. I cleared my throat and began. "*Thomas the Tank Engine: The Complete Collection* by the Rev. W. Awdry. Thomas was a tank engine who lived at a Big Station. He had six small wheels, a short stumpy funnel, a short stumpy boiler, and a short stumpy dome. He was a fussy little engine. . . ."

CHAPTER TWENTY-ONE

"From the top," Ms. Bryant said, emphasizing her displeasure by punching her fists down on her chai-colored pencil skirt.

The dance chorus was rehearsing the ice-fairy number. It was the point in the story where Penny—as Gerda in her quest to find her playmate Kay—was brought to me, said ice fairy. My fey little forest companions lead Gerda to my tinseled cottage—another team's set designs—where I warn her of, and provision her for, the perils ahead, all the while dancing my little fairy tail off. All Penny had to do was look lost and frightened, in this scene, anyway.

It was suddenly my turn to feel chilled when I sensed someone watching me. From the wings, Brigid's level-straight form emerged. I still was yet to warm to the celebrated stranger.

Ms. Bryant looked at her watch. "Let's wrap here for the day."

"Did I miss it?" I was surprised to see my dad hurrying in behind Brigid.

"We just finished," I said, relief running down my neck and even collecting in the cups of my sports bra. I wiped my brow with my forearm.

"What a shame," Brigid said. "Your father wanted to see you dance."

"Mr. Higginbottom would prefer we keep the rehearsals closed," Ms. Bryant said, walking over, her head angling to Brigid.

Clever, the way she made Higginbottom the heavy. Sure, he was the strict director type while she was his good-cop assistant; still, it was a way of confronting Brigid.

"But Mr. Higginbottom would surely make an exception for Kat's father," Brigid replied.

"Dad, really." I stepped in between the two women. It was comforting to think that there was possibly another person in the county who wasn't fawning over Brigid. "You'd just make me nervous. Can't you wait until opening night like everyone else?"

"If I have to," he said with a pout.

"Is Mr. Higginbottom in the choir room?" Brigid asked Ms. Bryant.

"Yes. He's working with Matthew on his songs."

"I'll be back," Brigid said to my dad in her best—though likely unintended—Terminator impression. "I have some music for him."

After the chill of Brigid's displaced air had settled, my dad extended his hand to Ms. Bryant. "Greg Leblanc, Kat's dad. Pleased to meet you."

"Sage Bryant," she said, shaking his hand. "Kat's design teacher."

"Hmmm." My dad stroked his chin. "Sage. An anagram of ages."

"I beg your pardon?" Ms. Bryant said.

My dad loved word scrambles, particularly those involving names. Penny still liked to talk about how he'd reworked Penelopa into *one apple* in mere seconds. Tina hadn't been quite as tickled with her Kerstina morphing into *a stinker.* She had been a good sport, though, and he eventually had her laughing at his weird skill. *Ages,* though; it reminded me of something Penny had reported about Ms. Bryant in her teacher profile article last fall.

"Is it true, Ms. Bryant, that you can guess anyone's age within a year?"

"I do seem to have an unusual ability in that area."

"Then how old do you think Brigid is?" I blurted out in a rush, my big mouth leaving my social graces at the starting blocks.

Ms. Bryant tapped her chin with her index finger.

"Well, now," she began. "I'm not sure . . ." She hesitated, her eyes fluttering up and down nervously.

"Where are your manners, Kat?" my dad asked. "Brigid may not appreciate this game."

"Sorry," I said, but thinking *Dang it all.*

"Though I'd like to play," my dad said with a cheeky glint in his eye. "How about me? How old am I?"

Ms. Bryant studied my dad while biting her bottom lip with her top teeth — very nice, very white teeth that they were.

"Thirty-eight. I'm sure of it. Though I bet you often get taken for younger. Partly because you're such a lover of games."

"Yes. Yes. And yes," my dad said. "Very impressive, but how did you know about the games?"

"The anagrams, of course. I guess we all have our quirky little talents," Ms. Bryant said.

Brigid returned from the choir room, looking as indefinable as ever. She and my dad walked me to my car, but I was lost in my own thoughts. I wondered about Sage Bryant's curious talent and even the way her very name was an anagram of it. I also wondered at her pegging my dad so accurately as a game player. And more than anything, I wondered just what kind of a game Brigid was up to here in Norse Falls.

CHAPTER TWENTY-TWO

Stanley insisted on throwing a small Valentine's party in honor of their postponed wedding date. He cooked live lobsters, my mom's request, in a pot so big that on stilts it'd make a decent water tower. There were only five of us: my mom, Stanley, Afi, Jack, and me, but it was nice to have a little diversion from the winter blahs.

"Everything was delicious," my mom said, placing her napkin to the side of the plate. "Thank you."

"And you're feeling all right?" Stanley asked. Though my mom had assured him, repeatedly, that her doctor encouraged an hour or two of low-key, around-the-house movement, he was still a nervous ninny.

"I'm good for a little while longer," my mom replied. "Besides, we haven't had the dessert yet. Kat, would you bring the cake over?"

The cake was carrot with cream cheese frosting and white chocolate shavings. Stanley had a sweet tooth, something I'd come to appreciate, given my mom's pregnancy-related salt cravings. I placed the cake in the center of the table and sliced into it with a large knife. Afi got the first piece, and then my mom.

"You haven't updated us on your trip," my mom said to Stanley.

I handed out plates.

"I didn't realize what a trek it would be," Stanley said.

"We have to fly into Iceland," Jack said. "From their international airport we'll transfer to a regional airport in Reykjavik, where we'll take a flight to Akurcyri, and from there a charter flight to Greenland."

"Into Akureyri?" Afi asked.

"Yep," Jack said, excitement lacing through his voice. I hadn't heard him this jazzed in weeks. "We'll arrive in Daneborg, Greenland, and from there we'll travel to the Klarksberg Research Station." Jack paused and glanced around the table. "By dogsled."

"Dogsled!" I said.

"Into Akureyri?" Afi repeated, clearly missing the connecting flight our conversation had taken. "That's not far from my hometown."

"Stanley, you didn't tell me anything about dogsleds," my mom said. "This sounds dangerous."

If not dangerous, at least archaic. And if the Ice Road Truckers could haul those abominable monster trucks over a frozen tundra, then why wasn't there some sort of bus service, or snow mobiles? Or how about that *Polar Express*?

"No. Not dangerous at all," Stanley said. "We'll be part of a large team, and escorted by members of an elite patrol."

"Brigid does it every year," Jack said. "She has assured us it's just a single day's journey. She herself has done far more intensive treks, clear north to the Greenland Sea."

My chin jutted forward at the mention of Brigid, particularly as it was yet another of her many fantastic — or was it fantastical? — life experiences. Plus, Jack had that all-too-familiar moony look, the one that, conversely, launched me into a sour mood.

"When do I leave for Akureyri?" Afi asked.

"Afi." I put my fork down. "Jack and Stanley are going to Greenland. They're only flying through Iceland."

"But when?" Afi asked.

"We leave at the end of March," Stanley said.

"The timing is perfect," Afi said.

"Perfect for what, Dad?" my mom asked, her voice thin with concern.

"For the festival, the Dance of the Selkies. Takes

148

place in Hafmeyjafjörður, my hometown, on April first every year."

"They won't have time for sightseeing," my mom said. "They're going on a research mission."

"Who said anything about bringing them?"

"I don't understand." My mom pushed her dessert plate away from her. "Who are we talking about?"

"Me, of course," Afi said.

"Dad, you're not going to Iceland," my mom said, as if this were the part of his announcement that was odd.

"Afi, did you say Dance of the Selkies?" I asked.

"Yes, I did."

"Selkies?" I repeated.

"Yep."

"Aren't those . . . ?"

"Magical creatures who once a year discard their seal pelts and take human form to dance by a silver moon."

"So, it's an old folklore the town celebrates?" asked the human Stork. As much as I had a new appreciation for fairy tales and the weird and wacky—discarding their seal skins and dancing? You didn't see me sprouting feathers and putting on an air show. Besides, it seemed like the sort of thing a mythical creature wouldn't want to publicize, never mind preschedule. I'd come to understand the advantage secrecy had over exposure to some of life's more mystical aspects.

"You must have some wonderful memories of those celebrations," my mom said, her face looking pale.

"What times we had," Afi said. "Feasts, and parades, and a dance in the festival hall." He pushed his chair back with a loud scrape. "I'm booking my flight in the morning." With that, he pulled his nubby old lopi sweater over his head, said his good nights, and headed out to his car with more giddyup in his gait than I'd seen in weeks.

Stanley assisted my mom up the stairs and back to bed, or as I had come to call it, command central. Jack helped me with the dishes.

"You think your *afi* is serious?" he asked, gingerly lifting a lobster shell by its tail and dropping it into the garbage.

"Nah. He probably just got excited by all your travel talk." Which reminded me. "And by the way, dogsleds? Doesn't that sound a little primitive? Not to mention bumpy."

"Where we're going is remote. That early in the spring and that far north, snow is a certainty. Sleds really are the best way to travel. Plus, what an experience. I'll be above the Arctic Circle. What an opportunity. For me. For my—"

"Your what?" Even though it hadn't come up again, I hadn't forgotten his New Year's resolution.

"My particular skill set."

"What about it?"

150

"To understand it better. To make proper use of it, or —"

"Or what?" I dropped a plate into the dishwasher. "Jack, please tell me you're going for research. Research only."

I heard Stanley's heavy steps coming down the stairs.

"Of course," Jack said, hunching his shoulders in innocence.

A few minutes later, he and Stanley headed into the thick chill of the February night, leaving me with the rest of the dishes and a lot of questions.

Later, after finishing an English assignment, I pulled out the Thomas book, as I had for two weeks straight. It was a gesture, a get-to-know-you period. It wasn't my taste in literature, wouldn't have been even when I was five. I myself had always gone for the gowned princess stories. And don't even get me started on what an impression the scene from Cinderella where the mice and birds embellish her old dress with beads and a sash had on me. Even back then I was a sucker for the swish of a skirt and a puffed sleeve. Thomas and his train-yard pranks were silly and a little repetitive, but I tried really hard not to let my voice reflect this boredom. I read two long stories that night, my voice high and clear, smiling even as I closed the book with an affected sigh. Nothing. I made a clicking sound with my tongue, wondering why the book wasn't working. I looked around my room. I loved my room. Dusty-pink walls, a vintage purple duvet, an ivory-painted, scrolled woodwork vanity, a dress form with a half-finished cape and matching skirt, and a huge cork-board with design ideas pinned every which way. It was my space and reflected my own personal style. But maybe that was the problem.

CHAPTER TWENTY-THREE

The next day, at the store, I found Afi leaning over Ofelia's shoulder and studying the screen of her laptop. Ofelia had a laptop? And Afi — a guy who still used an old-fashioned register and didn't even have cable, never mind Internet — was looking on?

"Hey, guys. What's up?" I asked.

"Airfares," Afi said. "Can you believe eleven hundred dollars to fly to Iceland?"

Afi was checking out airfares? "Yowza," I said.

"If it's the best you can do," he said with a shrug. "You said you needed my credit card."

Whoa, there. "Wait. What? Does Mom know about this?"

"Why should she? She's in no condition to fly," Afi said.

"Not to go with you. To say it's OK. You know how she likes to give her stamp of approval." *Uh-oh.* I just told a soon-to-be seventy-year-old man that he needed a permission slip—from his daughter. Afi was a sweet old guy, but nobody likes to be treated like a kindergartner, not even kindergartners.

"I don't need anyone's approval," Afi said.

"But when? For how long? And what about the store?" I asked.

"Ofelia here will cover for me. I fly out on March thirtieth."

"Why don't I call Mom real quick?" I said, thinking fast. "She knows all the best websites for cheap tickets."

Ofelia lowered the screen to her computer. "There're quite a few open seats on this flight. No harm trying to find a better deal."

As much as Ofelia still wasn't my favorite, I was grateful she was playing along. I snapped open my cell phone and went into the storage room to give my mom an earful of what was happening here. My mom sounded worried about Afi. She, like me, had assumed his homesickness was due to his upcoming seven-oh celebration. She sighed and said that she had enough to worry about without her aging father roaming around Iceland on his own, particularly as he seemed frail and sickly since the blizzard. The

154

blizzard. Ugh. The catalyst for so much that was happening right now.

"So what do you want me to do?" I asked my mom.

"Let me speak to him," she said. "Maybe I can talk him into waiting until summer, until after the baby's born."

I walked to the front of the store and handed the phone to Afi. I had been dying for my daily fix, a Caramel Macchiato, ever since Physics had been a lecture so boring it could put the theory of perpetual motion to rest. I bundled up and popped over to Starbucks.

When I got back, Afi and Ofelia were once again leaning over her laptop.

"Your mom says to call her," Afi said, handing me back my cell phone. "And she wonders if your passport is still valid."

"My passport? What do I need my passport for?"

"For spring break," Afi said. "For Iceland."

Somehow those two phrases were about as complementary as Nike and taffeta. My mind quickly connected the dots of what had possibly transpired, conspired even, in my absence. I quickly punched in the speed dial to command central.

"Hello?"

"Mom," I said, "what's going on?"

She exhaled in a slurry release of air. "Has Afi mentioned the trip?"

"Yeah. Kind of. But you're not serious."

"Maybe it's a good idea."

"Spring break in Iceland is a good idea?"

"You don't have other plans."

True. Technically. I did, however, plan to rest and relax in celebration that, by then, *The Snow Queen* production, and the ice fairy dance solo, in particular, would be history. And I hardly thought that flying to a climate where spring arrived at the beginning of July and hanging with a bunch of seal-cloaked, moonlight-dancing Icelanders sounded better than the plans I didn't currently have.

"Shouldn't I have some say in this?" I asked.

"Of course," my mom said. "I'm asking you to accompany your grandfather on a short trip. One week. I'd feel a lot better about it if I knew he had someone with him. To keep an eye on him."

She did have a point. Even I got nervous every time he headed out the front door for the short walk home, noticing more than once he set out in the wrong direction.

"I guess it's cool," I said. "To see where Afi and Amma were from. But I still think it'd make a better summer trip."

"I know, but for some reason it's important for him to be in Iceland for the festival."

After a long pause, I said, "It's valid."

"What is?"

"My passport."

Next, I called Jack to let him know of my own travel

plans. Though it looked like he'd already be safely installed in Greenland by the time I routed through Keflavik, Iceland's international airport, it was still kind of neat to think our itineraries were so similar. He was surprised and excited and then claimed to be a little jealous of my trip.

"You're jealous?" It definitely needed clarification.

"Don't get me wrong," he said. "I'm stoked about the research opportunity, but I'll be logging numbers into charts and graphs, and staying in military-style barracks, while you're at a festival, sightseeing, eating at restaurants, and enjoying the comforts of home."

"When you put it that way."

"And Brigid has warned us the food is awful."

It was my turn to feel jealous. Even the most casual of Brigid mentions made my toenails shrivel.

"Yeah, well, they pickle or smoke their fish, and hang their meat in Iceland," I said. "And you don't want to know what *slátur* is. Or *hákarl*."

"I've heard of both of them. But the Inuits in Greenland still eat seal blubber."

"It's a draw," I said. "Am I gonna see you later?"

"I'm going to try."

Which I knew meant no promises. One of my favorite Jackisms had always been his rock-solid commitment to things, but that had been when I was one of those things. Lately, all work and no play was making Jack a dull boy, and me impatient. I was in the mood to tell him so, but he hung up on me, claiming to have numbers coming in via fax.

As Ofelia and Afi had the store well in hand, especially given we were the only three in the place, I grabbed my backpack and warmest parka and headed out the back door.

I hardly ever used the back door. It was mostly for deliveries. And behind our side of Main Street lay the abandoned railroad tracks, now overgrown and pulled up in sections and used mostly by joggers and dog walkers. I was neither, but I picked my way along the patchy snow-covered rails. Something had briefly flashed through my mind when I had treated Afi like a kid. *Not even a kindergartner likes to be treated like one.*

A few minutes later, I found the Paul-Bunyan-size log I was looking for. It lay on its side like a fallen giant, three feet thick and worn smooth as marble. It ran along the tracks with the forest, its likely home, at its back and had presumably watched the busy trains bustle past, *clickety-clack,* for many, many decades. I laughed at myself. I was beginning to think like a *Thomas* character. Not too many girls in those books, and the few there were had subordinate roles: passenger coaches pushed and pulled by the bossy engines.

I took a seat on the log and stretched my legs out in front of me. It was very cold. I shivered, though my jacket was designed for modern-day explorers and adventurers. I pulled from my backpack the *Thomas* book and held it up as a teacher would to her class. I then set it on my lap, opening to a random page.

"You choose this time," I said out loud, my breath curling like a ghostly ringlet in the chill air.

Nothing. So what was I doing wrong? The right bait. No more pink walls. Asking him to pick. And then it hit me. Child Psych 101. I was *asking* him to pick. Julia had described him as headstrong, even contrary at times.

"Whatever you do," I said, "do *not* pick a story from this book."

I sat back, bracing myself with arms fully extended to both sides. Even through my fleece-lined mittens, the trunk of the old tree nipped at me with its icy bite. I wasn't sure how long I would last in this weather. Even Mother Goose had to have flown south for the winter. Then a wind blew from the east, rifling the pages of the book, the last two turning almost languidly until they settled on a story.

A huff was trapped in my throat. I didn't dare move. I looked down to find the pages flipped to the very back of the thick book and a story entitled "Ghost Train." *Of course,* I thought, mentally smacking my forehead. Something scary.

I grasped the edges of the hardcover and began:

"'And every year on the date of the accident, it runs again, plunging into the gap, shrieking like a lost soul.' 'Percy, what are you talking about?' 'The Ghost Train. Driver saw it last night.'"

When the story came to an end, I whispered, "Nice choice, Jacob," and closed the book.

CHAPTER TWENTY-FOUR

"Get in," I said, pulling alongside a startled Jack, just feet away from the spot in the school parking lot where he'd once pulled the same line on me.

"What?"

"Get in."

"I can't. I'm on my way to Walden." He braced himself against my car door.

This was not going according to plan. He was supposed to think my switch-up of last fall's kidnapping cute and clever and covered in awesome sauce.

"Get. In." I said.

He sighed, jogged around to the passenger side, and lowered himself into the seat. I took off before he could even buckle up, another turning-of-the-tables from last year.

"Where are we going? I need to call in if I'll be late." He pulled out his phone and began punching keys.

I grabbed his phone, swerving to the left with the maneuver. He tried to get it back; the tussle resulted in me sitting on it and us nearly having a head-on with a big black SUV.

"Give me my phone."

"No." I squirmed in my seat, possibly butt-dialing Bangkok. He crossed his arms and stared straight ahead but didn't dare go after the phone. He didn't like my driving under the best of circumstances.

We drove in silence for a long time. At least twice, I almost pulled a U-ie, aborting the mission, but something in my recent mindset—an overall resolve to be more proactive in everything—won out.

When we turned down the snow-banked lane to Elkhorn Lake, he finally spoke to me. "So, it's a full reenactment?"

"Something like that."

"Why?"

I pulled into a parking spot overlooking the fateful scene of our skating accident and near drowning. It was a bitter cold day. The wind skittered ripples of snow across the iron-banded surface of the lake. No skaters had braved today's conditions; we had the place to ourselves.

162

"Because"—the words *I'm afraid* edged dangerously close to forming—"I miss you. Can we walk?"

Though the wind bore down from above, making quick work of my warmest jacket as we followed the path down to the lake, another force was lifting everything from the fringe of my scarf to the wisps of my hair to my spirits. I could tell that the place was having a similar effect on Jack. His pace slowed, the trudge of his step was audibly lighter, and when he took my gloved hand, I could feel the warmth of his touch through two layers of wool.

At the lake's edge, I crumpled into him. Without uttering a word, we kissed urgently and greedily, a silent exchange of apologies and promises.

"Now I get the need for a field trip," he said, tangling my hair in his roaming fingers.

"Field trip? No way. This was an abduction. Never forget the lengths I'll go to."

"As if I could forget anything about you." With his hands on my shoulders, he spun me half a turn. From behind, he wrapped his arms around me. We then gazed out onto the lake for many moments.

"OK," I said. "I got what I came for, but now I'm freezing. Race ya!" I was fueled by the prospect of blasting the heater; he, by some macho can't-fail-gene—another of the Y-chromosome traits. He beat me; no surprise there. But I had the keys and dangled them teasingly. I found his cell phone on the driver's seat and tossed it to him before sliding in.

He waited until we were on the road, but punched in what appeared to be a speed dial.

"It's Jack. I know. . . . I'm sorry. . . . I'm not feeling well, but I should have called."

I barely recognized the groveler before me. He was even tipping his head forward in some sort of subconscious genuflect. As if Stanley wouldn't understand the need for a little personal time.

On an impulse — a naughty one — I leaned over and said, "Just tell Stanley the truth: that, for once, I won."

Jack's face went white. He half-choked into the phone, "It won't happen again," after which he snapped the phone shut, turned to me, and glared.

"What?" I said. "Like Stanley doesn't come running every time my mom snaps her fingers."

"Except that wasn't Stanley."

I gripped the steering wheel, not wanting to hear the rest.

"That was Brigid," Jack continued, "and, for the record, she's pissed."

The rest of the drive home was awkward. Jack kept scratching his right index finger against his thumb as he stared out the passenger window, his mood so foul he dirtied the glass. A part of me was livid that it had been Brigid's number Jack had on speed dial. Another part felt

bad that I'd put him in the position of lying to an authority figure. But the lion's share felt entirely justified. We
had needed to shut out the rest of the world and reaffirm
our connection. *Proactive* was the word I murmured all
the way home.

CHAPTER TWENTY-FIVE

Later that night, still a little let down by how my afternoon with Jack had ended, I crawled into bed with a bowl of popcorn, a big bag of Skittles, and two juice boxes. One advantage of having a bedridden mother was the let-go effect on me and the house in general. There were no less than three Coke bottles on my vanity; a pizza box lay on the floor next to my bed; and the six outfits I'd tried on for school that morning were scattered everywhere. I didn't think my guest would care. Over the past week, I'd felt Jacob's presence growing stronger. Sometimes it would be the faintest hint of a child's voice splashing with the milk over my morning Cocoa Pebbles. Or the way I'd swear it was a chubby finger turning my chin so as not to miss a big truck or a fast car. And as much as I knew I'd somehow summoned him, I didn't know how to proceed. What I wouldn't have given for advice. Hulda's would have been ideal. The very depressing news on that front was "no change in her condition." Frustrating, but better than a turn for the worse, I supposed.

I stuffed a handful of popcorn into my mouth, powered on the TV, and scrolled through channels until I got to the Cartoon Network. Ofelia had crossed my mind as a confidante, but the way she continued to ingratiate herself with my family still had me uncomfortable. Not only was she Afi's go-to gal, but it had furthermore been decided that she'd stay with my mom while Afi and I were in Iceland. She'd even offered, so my mom said. The whole thing smelled as fishy to me as the oil-packed tuna my mom craved. Given how she'd wheedled her way into our family's business, and now even my mom's trust, I was not about to confide in her. And I ignored every esoteric cock of her head or googly-eyed look she gave me.

With my teeth, I stripped the cellophane from the juice box's straw and pushed it into the tiny foil-covered hole. Next, I did the same with the other juice and set it on my bedside table. For the briefest of moments, even old Grim had seemed a possibility for guidance. Though the way her disapproving once-overs and rankled jabs undermined my temporary authority at every opportunity, I knew she was out of the question. It was more likely she'd have my Stork wings clipped in some painful and humiliating way for what I was doing.

Just what was I doing? Jeez. I barely knew. And as much as I had a conviction that I was finally putting my gifts to good use, I was on my own. Winging it—ha, ha. With a questioning shrug, I opened the bag of Skittles and spilled a big pile of them next to the juice box on the nightstand. *Who cares about plates or napkins? Not us; right, Jacob?* And if he could overlook the pink and purple in my room, I could overlook a few table manners.

We watched two shows. I was so preoccupied with my own thoughts I don't even remember what was on, but occasionally it'd seem like the bed shook ever so slightly. Jacob laughing at something? Jacob squirming to get to the goodies? Once the credits rolled, I turned off the TV. And so concluded the entertainment portion of our evening.

I sat back against my headboard and concentrated harder than I ever had. Harder even than that algebra final, after which I stood and fell to my knees because my darn legs—both of them—had gone to sleep. *Listen to me, Jacob,* I repeated over and over in my head. I knew, somehow, this wasn't getting the job done. How many adults had tried to get his attention with that line? Probably a few, right? I tried again. *Peep! Peep!* doing my best impersonation of a bossy little engine. My right ear tickled with the lightest of whispers.

Let's play a game. A game where you go for a train ride, Jacob. Thomas will be the engine, of course. And you'll be the passenger. Would you like to do that? If you would and if you're ready, you have to let me know. You have to tell me tonight while I sleep. And, Jacob, you have to tell me the name of the coach you'd like to ride in. I know Thomas usually pulls Annie and Clarabel, but you could pick your own. Do you understand, Jacob? You get to pick the passenger car.

After that, I wasn't sure if I felt sleepy or was in some kind of weird stupor. My lids were so heavy they felt like slabs of concrete pinning me to the pillow, but my arms and legs felt tingly, like carbonated water, not blood, was fizzing through my veins. I may have burped. And somewhere far off I heard the rumble of a train and then a whistle.

CHAPTER TWENTY-SIX

Through the train's half-open window, the sun splashes over my arms and up onto my face. I turn to take in the scenery: baby-blue sky, cotton-puff clouds, and leafy green trees. We take a bend and pass under an old stone bridge, and then the seaside rolls into view. Turquoise waves lap at a pebbled beach. The setting is happy, the hues are vibrant, and the music bright and cheerful. I look down at my lap, my hands folded neatly, one per-fectly peach-colored fist over the other. I lift my right to examine the flawless tone, and I gasp. One thumb and three fingers. Three fat nail-lacking fingers. I turn to the glass of the window finding my reflection easily, but, again, I'm startled. As expected, they're my features: white-blond hair, pale blue eyes, even my new pink top, but all of it, every last detail a cartoon. And I've never felt better, more lively, more invigorated — or more animated. I am, after all, a drawing.

Sunlight dapples over the waves with a sparkle that snaps. I hear the *click* and the *clack* of the happy train that, as if sensing my approval, blows its high whistle.

I stand and look about. No one else is in the passenger coach with me. I walk forward, pulling open the door to the forward car. No one in the next coach, either. I push my way through this empty passenger coach, and then another. At the front of the third, I can see into the engine — the bright blue engine. I see Jacob, his cartoon image anyway, busy at the controls — too busy at his engineering duties to notice me.

The train slows, and a station comes into view. Once the train glides to a screeching, hissing stop, my no-cap knees descend with two easy glides to the spotless platform. From this gleaming, vine-covered depot, I watch as the fussy blue engine pulls away with a *Peep! Peep!* The coaches clatter past. Annie's name painted in script on the side of the first coach, followed by Clarabel. The third coach is painted a sunny yellow, but I'm alarmed to note it has no name painted on its side. I run with stiff legs to keep pace with the train, but it quickly passes me. Then on the back in a loopy cursive, there it is — Julia. Onto the gated back end of the train steps Jacob. He waves as the train pulls into a tunnel and disappears behind a final puff of steam.

CHAPTER TWENTY-SEVEN

Waking following one of my Stork dreams was always disorienting. Even to call them dreams was somewhat of a misnomer. They were more altered state than REM cycle. This one, though, with its picture-book quality, was a brain-boggler. I was keenly aware that what I was doing was risky, a wildcat maneuver in a flock of jittery birds. I had no idea if there was a precedent for my actions. Was I the first to ever actively recruit a soul and reconnect it with grieving parents? If it had been done, what was the outcome? If it hadn't, what was the risk? And should my manipulation be discovered, what would happen? So many worries and doubts were banging around my head that I could hear them. The slightest shake, and I clanged like pots and pans. So why, aware of all that was at risk, was I so committed to proceed? Why was I excited? I felt that same post-Stork-dream sense of elation and purpose and even a little bit of that check-me-out self-confidence that put a rocket behind my heels for a full day. I even dressed differently following a Stork dream, usually representative of its theme. Today, I chose primary colors: a red jacket over a yellow-and-red polka-dot cotton blouse, an above-the-knee denim skirt with white knee socks, and jay-blue, ankle-high suede boots. I bounded up the front steps to our small-town high school feeling as bold as the palette I wore. Yeah, I got looks, but they were fleeting. My classmates at Norse Falls High were used to my fashion sense by now.

In the hallway, on our way to fourth period, Jack sniffed out my fidgety mood.

"Is something up with you today?"

I pulled my hand out of his, as if skin contact had somehow been the giveaway. "It's kind of a big day," I said.

"Anything you can tell me about?"

Like I wasn't in enough trouble already. Like I hadn't seen blabbermouth Dorit scalped of her life's purpose and pride before us. Like I hadn't already prompted Jack into a misuse of his powers. Like I wanted to admit even *that* hadn't taught me a lesson.

"In Design today we start taking Penny and my

winning drawings from concept to pattern to costume." It was something I was both proud and excited about, but it wasn't technically what had me firing like a pinball machine.

"Clear the runway," he said.

I knew he didn't mean to trivialize something that I'd worked hard for, but it was there in his flat tone: condescension. And as much as it wasn't the real thing that had me lit up, was just a dumb duck of a decoy, I still took offense. Maybe it wouldn't solve the global warming problem, but it was going to be a very appealing use of velvets and fur trims.

"Well, we can't all be a part of Brigid's super-elite climate commandos, now, can we?" I caught a quick glimpse of Jack's startled face before I marched off in a huff. In addition to making me one ball of nerves, this particular round of Stork duties had me so hot-tempered, flames were spouting from my nose. I smelled smoke.

Going off on Jack like that put me in a foul mood for the first half of class, even though Ms. Bryant had distributed booklets of our costume designs to everyone. Finally, Penny's sunny aura lifted my spirits, and I was honored to have our drawings so praised and complimented. The next step in the process was for the class, working in teams to create patterns from our drawings, sized to the individual playing the part. Penny and I naturally chose her character, Gerda. Even though our designs for the

Snow Queen, Monique's character, were the most elaborate and ornate, I was pleased to be working on Gerda's. For the Snow Queen we'd chosen icy white silks and shimmery blue taffetas, whereas for Gerda, the resilient and plucky young heroine, we'd gone with crimson velvets and gold and plum brocades — all colors that would suit Penny's copper-colored hair.

After class, I looked all over for Jack, but he'd apparently left early for the day, though I only heard this via editor in chief Pedro. Jack's phone had gone straight to voicemail when I tried to get hold of him.

I had a dance practice after school. After that, I stopped home to check on my mom. Stanley had driven her to a morning doctor's appointment, but then had a training session all afternoon. I assumed that was where Jack disappeared to, but I still hadn't gotten hold of him. I did know that those who had been chosen for the Greenland trip were expected to be familiar with basic field procedures, to have experience with the monitoring equipment, to know basic first aid, and to have a few cold-weather survival skills. It all had me a little curious as to how and why a high-school senior had ended up as part of this group. My mom reiterated that such an honor spoke very highly of Jack and that it had been Brigid's, not Stanley's, decision. She obviously thought this would make me happy or proud. Instead it made me even more suspicious. Not that I didn't think Jack more brilliant than the sun, but I was supposed to, right? I couldn't help wondering just what it was about Jack that had Brigid singling him out. I didn't like it, and I didn't like Brigid.

I made us a quick dinner of spaghetti with jarred sauce. It was my go-to meal. We had it about three times a week, but my mom was too appreciative of all my help to complain. In truth, even I was tired of it, but not as tired as I was of being the kitchen wench. I rinsed and stacked the dishes in the sink and then told my mom I was going to go check on Afi, though I really didn't need to invent an excuse. My asleep-by-nine mom was way past trying to keep tabs on me.

At the store, I found Ofelia alone.

"Your *afi* went home hours ago," she said. "I was just about to close up."

"You'd just have to turn around and come back again," I said, fake-clawing at my head.

"Oh," she said. "Are we meeting tonight?"

"Yep," I said, scratching for real this time. "I'm sending the signal right now."

It was late, way late. I was giving my sister Storks a mere half hour to report to duty. Grim would go barbarian with rage. As much as I knew I was way too far down this road to turn back, I'd procrastinated out of fear and nerves. What the heck was I doing?

"How odd," Ofelia said, fixing me with one of her weird kindred-spirit stares. "Because I didn't get . . . I mean there wasn't any . . . Oh, listen to me rambling." She checked her watch.

She made it seem like she usually had some kind of advance notice or forecast of these things. But how could she? It was my turn to stare at her. She soon invented an excuse to pop down and let her sister at the bookstore know to head home without her. Worked for me. I was grateful to have the last twenty-five minutes pre-meeting to myself, even though I was too nervous to do much more than google heart-attack symptoms on my iPhone.

At nine straight-up, the Storks began filing in. Last to arrive was the very put-out, red-faced Grim. Man, she liked to turn her entrance into some sort of death march. What had I taken her away from, anyway? It sure wasn't charm school, and it sure wasn't beauty sleep.

I watched as Birta walked in with a gleaming leather book tucked under her arm. I also saw that we had new bowls of medicinal herbs and brand-new candles running the length of our table. I waited until everyone was seated before I began. "Fru Birta, I notice you have a new book."

"It arrived just the other day. Special delivery."

"And our herbs and candles, so nice to see them replenished, too."

"*I* took the liberty of ordering those, as it appeared no one else would," Grim said. There could be no mistaking who the "no one else" was.

"Thank you, Fru Grimilla," I said. "As always, you

go above and beyond." I probably shouldn't have thought *and behind my back*. Ofelia giggled and then tried to cover it up with a hacking cough into her fist, but Grim wasn't fooled. She clubbed us both with a bullying look. *Great.* Like I needed to piss Grim off right before I launched into my riskiest move ever.

"I have, myself, called this meeting," I said, "with a soul to place." I took a deep breath. "A boy: willful, and playful, and a lover of travel. There are three potential vessels. The first is a highly efficient individual who works well with people." *Carrying them, their little cartoon figures anyway, from station to station. Answers to the name of Annie.* "The second is a very sweet-natured woman who works as a . . . coach." *They'll think basketball, soccer, or some other sport, right? Not Clarabel, Annie's sidekick and Thomas's passenger train.* "And, finally, a woman who has recently suffered the loss of her only child. Her strength, and courage, and capacity to still love are proof of her character. My recommendation is, wholeheartedly, the third. Your show of votes, please," I said quickly, before Grim could interject.

Everyone, Grim and Ofelia included, supported my recommendation with a wag of three fingers, though Ofelia stared at me with full-moon eyes. Even as I was thinking all the little asides about Annie and Clarabel, I knew it was dicey, but how do you stop your thoughts? It was advanced mind control, way beyond my rookie skills.

"In conclusion, then, Fru Grimilla, is there any change to Fru Hulda's condition?"

"None."

"And anything any of us can do?"

"No."

"Then, I wish everyone a pleasant evening." I bowed my head in a very Hulda-like manner and said, "Peace be."

Borrowing Hulda's traditional closing remark was an olive branch for Grim's benefit. Seeing as she hadn't been a dissenting vote had me feeling generous. So much for my token. Grim passed behind my chair and said to Fru Svana in a loud voice, "A mere half-hour notice. I guess some of our members think we have nothing else to do." I heard my peace offering snap under Grim's ugly black clodhoppers.

And the look Ofelia gave me on her way out. Good God, it was ghoulish. I hadn't fooled everyone.

CHAPTER TWENTY-EIGHT

"This cannot happen tomorrow!" Mr. Higginbottom yelled like the diva-possessed creature he had become.

A stageful of blame-filled eyes turned toward me, the primary offender. Technically they turned down on me to where I lay in a crumpled heap, having just fallen during my dress-rehearsal solo. Crap. Twenty-four hours to go until opening night and my legs had deserted me, leaving me with two clumsy stand-ins who didn't know the dance, or who just possibly—like me—had had enough. Neither I nor my impostor legs were in any hurry to get up.

"From the top," Mr. Higginbottom called, smacking his clipboard against his thigh.

I scrambled to a stand.

For the past three weeks, rehearsals had taken over my life like an invading army. Mr. Higginbottom was a perfectionist. A good thing, in my humble opinion, for exact sciences like calculus and microbiology. Bad for anything dependent upon high-school kids learning their lines, hitting their marks, and nailing their dance solos all day, every day.

And if tomorrow's show wasn't enough to have my nerves skittering like live wires, there was plenty else to fret about. Ofelia had been avoiding me ever since my placement of Jacob. It wasn't like I missed her or her nosing into my thoughts, but I couldn't help but question the reasoning behind that old saying, "Keep your friends close and your enemies closer." But how did you even figure out which category they fell into if they were avoiding you?

Also weighing on me was the fact that I hadn't heard anything about a pregnancy announcement from Julia. Not that I was in her friends-and-family network, nor that she would be announcing anything this early, but, still, I wanted to know if my enterprise was operational.

Luckily, I didn't have all that much time to dwell on it; I was simply too busy with school, planning for the only-days-away Iceland trip, taking care of my still-bedridden mother, and trying to keep track of an even-busier-than-me boyfriend.

Somehow, I got through one fall-free version of my

dance, a small miracle given the ridiculous contraption of wired wings, gauzy layers, heavy glittery doodads, and eye-lashing ribbons that Penny and I had designed. *Note to self: Next time, junk the jewels and ban the spangles.* Finally, Mr. Higginbottom felt he could move on to Penny's pivotal encounter with the evil Snow Queen.

I sat in one of the seats of the auditorium unlacing my slippers when I was startled from behind.

"What happened to you up there?"

Only Brigid's "What" sounded like *Vot;* still, I turned in surprise.

"Nerves, I guess," I said.

"I wouldn't have expected it from you," she said. "I thought you were made of tougher stuff: more mettle, more grit."

My head bobbed forward in shock. Who said such things to someone so close to opening night?

Brigid's mouth opened in a broad smile. "It is stage tradition not to boost or plump the ego before a big show. We never say 'good luck'; we never compliment. It is kiss of death onstage. You know this surely from the expression, 'Break a leg.'"

I honestly couldn't stop gaping at the woman. "Break a leg" was in no way funny to someone who had just taken a face-plant in front of the entire cast and crew. And "kiss of death"? I didn't care frick or frack about stage traditions, but death omens — now, those I took seriously.

"Don't worry about me," I said, smiling, as much as I could, anyway, while inwardly hissing. "I'll be full of grit tomorrow."

"Good," Brigid said. "And how do they say it here? Knock 'em dead."

From the director's table, Mr. Higginbottom called Brigid over. I watched her walk away, shivering at another mention of the snuff of life, but at least this time I wasn't on the receiving end. Because if it came to it, I had mettle. Heavy mettle.

CHAPTER TWENTY-NINE

From behind the curtain, Penny and I peered into the crowd. The hum of the orchestra buzzed like a swarm of insects with the tinkle of light conversation layering the air. Front and center were the families of Monique, Penny, and Matthew. My small squad of fans — Jack, Afi, my dad, Brigid, and Stanley — had also scored front-row seats, but slightly stage left. The absence of my mom made me sad. At least dutiful Stanley had his video camera at the ready for her own private viewing. The doctor had nixed her plans to attend; moreover, he had further restricted her activity and had increased her checkups to twice weekly. Not to be left out entirely, my mom had invited a small group of us back to the house after the show for her private showing, pizza, and a send-off toast to tomorrow's travelers. Jack, Stanley, and Brigid flew out the next morning.

"I hear it's a sold-out show," Penny said.

"May as well make it worth our while," I said, trying to sound confident.

"Good luck tonight, girls," Ms. Bryant said, placing a hand on both of our shoulders.

Uh-oh, I thought ever so briefly. But how on earth could anyone as sweet as Ms. Bryant be the kiss of death?

The conductor then raised his stick, and the overture began. Penny and I squeezed hands and hurried off to take our spots onstage.

The curtain opened onto the "Happy Village" number. It was the first of five chorus routines, not counting my solo, where I was a prominent dancer, albeit a reluctant singer. It was a good scene for everyone to work the jitters out as we sang and danced together. I played a shopkeeper who swept my storefront while waltzing with my broom and then offered sugary treats to the angel-faced Gerda and rough-and-tumble Kay. It felt great to get this first performance under my belt and was a good omen — I hoped — for my looming solo. And once I got into this first number, I was able to trust my legs to muscle my mind out of the proceedings. I snuck only one quick glance at the front row, not wanting to jinx myself in any way. Despite the darkness of the house

185

and with just that fleeting glance, I spied Jack grinning like a chimp. Seeing him so fixated — on me — my hopes soared, but I also noticed he was sitting next to Brigid.

The next scene was a first-of-the-season snowfall into which all the village children ventured out with happy faces and trailing their pretty sleds. I was a village child; my sled was cherry-red; and my costume — thanks to me and Penny — was an adorable fur-trimmed velvet. I loved it. It alone made me prance, though the music helped. As did just watching Penny bloom before my eyes. She was a natural and nailed her scenes with an effortless presence and a pure, sweet voice. She had undeniable star quality, something I'd personally seen, but now the whole school was witnessing it.

And Matthew. Another with hidden talents. In the closing scene to Act One, Gerda and Kay arrive hand in hand with their his-and-hers sleds. We — the village children — frolic and delight in the falling snow to a song called "Sledder's Hill." With the conclusion of the song, Monique, the abominable Snow Queen, makes her entrance in a stately, horse-drawn sleigh. Monique may have had to wait through most of Act One to make her entrance, but even I had to admit that she made one impressive ice witch. She belted out her introductory number, "Who Dares Follow My Sledge?" with such moxie that I was surprised we all, like lemmings, didn't trail after her. Only Matthew, as was scripted, did; the act closed with him hitching his little metal-runnered sled behind her grand and glistening horse-powered vehicle and being led away with a confused Gerda calling after him.

During intermission, we all crackled with the excitement of having a flaw-free Act One. The girls' dressing room was a hive of activity, with changes of costumes sailing over heads and touch-up clouds of powdery makeup dusting the air. Ms. Bryant had the burden of keeping us calm and getting us back onstage for Act Two. It was a testament to her likability that she protected both the costumes and her popularity, and had us waiting in the wings for our cue.

Act Two began with the enchantress Snow Queen enticing young Kay from his small sled into her larger, warmer, cushier sleigh. The moment she touched him, he went cold and fell into a stupor while she raced north across a frozen landscape. Her song, "To the Land of Frost," told of her destination: a barren snow castle in need of an heir. I didn't like the song, and not just because, when it came right down to it, I wasn't all that crazy about Monique. I had developed a sensitivity to the word *frost*. Naturally, I associated it with Jack. Somehow even this fictional, children's-book usage made me shiver. Then again, my current costume was the infamous ice fairy getup. What it lacked in skin coverage it made up for in cumbersome beads and baubles. And the flap-happy wired wings were like a portable fan. My lips were blue before the cerulean gloss was ever applied.

Gerda's journey to find Kay began with the next scene. Her venture took her north, first following the creatures of the forest, and then encountering my fey attendants, who brought her to me: the ice fairy. Maybe I felt "in the moment," having reflected upon my aversion to Monique singing about frost. Maybe I was so cold in the gauzy sleeveless contraption that I needed to generate body heat. Or maybe I let go and allowed the dance to lead me, instead of vice versa. Whatever the catalyst, it was my best dance ever. I felt lithe and graceful and ethereal. Castmates descended upon me the moment I came offstage, hugging and high-fiving me, Penny the most zealous of them all. And trust me, the girl is way stronger than she looks. All in all, it went better than I had dared to imagine, especially considering my only goal had been not to fall on my face.

The rest of the show was spectacular. Penny, Matthew, and even Monique were crazy-good. The frenzy backstage, after the curtain call, was wild and untamed. We exhaled, in unison, a sigh of relief. Friday's performance down, and only the Saturday-matinee and Saturday-night shows to go. I practically floated toward the dressing room.

"Congratulations," Jack said, meeting me in the small passageway outside the changing room. "These are for you." He held out two dozen ribbon-tied yellow roses.

"Jack. These are too much."

"Those are actually from your dad. Mine are underneath."

Upon closer examination, I found three cellophane-wrapped red carnations under the giant bundle of roses.

"Thank you," I said.

"It was a great show," he said.

"It was. Penny did great."

"So did you. And I bet you were relieved to get it over with, you know, without falling like in rehearsals."

"Where did you hear that I fell?"

"From Brigid. She said you were overthinking your performance, that you had to trust yourself."

It wasn't myself that I didn't trust.

"What else did Diva Fonnkona have to say?" There was an edge to my voice, one I would have liked to push Brigid over.

"Don't get defensive. She liked it, said it was good for a high-school production."

"Good?"

"Last I checked," Jack said, "good was a compliment. Oh, yeah, and she liked the costumes."

I wondered if Jack realized that none of his comments were his. Was it the former editor in him citing sources? Or was it an influence of a more insidious nature?

"Speaking of costumes," I said, "Ms. Bryant wants them all off our backs and checked into Wardrobe immediately."

"Hurry up," he said. "It's our last night together."

"What?"

"I fly out in the morning. You know that."

Of course I knew that, but I didn't like the way he had phrased it. Not one bit.

CHAPTER THIRTY

The send-off party for the following day's travelers began innocently enough. As parties sometimes do, it divided by age. The adults were in the living room watching the video of the performance, while my friends and I hung out in the kitchen eating pizza.

"Are you ready for tomorrow, Jack?" Penny asked.

"I'm ready."

"What time's your flight?" she asked.

"One p.m."

"How long is it?" Tina asked.

"With two stops, almost thirteen hours. And that's just to Iceland." Jack ran his fingers though his hair. "From there, we transfer airports and still have two more flights to go."

"Sounds grueling," Tina said.

"Especially for a first-time flier," I said.

Jack dropped his head and tossed his crust onto his plate.

"It's your first time flying?" Logan said. Logan was a cast member and one of Matthew's band buddies. To me, he seemed loud and coarse, but everyone, Penny included, thought he was hilarious. "Welcome to the twenty-first century, dude."

Hilary, a chorus member and Penny's understudy, giggled.

"I appreciate it," Jack said to Logan, but it was me he locked eyes with.

Jeez. All I'd said was that it was his first time. It wasn't like I'd blabbed, or worse, teased, about his actual fear of flying. Weeks back, when he'd admitted it, I'd known it was a big deal. The guy didn't admit to many weaknesses. From the look he raked over me, I knew he felt betrayed. Like I'd turned state's evidence against him, or read excerpts from his diary out loud. I forgot, sometimes, how buttoned-up Jack was, but in this case he was overreacting. I hadn't sold him out.

"There's this thing called the Internet," Logan said. "You ever hear of it? And phones: they're mobile now. You can take them with you, even on that big air-o-plane you'll be on." Logan was on a roll. Hilary tittered into her cupped hand.

"Did you guys hear about the dogsleds?" I asked in a subject-changing ploy.

Not everyone had, and Jack was way more comfortable with this topic. He described the plans for their Iditarod-like portion of the trip. It was evidence of our respective distractions that even I hadn't known that though he would basically be a passenger on the sled of an experienced musher, part of his recent training included basic dog-handling skills. I had not known that *hike* was the more commonly used command for go, not *mush*. Right was *gee* and left was *haw*. And *leave it* was the command for the dog to stop sniffing at an item, animal, or other temptation.

Speaking of temptations, I decided it was dessert time. My mom had gone to the trouble of ordering a chocolate-on-chocolate sheet cake with a big fat loopy *Bon voyage* scrolled across the top; a red, white, and blue map of the United States in the bottom left corner; a green map of Greenland in the top right; and a little plastic plane flying between them on a broken-line trajectory. I set the cake on the island and was fishing forks and spoons out of a drawer. Penny, Tina, Matthew, and the others were bunched up at one end of the island downloading pictures from Tina's camera phone onto Matthew's Facebook page.

"I smell coffee," Brigid said, stepping into the room.

She had removed the long jacket she'd worn earlier, revealing a low-cut, tight-fitting sweater. A new silver snowflake necklace wasn't the only thing it showed off.

"I just wanted to congratulate you all on a wonderful performance."

We'd been upgraded from "good" to "wonderful." Whoop-de-do. More to the point, I wondered who was putting on the show.

A chorus of "thanks" echoed through the small kitchen. Matthew and Logan, I noticed, went from baritones to altos.

"The coffee's not quite ready yet," I said, "but I'll bring it into the family room with the cake."

"Sounds perfect," Brigid said with a parting wave.

"Did you guys get a look at that body?" Logan asked. "*Hello!* You are one lucky dog, Jack."

"What's that supposed to mean?" I asked, looking for a cake server in our utensil drawer.

"You got room in your suitcase for me?" He punched Jack in the shoulder. "Because she is smokin' hot."

Jack didn't reply, lucky for him. Unlucky for Logan, I opted to go with our largest knife in lieu of the wimpy cake server.

"Logan," I said, holding the knife in front of me. "I hardly think —"

Logan cut me off. "What's the bunk assignment like? Did they teach you about shared body heat in your

194

survival training? 'Cause a guy would warm up nicely cozying up between her —"

"Logan," I said in a tone that conveyed everything; the slash of my knife through the air was probably unnecessary.

Matthew and Jack choked back laughter in some kind of bro-spiracy.

"Easy there," Jack said. His eyes dropped to the knife.

Like I would really use it. Like I needed anyone — Jack in particular — telling me "Easy there." It was condescending and insulting. And Logan *had* been inappropriate.

"What if she hears you guys?" I said in a sulk.

"She didn't hear anything," Jack said.

"Which makes it OK?" I asked, dumping cake slices onto plates. I deliberately served Jack the piece that was upside down and misshapen. I then carried a tray out to the adults in the front room. When I returned, Jack had his coat on.

"Tomorrow's an early morning," he said. "I should be going."

I found my own parka in the pileup of belongings and followed him toward the foyer. He briefly mumbled a "Good night and thank you" to my mom, but overall his departure was abrupt and kind of rude.

"Wait up," I said, stumbling behind him down the porch steps.

He paused at the driver's-side door to his truck, which was parked in the driveway, but didn't say anything.

"Are you OK?" I asked.

"I'm fine."

"It just seemed like—"

"I said I'm fine."

His tone definitely implied otherwise.

"So why are you taking off, then? We didn't even get any time alone."

"I'm not done packing."

"Are you sure you're all right? Is it the flying thing?"

"No. Though I really don't appreciate my lack of travel experience being thrown in my face."

"Thrown in your face? It's not like I said you were scared."

"I'm not scared." His voice was gruff.

"I never said you were. And maybe I don't appreciate you drooling over Brigid with a pig like Logan."

"You're overreacting."

"I am not," I said.

"Yes, you are."

The front door opened, and Brigid stepped onto the porch. Her timing couldn't have been worse. Jack kissed me quickly on the lips and pulled away. Honestly, I'd been kissed by a dolphin at SeaWorld with more passion.

"Take care of yourself," he said, pulling at the truck's door handle.

"I will," I stammered, too stunned to properly react. *Take care of yourself?* What the hell did that mean?

Brigid approached us and stopped.

"Katla," she said, using my full name for the first time, "it has been a pleasure to know you." She shook my hand with gloved fingers. "And, Jack, I will see you tomorrow."

"Looking forward to it," he said, his eyes bright and eager.

Though he gave me another brief kiss—on the friggin' forehead—his gaze seemed to follow Brigid as she walked down the driveway and out to her street-parked car.

Before I knew it, Jack was behind the wheel and backing down the driveway. My eyes chased between Jack's truck and Brigid's rental, and I remembered the dog-mushing command Jack had taught us.

Leave it, I thought with a snarl.

CHAPTER THIRTY-ONE

Following our last show, the curtain dropped and the stage exploded in hugs, tears, whistles, and cheers. I made the rounds, going through the motions, but I was not one of the revelers. My matinee and Saturday night performances went fine — just fine — not great. I didn't fall or screw up, but I didn't dance like I had on Friday, either.

The problem was Jack. I missed him. I had expected to, but it was more than that. Our good-bye had been distant and cold. First cousins in a fair number of states could legally display more affection. Worse, I honestly didn't know where we stood. "Take care of yourself"? It sounded more like a kiss-off than an accompaniment to a see-you-soon kiss.

I kept trying to convince myself that it was just nerves. His fear of flying getting the best of him as take-off loomed. But the way he had laughed at Logan's remarks—I'd never seen that side of Jack before.

Penny practically tackled me with her post-Gerda hug. "Are you coming to the Kountry Kettle?" she asked, her cheeks wet with happy tears.

"I can't. You know Afi and I start our trek to Iceland bright and early."

"Speaking of treks, what about Jack? Did you talk to him before his flight?"

"No. I didn't get a chance." Because he hadn't called me. Prior to boarding, Stanley had called my mom briefly, but Jack, he said, had wandered off.

"Are you sure you don't have even a half hour to come out and celebrate with us?" Penny asked.

I shook my head no, but, in truth, it wasn't the time I lacked, more like the right frame of mind.

My mood was no better the next morning as I threw the last bits and pieces into my suitcase. I scooped a brush, a pocket English-Icelandic dictionary, and my makeup case from my dresser top, when a small black velvet pouch caught my eye: the runes from Jack's grandmother. The sack sat where I'd dropped it the morning after returning from the blizzard fiasco, in a lopsided pottery bowl I'd made in seventh grade. Somehow, their association with my horrible blunder had prevented me from researching the moonstone rocks and their engraved symbols, or even handling them. My hand hovered over the crude bowl. Sure, I expected Iceland to be a little backwater, but an ancient alphabet carved into small stones — what did I think I'd trade them for, a handful of magic beans? I hardly knew, but my greedy fingers — ignoring the TSA baggage restrictions running like a news banner at the bottom of my thoughts — snatched up the pouch and tossed it into my suitcase. Next came a good-bye to my teary mom. She, at least, had pregnancy hormones and cabin fever to blame for her crazy emotions.

"Now, remember," she said, her voice thin, "call me, for any reason. Don't worry about the expense."

"OK."

"And take care of Afi. Make sure he eats right. He's been looking so thin."

"I will."

"Give me a hug, then."

Despite the big tummy bulge, she seemed small and weak as I leaned over her bed. Taking care of her, I knew, was a big job. I just hoped Ofelia was up to it. Ofelia. Just thinking about her gave me an uneasy feeling.

"How're we doing in here?" Ofelia said, appearing suddenly in the doorway to my mom's bedroom. The uneasy feeling grew. Dang, her mind-reading thing was creepy.

"I'm just about ready to head out," I said. "Afi's probably sitting on his suitcase in his driveway."

"No, he's not," Ofelia said.

My mom gave her a quizzical look; the look I gave her required a stronger adjective.

"He seems way too smart a fellow to sit in the cold," Ofelia said, trying to cover her tracks.

"OK, Mom," I said, lingering in the doorway. "It's just a week. We'll be back before you know it."

"Love you," my mom called out to me.

"Love you back," I said, backing into the hallway.

Ofelia followed me downstairs.

"Don't worry about your mother," she said. "I'll take care of her."

Take care of, I rolled it around my mouth like a marble. It sounded like something Tony Soprano would say. And definitely not helping my overall mood.

"Thank you," I said, wheeling my suitcase toward the back door.

"Katla," she said, "there is something I feel needs saying."

Kind of a long-way-round *listen up,* but it got my attention.

"What is it?"

Ofelia squinted and lowered her head. "I had not realized the strength of your calling. It is . . . What I mean to say . . . I would never forgive myself were I not to—"

"Ofelia, just tell me."

"A warning," she said in a gravelly voice. "You are more than a deliverer of souls, and more than a summoner of souls."

Again, Ofelia hesitated, giving me time to ponder the difference. So she suspected what I had done for Jacob. What I hoped I had done. There still had been no news on that front.

"OK," I said.

"Special ones may appear to you." Ofelia gripped my shoulder. "Be careful. A pact once made cannot be broken."

Oh, boy. And great. Because I needed one more thing to add to my load.

"No need to worry," I said, tucking my heaviest parka under my arm. "I'm on vacation, remember?"

CHAPTER THIRTY-TWO

I couldn't believe I was in Iceland. It had been a long, hell-ish journey. Afi had been so slow we almost missed our connecting flight in Boston, and we hit some scary turbu-lence over the Atlantic, but we were here. Iceland. Even its name was formidable. One of my favorite things about flying was the bird's-eye view it afforded. Unfortunately, I barely got a peek at the terrain as we descended from clouds into an early-morning fog so thick it would make a pretty decent packing material. Once through cus-toms and baggage claim, we hopped a bus for the trans-fer from the international airport to the regional airport some thirty miles away. It was a cold, rain-soaked day.

From the bus windows, I looked out onto a barren volcanic landscape. It was not the happy little village scene I'd expected. Soon, though, we came into the downtown area of Reykjavik, Iceland's capital and largest city. I was surprised at the number of modern buildings—again, not the Iceland I'd expected. Finally, we arrived at the regional airport and soon began the business of check-in and boarding; the allure of travel had long since lost its appeal. At least this last flight was short.

When Afi had said his cousin Baldur would pick us up at the airport, I had thought that was his name, not a description. Turned out it was both. The guy looked like Afi, except Afi had a shock of white hair, whereas this guy was as bald as his name suggested. Except for the wired eyebrows and tufts growing out of his ears, that is. I supposed if you'd lost a whole head of hair, you'd be inclined to preserve it elsewhere. I liked his eyes, a blue so aqua they splashed. He was tall, like Afi, but stockier, with a belly that suggested a healthy appetite. Afi and Baldur hugged and slapped backs like a couple of linebackers. Then it was my turn for a hug. Baldur embraced me and said, "Aye, she's an Icelander, all right." Which I supposed was good, because his eyes twinkled as he said it. They jabbered away in Icelandic. I didn't catch a word. Then again, there were only about five that I knew. And I didn't think now was the occasion for "the toilet, please," or the "I'm not hungry, thank you," that I'd expressly learned.

The idea of unwittingly chowing down on sheep's head or fermented shark meat still had me freaked.

For a pretty big guy, Baldur drove a little munchkin car. I scrambled into the backseat, holding my suitcase on my lap, trunks and hatchbacks apparently being another example of the U.S. super-size-me culture. It was the last day of March, technically spring, but there were still patches of snow on the ground. What struck me the most were the cloud-capped mountains hovering over us and the volcanic island's lack of trees. Minnesota had spoiled me for trees.

Baldur pulled out of the tiny airport's parking lot and headed north. "So, Katla," he said in pretty darn good English, "welcome home."

My breath caught inwardly with the word "home." I hadn't known how to describe it, but as soon as we had landed here in Akureyri, I'd had the oddest sensation of *déjà vu,* which I knew from my French grandmother translated literally as *already seen.* Here, in Iceland, I had the feeling that I'd *already been.* Except I hadn't; my international travel consisted of Cancun, Vancouver, and Paris.

"Akureyri," Baldur said, "is considered the capital of northern Iceland and is at the base of the Eyjafjörður."

I'd studied the maps before leaving, but a pastel drawing could never do this justice. The Eyjafjörður was a long, fingerlike inlet, a fjord, that cut deep into the coast of Iceland off the Atlantic Ocean, offering a protective harbor for a centuries-old fishing industry.

"The first Vikings arrived here in the year 890," Baldur said. "And Akureyri has been a market town ever since. There is even reference to the old section, Oddeyri, in the Sagas."

Impressive, sure, but didn't explain why it felt familiar to me. I knew for a fact the Sagas were not in my bookcase at home, nor did I think too many movies had been set in the area. Baldur explained we were on the Drottningarbraut, the road skirting the west side of the fjord and heading north into town. To my right, the inky-blue waters of the fjord were visible. Soon, scattered buildings came into view, and then the town itself. The architecture was typically Scandinavian, with scattered, brightly painted wooden buildings of canary yellow, electric blue, or whitewashed with metal roofs of leaf green and brick red. And it was larger than I expected: a bustling town with many shops, restaurants, and businesses.

As if on cue, Baldur slammed his hand to the steering wheel. "Aye. Traffic," he said.

The "traffic" consisted of five vehicles in front of us at a red light. Seriously? The guy wouldn't last a minute on the 405 in LA. Baldur did not live in Akureyri, which, with a population of 17,000, was far too "crowded." He lived in the much smaller town of Hafmeyjafjordur, thirty miles farther north along the fjord. My eyes soon said good-bye to the vibrant Akureyri and to daylight itself. It really had been a long journey, and as much as I was fascinated by my ancestral land, I was blotto. The last thing I remembered was laying my head back against the window, with towering mountains to my left and the glassy blue fjord to my right.

The next thing I knew, we were rolling to a stop in front of a small white house. I blinked my eyes several times. How long had I been asleep? How far had we gone? Thirty miles, I'd been told, about forty minutes, but surely it should take a lot longer than that to get to the end of the earth. Besides the white house, set on a hill overlooking the fjord, there was nothing else around.

"Where are we?" I asked.

"Baldur's house," Afi replied.

"Where is everybody?" I was groggy and confused.

"My wife, Vigdis, should be home," Baldur said.

"No, I mean the town. Afi's hometown, where is it?"

"Ah," Baldur said. "It's back down the road a ways." He climbed out of the driver's side and pulled the seat forward. "Vigdis and I like the peace and quiet."

As if living on a slab of volcanic rock in the middle of the Atlantic Ocean wasn't enough solitude. And I had thought Norse Falls was remote. What did they do for a gallon of milk?

Baldur hoisted first my suitcase and then me out of the minuscule backseat. I popped out like a stubborn cork, not my most graceful move, but after more than twenty-four hours of transport, I was happy to be on solid ground—even if it was a cliff house above an icy Atlantic fjord.

Vigdis soon joined us in front of the home. She was short with dark hair, a round face, and shiny brown eyes. She pulled Afi and then me into hugs; they probably didn't get many visitors out here, certainly not family from the U.S., anyway. I supposed the occasion called for an embrace, though I was sure my ribs would be sore. The woman was one serious bone cruncher.

Vigdis took my hand and led me into the house like a toddler. Normally, I would bristle at such disregard for personal boundaries, but something about Vigdis's high, round cheeks and gummy smile had me suspending rules. That and an exhaustion level exceeding EPA guidelines: without sleep, I was a walking zombie. She led us up the path to the front door. The house was one story with an arched red door and a green corrugated roof. To one side of the path was a small detached garage, and to the other, old stone steps that descended downhill and toward the rocky shoreline.

Once inside the home, Vigdis pulled kitchen chairs out for Afi and me around the long, battered farm table. Even with the short nap in the car, the travel, compounded by the time difference, was pulling me, like an undertow, out to sea. It was two in the afternoon on a clear, bright, although chilly, day, yet my body was telling me differently. Vigdis set out coffee and a platter of meats and cheeses, but I had no appetite.

Finally, she punched her fists down on her thick waist and said, pointing at me, "This one needs a bed."

The bed, though only a twin, looked like a cocoon of feathery softness. Still wearing my travel clothes, I fell upon the tiny guest room's mattress, grateful for the beauty of a down-stuffed duvet and central heating. I remembered how Jack had said he was a little jealous of our vacationer's itinerary and comforts-of-home stay. Home. It made me think about my mom and Jack. My mom I could picture, remote in hand or fanned-open book poised atop her ever-growing tummy. But Jack. It bothered me that I had no visual on where he was or what he was doing. If my sleep-deprived mind had the facts straight, he'd arrived yesterday in Daneborg and had set out today by dogsled for the Klarksberg Research Station. It rankled me even more that we'd parted on such confusing terms. Was he mad at me? Was he not speaking to me? I pulled the lavender-scented duvet to my chest and surrendered to a much-deserved nap.

CHAPTER THIRTY-THREE

I woke to the eeriest sound ever. Nothing. Never before had I been so aware of absolute silence. And it was dark — the kind of dark you could put on a scale and weigh. I sat up, thinking that it had to be the middle of the night. I was still in my travel clothes, so I must have slept through the afternoon, dinner, the evening, and — by the looks of it — midnight. For several moments I remained still, assembling the jigsaw of recent memories. I was in the guest room of Baldur and Vigdis's cottage by the sea, in Hafmeyjafjordur, Iceland — Afi's hometown. So, that was the where. I just needed to figure out the when. My toes located the fleece lining of my UGGs, and my outstretched hands found the desk chair over which my parka had been thrown. The central heating I'd been grateful for a few hours ago had been turned way down. I snuggled into the warmth of my jacket and slowly paced off the few steps to the bedroom door. It opened with the tiniest of creaks, and I stepped into the small hallway and toward the kitchen. From the large above-sink window, a shaft of moonlight illuminated the battered table and four simple wooden chairs. A digital clock on the stove showed the time as 3:47. Mystery solved: everyone was obviously in bed.

I stood in the kitchen, looking out the window. The moon was a huge metallic ball. Were we closer to it this far north? My mathematician mom would have buried me with formulas about the earth, its axis, and rotation, but, honestly, it had never appeared so accessible to me before, had never appeared so enticing. Like in the movies, I heard music and assumed my mind was inventing a sound track to intensify the moment. Soon, I realized I really was hearing music. But from where? Everyone was asleep. Besides, the melody was odd, both eerie and compelling. It seemed to be coming from outside. Under the sink, next to a plastic bottle of dish soap, I found a flashlight. I clicked it on, brushing its light across the empty room. In a kind of dream state, I walked the few steps to the kitchen door, silently lifted the latch, and followed the old stone steps down the hill and under the silvery light of that giant orb.

The steps were about a thousand years old: cracked

and overgrown with weeds. The path wound its way down the hill, skirting brush and bushes and a few forlorn trees. Strangely, I didn't feel the cold, though my labored breathing hung like tinsel in the night air. Everything stilled as if yielding to the plaintive song. Even the waters I knew were at the bottom of the hill seemed at rest. The steps came around a series of large boulders, and I found myself on a stone-filled beach. Had I awakened the sleeping fjord? It roared to life with an urgent press of waters upon the rocks, quelling even the music. A plunk of water, like a stone being dropped, drew my attention down to the shoreline, and I swept my flashlight over the area. Were this LA, or even Minnesota, my hackles would be up, but this was Iceland. Did they even have bad guys? Or bears? Or anything scarier than Björk's fashion sense? I walked closer to the shore. I heard a big splash, and I directed my small beam of light toward the sound that rippled with an echolike reverberation until it morphed into something like laughter, an almost girlish giggle. Then I saw the flash of a tail. It looked like a big fish — as big as me.

Holy crap! I dropped the flashlight and gasped. What the hell was that? I bent down over one of the giant boulders at the shore and peered into the water. What had I seen? What on earth had been there? I clumsily stooped to retrieve my light. By the time I stood up again, whatever it was was gone. And whatever trancelike state I had been in was gone with it.

The cold suddenly bit into me. My gloveless fingers went numb, and I had to draw the flashlight up and into my sleeve so as to shelter my aching hands from the whip of the wind. I scurried up the stone steps, eased the kitchen door open, and tiptoed through the house and back into the comfort of my small guest room. Still in my original travel clothes, I once again lowered myself into the safety of the down-filled duvet. I'd probably heard the wind whistling over the waves. I'd probably seen a dolphin, or a seal, or just a big ol' ocean fish. Dolphins had funny vocalizations, didn't they? Ones that were laugh like. More likely, I was still groggy from travel and allowing my imagination to get the best of me. For a very long time, I lay awake purposely thinking of other things. *I hope Mom is OK. Has Jack been thinking of me?* I listened for sounds of life in the house. I needed a shower, and I was starving and wanted breakfast. I just hoped it wasn't fermented shark meat—or fish of any kind, for that matter.

CHAPTER THIRTY-FOUR

Finally, I heard sounds from the kitchen and, more importantly, smells: coffee and sausage. My stomach barked at me from neglect. I wasn't quite sure, given the time difference, but my rudimentary calculation tallied more than twenty-four hours since my last meal. I picked a brush through my matted-to-face hair and contemplated putting on a new shirt, but the promise of food was just too tempting. I walked quickly down the hallway, only slowing my pace at the kitchen archway. I didn't want to appear ravenous, though I was.

Vigdis, spatula in hand, was at the stove. She turned, her appearance taking me by surprise.

"Vigdis?"

"Ah. Good morning, sleeping beauty."

Funny she should mention a fairy tale when she looked like she'd just stepped out of one. She wore a white lace-trimmed cotton blouse with puffed sleeves and a gathered neckline, over which was an elaborately embroidered lace-up vest. Her black full-length skirt was topped with a white lace apron; and she wore a funny black wool cap with a huge silver tassel that hung above her left ear.

"Good morning," I said. "I like your outfit." Something had to be said about it, and I did like it. It was unique, anyway. I always gave props for originality.

As if on cue, Vigdis said, "For the festival today. Is custom to wear traditional Icelandic *upphlutur* costume." She held the spatula away from her body and stepped to the side, making her long skirt sway. "I'm glad you like," she said, pointing with her spatula to a garment bag hanging from the knob of a breakfront cabinet. "Yours is all ready to try on. I hope is good size."

I stepped toward the zip-front plastic bag. I had always been a sucker for dress-up. Halloween, for me, had never been about ghouls or candy. And as a child, no treasure box full of cash and coins could have tempted me over an old trunk of scratchy gowns, boas, and cheap costume jewelry. "For me?" I opened the bag and fingered a red woolen lace-up vest adorned with embroidery.

"Yes. If you like?"

"I like," I said, lifting the hangers off the hook and holding the garment bag against my front.

"Breakfast first," Vigdis said, taking the bag from me and draping it over a chair.

I took a big-bad-wolf style inhale, taking in all the savory smells. "Thank you. I'm starving." No sooner did a fried egg hit my plate than it disappeared. I ate three, maybe four. Vigdis was wickedly quick with that spatula of hers. Sausage links, too, were eaten too quickly to count or even ask just what was stuffed in the casings. I didn't suspect fish, anyway, which reminded me of my wee-hours stroll. What to even think about that?

I dropped my napkin over my plate and carried it to the sink. Now that my stomach had stopped whining, my heart got a word in edgewise. Jack. Thoughts of him haunted me, and I wondered, for the millionth time, if I was on his mind, too.

"Did anybody call for me yesterday, while I was sleeping?" I asked.

"Your mother," Vigdis said. "She wants you to call her back. Don't worry about the time. She said she can't sleep anyway."

"But it would be the middle of the night there."

Vigdis waved the spatula back and forth. "If it were me, I'd do as she says. Her orders were very clear."

I had to smile at the thought of command central stretching clear across an ocean.

Despite my mom's orders, it was still Jack I wanted to contact. "Do you have Internet here at the house?"

"Sorry. We're too old for all that new stuff."

"In town?"

"Sure. At the library. At the café. I see everyone on their computers."

I had an e-mail address to Klarksberg Research Station that would go into their office. So even if I could get a message to him, it wouldn't be very private. I also had a phone number, but I couldn't exactly reverse charges to Greenland from Iceland. For now, I'd just have to hope my mom had news of Stanley and Jack.

"I guess I will call her. And then take a shower."

"Of course," Vigdis said, dunking my practically-licked-clean plate into a sink full of suds. "Come. Use the phone in Baldur's office."

Vigdis led me to a small room that had a view out to the shoreline. Had I really stumbled around out there in the middle of the night?

"Vigdis," I asked, "how far away is your closest neighbor?"

"A couple kilometers, at least."

Which ruled out an insomniac neighbor with the late-night giggles and a boom box.

I don't know why I was reluctant to admit I'd ventured out last night. I'd even gone so far as to carefully replace the flashlight exactly where I'd found it.

Vigdis pulled the office door behind her, giving me privacy for my phone call.

The international operator connected me to our home phone, and I heard my mother's voice accept the reversed charges.

"Hello?"

"Hi, Mom."

"Oh, Kat. I'm so glad to hear from you."

"Is everything OK? Did I wake you?" She sounded so small and far away.

"No, no. I can't sleep, but nothing to worry about. How was the journey?"

"Long. Exhausting."

"How's Afi?"

"Still sleeping, I guess. It's early here. Though I'm not the one to talk; I pulled a Rip Van Winkle and pretty much slept through yesterday."

"The time difference can be disorienting," my mom said.

"Have you heard from Stanley?"

"Yesterday. Just briefly."

"What did he say? Did Jack pass along any sort of message?"

"They sounded busy. Also tired from the long travel days. And apparently the dogsled trip was grueling."

"So no message?"

"No."

"He said he'd find a way to get hold of me," I said, hearing the pout in my voice. He had, but in the weeks leading up to our trips, not at that botched good-bye.

"Stanley said—"

"What?"

"Jack's been very quiet. A little . . . he didn't quite know how to describe it, but said he was a little withdrawn. He even wondered if the cold was getting to him. It's not an easy adjustment, so Stanley says."

The cold? Anybody else, Stanley or my mom, might believe in such a theory. I knew better. Our fight could have him sulking; a breakup—if that's what it was— could do the trick, too. Neither of those scenarios did much to lift my spirits. I racked my brain for other causes. "Maybe he's coming down with something? Is there a doctor where they are?"

"Stanley didn't think it was physical. Anyway, he said Brigid has been spending a lot of time with Jack. Doing what she can to help him adjust."

Adjust? To what? Her? Away from what? Me? I did not like the idea of Brigid playing nurse to Jack. Not one bit. I seriously needed to hear from him.

"Do they have Internet access where they are now?" I asked.

"Yes."

"Can you e-mail Stanley? Have him tell Jack to send

me a message. I'm going to find the café with Internet access in town today. Please?"

"Of course," my mom said through an odd groan, long and loud.

"Are you OK?"

"I think so. This baby, though, is jumping like a fish."

"Are you sure you're OK? What does the doctor say?"

"I have an appointment today."

"Is Ofelia handling everything?" I asked.

"She's a godsend."

As much as there was still something weird between me and Ofelia, I was glad someone was there for my mom. Her groan had sounded primordial.

The hot shower felt great, but I couldn't help stressing out about my mom's condition and what Stanley had said about Jack. Quiet and withdrawn? The guy had viewed the trip as the opportunity of a lifetime. He wasn't the type to let anything get in the way of his personal goals. I hated not knowing what was going on, hated being out of touch, hated not being able to look into those deep blue eyes and fall into them. Because I did, head-over-heels, every dang time. I missed him so much. I wanted to know that he missed me, too. I wanted to say sorry and hear him say it back. And I wanted to be the one cheering him up—not Brigid. Despite cranking the hot water in the shower to full blast, I felt a chill run down my spine like an arctic front coming in fast and hard.

CHAPTER THIRTY-FIVE

In the comfort of the small guest room, I tried on the costume. I loved it. The heavy gathered skirt, although a scratchy wool, had a good swish quality to it, one I wouldn't have thought possible for such a sturdy cloth. Icelandic sheep: another example of the island's against-the-grain tradition. And the cap's silver tassel was silky smooth as it brushed my face. Clothing with moving parts—yes, now. And the small over-the-shoulder satchel was a very practical addition. I ran my finger over the worn brown leather. This was no modern costume reproduction. It was faded in dappled patches and as soft as a butterfly's wing. Into it I stuffed a wad of Icelandic bills and a lip gloss. I was just about to toss in the pocket dictionary when the black velvet pouch of runes caught my eye. I'd yet to open the bag since receiving it; the engraved markings meant nothing to me; and I still suspected my fingers of some sort of betrayal in packing them. *Modern dictionary practical; ancient alphabet useless,* were the words I heard in my head. Again, my double-crossing fingers grabbed the bag and stuffed it into the satchel.

Voices alerted me to Afi and Baldur's presence. I hurried to find them in the front room with Vigdis. They, too, were dressed for the occasion. Both wore black knit caps with silver tassels, white shirts, dark vests with two rows of buttons, red neckerchiefs, short knicker-style pants, dark knee-high socks held up with tasseled garters, and funny pointed shoes.

"Afi, I love the look."

He tugged at his knotted red scarf. "Thank you." He looked at me, nodding his head. His eyes were glassy. "You look like my long-departed sister, dressed as you are."

"I'll take that as a compliment," I said.

"There's none higher," he said, winking and wiping the corner of his eye.

"We make a fine group," Vigdis said. "A very good start to a festival day."

"So what's the schedule of events?" I asked.

"There's a luncheon hosted by the church, then speeches in the square, then games to build appetites for the big dinner at the festival hall, and, of course, the dancing. Most important is the dancing."

Holy cow. All that in one day? Vigdis and Baldur hardly looked like endurance athletes, but I honestly wondered if I'd be able to keep up. Already they were idling high with adrenaline coloring their cheeks and tapping their toes.

"Do you think there will be time to find that café with Internet?" I asked. "I want to send an e-mail."

"Of course," Vigdis said. "We'll drop you off on our way to the church. I will be busy with duties, so you take your time. Explore the village. Then come have a nice lunch."

As promised, Baldur's little sardine-can car dropped me off at the small restaurant. Once in town, my costume didn't feel like such a good idea. The café catered to a young crowd, a hip crowd. So far, I seemed to be the only one under thirty dressed like the St. Pauli Girl. I made my way through the crush of small tables to an open seat in the back. I was definitely getting looks and comments. The language barrier didn't help. In fact, it fueled my imagination. Was *gofka* Icelandic for freak, or for punked?

At least I had the promise of an e-mail from Jack to take my mind off the pointing and staring. I fired up my laptop and opened my Hotmail account. My heart fell with the realization that my in-box was empty. A waitress appeared at the table and rattled off something

223

I didn't understand. I supposed if I looked like I'd just stepped off the cover of an Icelandic travel brochure, her assumption that I could handle a basic sentence was fair.

I replied with two of the roughly ten words I knew, *"Kaffi, vinsamlegast."* And just hoped I'd asked for coffee, please.

I typed a quick e-mail to my mom, hoping she had her laptop on her belly.

The message read,

Mom, did you send Stanley a note for me? Asking
Jack to send me an e-mail? Hope you're feeling
better. Love, Kat.

Just as I hit the send button, the waitress delivered the coffee and a small jug of milk. As I stirred a spiral of white into the steaming cup, my computer dinged. Man, did I love my ever-dependable Mom? And I had an ever-growing appreciation for command central.

Her reply read,

Dear Kat, Stanley promised to pass your
message on to Jack. It does sound like they're busy,
spending many hours in the field. If you want to try
yourself, here's the e-mail: info@klarksbergstation.
net. In the subject line, put attention: Jack Snjosson.
It won't be very private, but they do seem to go
through. Enjoy the festival. Love to you and
Afi, Mom.

I took a sip of the coffee. Dang, it was strong. A cup of joe my dad would definitely appreciate. I typed in the e-mail address my mom had given me and Jack's name into the subject line. The gist of my message was: Where are you??? E-mail me back!!! I can't breathe.

I had just hit send when I felt a tap at my elbow. From the table next to me, a young guy with big blue eyes and sandy brown hair said, *"Gobbledy orforick goop. Ekka mejr goop"* — or at least that's what I made out of what sounded like complete gibberish to me.

"Sorry," I said. "I'm not Icelandic."

"Not Icelandic?" he said, switching into English. "But you're dressed for the festival."

I looked around the café. Two others up front, thank God, were also dressed like Hansel and Gretel.

"I guess I thought everyone else would be, too," I said, adjusting my little woolen cap.

"But, you wear the silver tassel," he said, pointing at the thick silken tail-like thing hanging over my left ear.

"So?" I asked.

"On festival day, only the *selurmanna* wear the silver tassel."

"The who?" I asked.

"The *selurmanna*," he said, still pointing. "The seal people. Your cap is a sign."

Talk about *déjà vu*. Once again, I found myself in the

uncomfortable position of someone pointing at my head and calling it a sign. And cap? That's what the Storks call our ridiculous means of communication.

"It's not a sign," I said. "It's just a hat."

"But where did you get it?" he asked. "They are very obscure."

Which, at least, explained the looks and whispers I had attracted upon arrival.

"My *afi* and I are staying with his cousin and his cousin's wife. They're all wearing them, too."

"Then you are a descendant of the *selurmanna*."

Jeez. Like I needed more branches sprouting from my crazy family tree.

"What does that mean?" I asked, knowing — but not caring — how dumb I sounded.

"Ancestors who can trace their lineage as descendants of Finnur, a legendary forefather."

That was a relief, more a matter of first dibs than something fantastical. His use of the word "obscure" probably one of those lost-in-translation moments; *rare* was probably the word he was looking for. Though his English was pretty darn fluent and his accent very light.

"So kind of like an Icelandic version of the pilgrims," I said. "Was he a Viking settler?" At least I had a smattering of Icelandic history and felt confident that this was a good guess.

The guy laughed, smacked the table, and said,

"Nothing so common for Hafmeyjafjörður, not according to the legends." He gestured with his arms in a floppy circle. "Here is considered a place of old mysteries. Here it is believed the *huldufólk* walk the earth. Here the *vatnfólk* still swim the seas." He then winked, as if making light of it all.

Just as I was about to ask for an English-please translation, my in-box chimed. I quickly pulled up my Hotmail account and saw that I had an e-mail from Klarksberg. As I opened the message, I heard the chair next to me scrape the floor and watched my chatty neighbor stand and wave to someone across the room.

"Enjoy the festival," he said to me as he walked away.

I wanted to yell "Wait," get a little more backstory from the guy, but I also wanted to read the e-mail immediately. Someone in Greenland was sitting at a keyboard. *Jack? Please let it be Jack.*

My eyes scanned the message. My hopes drained with a glug. It read:

Dear Kat, your message to Jack has been brought
to my attention. Sorry to say that he is currently
unavailable. I will get it to him at the first possible
opportunity. Will explain more later. Pressed for time
now. Best to you and Afi. Stanley.

I read it three times, but still sat staring at the screen like some sort of code had been embedded in the short missive. *Unavailable?* Weren't there, like, twenty of them, tops, at the base? What? Was he in the bathroom? In the shower? How long could either of those take? Which brought me to *at the first possible opportunity*? *Pressed for time*? They were dealing with climate change, right? Small gradual changes over the history of the planet. Hardly anything with a detonator attached to it. So why the hurry?

I closed my laptop with a snap. I hardly knew what to stress about first and most. My talkative neighbor calling my silver tassel obscure and a sign and calling the town a place of mysticism, or reports coming in of Jack being withdrawn, under Brigid's special care, and now unavailable. I left the café with more than my strange cap weighing on my mind.

CHAPTER THIRTY-SIX

I found the church easily enough. It helped that it was set high on a hill and that the noon bells were louder than jet traffic over LAX. Though church bells were much more melodic. I followed the crowd into what felt like a meeting room or banquet hall. Rafters of rough timbers towered above, and the plaster walls were thick, with few windows. It felt like the real deal: a Viking longhouse, not some Disneyesque recreation. In the center of the room, there were long tables covered with crisp white cloths, while colorful paper lanterns and silvery netting hung from the ceiling and flags and coats of arms decked the walls. People carrying plates of food milled about. Finally, my attire allowed me to blend. Everyone was dressed as if stepping out of a Hans Christian Andersen tale. Silver tassels, however, were few and far between. Vigdis's shiny round face was easy to spot. She waved at me from her place in the serving line, where she wielded a large spoon over an even larger serving dish. I found Afi and Baldur sitting at the far end of a table sipping coffee, with dirty plates pushed to the side.

I sat down at an empty seat.

"Uh, Afi, is there something I should know about this silver tassel?" I asked, fingering its shimmery fringe.

"It's for the pure Hafmeyjafjörðurs," Afi said.

"But what does that mean? Some guy at the café made it sound like it was unusual. And another thing: who are the *huldufólk* and the *vatnfólk*?"

The table got very quiet. Baldur cleared his throat; Afi stroked his chin.

"Afi?" I asked.

"These are old legends, Katla. Stories, really."

Like I hadn't heard that one before.

"Go on," I said.

"The *huldufólk* are the hidden people," Afi said.

"Hidden how?" I asked.

"Magical beings who are invisible to humans," Afi said with no more inflection than a weather report.

"And the *vatnfólk*?"

"The water creatures of which mermaids, mermen, and the selkie belong. *Hafmeyja* is even the Icelandic

230

word for 'mermaid.' Our town, Hafmeyjafjörður, translates to 'Mermaid Fjord.'"

Again, Afi spoke so matter-of-factly. I kept waiting for him to crack a smile, slap a knee. Nothing.

"Hungry?" I looked up as Vigdis slid a plate of food in front of me.

I was, but I also considered food, like ancestors, a don't-surprise-me topic.

"Thank you," I said, trying my best to sound convincing.

"Is my specialty, rhubarb-filled pancakes and *blóð-mor* sausages," Vigdis said, beaming at me with pride.

I hoped it was the pancakes she was pushing, because, personally, I didn't want *any* blood in my sausages — *more* was simply out of the question.

"You'll have to eat fast," Vigdis said, "because next comes the minstrel out in the square."

"The minstrel?" I asked with a mouthful of pancake that was warm, and honey-infused, and disappearing quickly.

"Ah, yes," Vigdis said, nodding with pleasure at my appetite. "The village minstrel will recount the story behind our festival. So many come from afar that is helpful to give the history. And for some years now is all done in English. You're not the only tourist here today. We've become quite the attraction. Eat up, eat up," she urged. "Is starting very soon."

231

I dropped my napkin over two untouched blood-filled sausages. "Let's go, then. I'd really like to hear the stories." It was true. If I was going to walk around town with some symbolic silver tassel, I supposed I needed the 411 on it.

After stashing my laptop in Baldur's tiny trunk, I followed Afi, Baldur, and Vigdis down the steep hill and into the town's square. It wasn't far from the café where I'd been earlier, but this was definitely a much older part of town. The shop fronts had a Nordic charm, with their bright colors and ornate trim. Some had medieval-looking turrets; others had pointy spire-like roofs; one even had a clock tower. And old-fashioned wooden shop signs hung from iron brackets. Over cobblestone pavers, we followed the festival-goers into the open square, where a stage had been set up.

Scattered through the crowd were the obvious tourists dressed in jeans and modern attire. Somehow, against this idyllic backdrop, they were the ones out of place.

Soon, an official-looking gentleman took the stage. Though his costume was also period, its high ruffled collar and big brass buttons down the front of a tailed coat spoke of authority. He introduced himself as the mayor and then, with as much pomp as he could muster, declared the festival open. The first order of business was the selkie legends.

The minstrel climbed onstage, and I almost took

cover. Talk about hulking. He was tall and built. He wore heavy brown woolen stockings, a mid-thigh-length bright green tunic with gold braiding, a red cape, a wide leather belt and thigh-high boots, and a leather cap with fur trim. Yowza. His long dark hair and beard were thick and, quite honestly, in need of some very deep conditioning. He looked like a cross between Hagrid and one of the beasts from *Where the Wild Things Are.*

He opened his arms in a gesture of welcome. "Once upon a time," he began.

I relaxed. That's how children's books began. Fiction, from long, long ago: that, I could handle.

"God in heaven cast out those angels who merited neither salvation nor damnation." He brought his hands to his side, hooking his meaty thumbs into his belt. "They tumbled to earth here on this Icelandic fjord, where their celestial traits set them apart from God's children. Some fell into the waters and became the *vatnfólk,* the sea creatures, of which there are many. Others fell to the earth and became the *huldufólk,* the hidden people, also taking many forms. Of all the creatures, there's but one with the ability to inhabit both land and sea. The selkie alone can shed its seal cloak to reveal a human form. Once a year, in atonement, the selkies come ashore here, the place of their fall." The minstrel gestured in the direction of the fjord with his muscled arms. "In a cavern by the water, they dance with their long-lost cousins, the *huldufólk,* for one night, and then return to the sea, always seeking a return to God's good graces."

So far so good, I thought. An annual beach party: a kind of dancing-with-the-fallen-from-the-stars. After an Icelandic winter, I was certain the locals would invent any excuse to celebrate.

"For countless generations, the townsfolk knew of this night and respected the privacy of these mystical creatures. One winter, though, ten hundred years ago, times were very hard and there were many hungry mouths to feed. A hunting party of menfolk waited on the rocks for an opportunity to slay the unsuspecting seals. One among this group, Finnur, a poor, unmarried fisherman, could not lift his eyes from the human form of one of the selkies. Legend says she had hair the color of fire and eyes the color of emeralds. Even the selkie-men sought her out, calling upon her to dance: 'Lovely Leira, charm of the sea, Lovely Leira, dance with me.' So enraptured was Finnur that he could not bear to see her hunted. Even after watching her shape-shift back into her sealskin, Finnur was captivated. To protect her from the hunters, he shielded her and her fellow seals with his own body."

Still sounded OK to me. And as romances go, boy meets seal was an interesting twist. The hammy minstrel definitely had my attention.

"That night, Leira and the other selkies escaped, while a wounded Finnur could only watch helplessly as the beautiful creature slipped away," the minstrel continued. "Afterward, Finnur was shunned by the villagers and forced to live in a small hut many miles from the town. Here he lived another summer and winter, but very lonely and with a heavy heart. The following year, the night of the dance of the selkies, he returned, hoping for a glimpse of the lovely Leira. Crouched behind some rocks at the entrance to the cavern, Finnur was approached by an elf, one of the *huldufólk*. The elf said:

'Many a selkie here tonight
Owes unto thee its life.
In gratitude, we offer thee
The most precious of all as wife.

For seven years, bearing seven children,
A wife to you she'll be.
Then, Leira, to whom the waters are home,
You must vow to return to the sea.'"

The minstrel paused, locking eyes with many in the crowd. I looked around. Even Baldur and Vigdis, who must have heard the story year after year, were pink-cheeked and attentive. The beefy bard sure knew how to tell a story. I, too, was eager for the rest of the tale.

The minstrel continued, "The young fisherman eagerly consented. He was then invited to dance with the red-haired, green-eyed beauty. After a jig, the elf presented to the young man a sealskin, and instructed the fisherman to lock it away until the pact was done, but cautioned that on the night of the selkie dance, eight years thereafter, the pelt, and her freedom, were to be returned. As prophesied, over seven years, she was a loving wife and bore him seven children: seven girls, in fact, each as beautiful as their mother. During their final winter together, Leira, again, grew round with child, and Finnur, who longed for a son, was certain that Leira carried a boy. Yet on the eve of the dance, it was clear that the child was months from birth. Finnur begged his wife to abide by him until the child was born, after which he'd return her sealskin and her freedom. Leira, understanding the solemnity of the vow, insisted that Finnur take her, and her hidden sealskin, to the dance.

"In the end, an anguished Finnur locked Leira, his daughters, and the sealskin in the hut and hurried to the dance in hopes of bargaining with the *huldufólk*. The elf was furious that Finnur had broken his vow and would hear nothing of a delay. The angrier the elf became, the greater the winds whipped, until a huge squall brought driving rain and waves the width and breadth of giants. Fearing for his family during such a storm, Finnur rushed home to find his hovel reduced to flotsam, his seven distraught daughters clinging to one another in fear, and his wife and her sealskin washed out to sea. Nor was it only the family of Finnur who bore the brunt of that storm. Villages up and down the length of the fjord were washed away that fateful night. Finnur took to the sea in his fishing boat, never to be heard from again. To this day, storms bring stories of a mist-shrouded skiff and ghostly form tossed by the swell of an angry sea. And the seven daughters—half-selkie, half-human—were adopted out to the kind families of Hafmeyjafjörður. Legend holds that the descendants of these sisters are sometimes more water creature than earthly being. And any who can trace an ancestor to one of these seven sisters are considered the *selurmanna,* the seal people, and wear the silver tassel to the selkie dance."

At the conclusion of the minstrel's performance, I turned to my grandfather. "Afi, how is it I've never heard of the seal people before, especially if we're descendants? And just what does that mean? It couldn't possibly be a true story."

"Town records indicate there were seven sisters, daughters of one Finnur Haldorsson." Afi scratched at his head. "The rest of the story, well, I suppose that as it passed from generation to generation, it grew, as such things do."

"So there're no selkies swimming in your gene pool?"

Afi laughed. "Our breed's a long line of mariners, whalers, and fisherman, but two legs and two arms had every one of them." He pushed up the sleeve of his thick woolen sweater and pointed to a bulbous blue vein that ran from the back of his hand over his wrist. "Though I've always said it's seawater, not blood, coursing through these old veins of mine. But the *selurmanna* and the selkie dances—all the makings of a good story and a good celebration. No?"

"So far so good," I said. "What's next?"

"The games," Afi said.

"What kind of games?" I asked.

Afi chuckled. "Like nothing you've seen before."

He was right. We followed the crowd down to the waterfront, where, upon a large grassy clearing, a Viking encampment had been recreated. Colorful banners and flags flapped in the wind of the early-spring day. Though snow lay in scattered piles and the air temperature was in the low forties, tops, a weak late-afternoon sun did its best to brighten the scene. I myself zipped up my white down-filled parka. Afi, as well as most of the crowd, seemed unbothered by the brisk day.

Again, I was impressed by the scale of the event. A lively village lay before us. Simple stick hovels and canvas tents horseshoed one side of the perimeter, from which merchants and artisans sold their wares. We walked along, inspecting the many objects for sale. Shields and crude swords were popular items. Afi explained that later there would be a contest of Viking war tactics. Though some of it was clearly child-size and cheap reproductions, there were a few vendors who appeared to be hawking the real deal. I also noticed quite a few hooded capes made to look like sealskin. Leather belts, pouches, and saddlebags were spread over blankets and hung from makeshift display fronts. Fur-trimmed vests, chain-mail tunics, Viking helmets, Nordic sweaters, and sheepskin coats were also being sold by authentic-looking shopkeepers. Afi struck up a conversation with one of the wool vendors, while a table of jewelry, a few tents down, caught my eye. Behind the table sat a woman and a girl about my age. The woman wore layer over layer of bright peasant-style clothing, bangles up and down her arms, and a head scarf. Daggerlike slashes of eyeliner and smoky-blue shadowed lids intensified her brooding stare. She was either playing the part of a gypsy or was the true article. I guessed the latter. The girl had dark eyes, coal-black hair, and an all-black palette that was hard-core goth; even her lipstick and the tats inking her arms were midnight black. I smiled at her; she scowled back in return. *So much for customer service.*

I picked up one of the medieval-looking crosses on a thick leather band. With my Doc Martens and against a simple white T-shirt, it would look great. As I was running the krona-to-dollars calculation in my head, I spied a pile of stones much like the ones stuffed into my leather satchel. My free-thinking fingers reached out and palmed a few of them, like dice.

I heard the woman jabber something at me.

"Sorry," I said. "I'm American."

She looked at me, up at my cap and tassel, and then turned and squawked something at the girl.

"My mother wonders if you'd like to have your runes read," the girl said. Though it was technically a question, or maybe even an invitation, her tone couldn't have been more disinterested.

"My runes read?" I asked. I had thought they were an alphabet, not a fortune-telling device.

"With the aid of the runes, an *erilaz,* like my mother, can tell the future."

I figured it was a trick to get me to buy something. As a con, the woman likely dished out bogus fortunes and then asked for a fistful of krona in return. "I'm good," I said, unhooking the strap to my leather satchel and pulling out my velvet pouch. "Already have my own set." I shook a few of the rocks onto my palm.

Goth girl's lashes batted up and down. She spoke so fast and with such a hiss, I wondered if runic was a spoken language.

"May I see them?" the girl asked, but before I could respond, she grabbed the pouch and the few stones from my palm in a very swift, very deft move: a sort of reverse shoplifting. While holding them, the girl closed her eyes and then, as if goosed, her eyes popped open.

"Where did you get these? They're very old."

"They were a gift," I said.

Gobbledygook was exchanged between the two. I

couldn't be sure, but it seemed like the conversation ended with gypsy mom telling goth daughter to shut up. Some things don't need a translator.

"My mother will read them for you," the girl said. It wasn't a question.

The woman shook a large white cloth from her pocket and spread it out on the table in front of me. One at a time, I was instructed to pull runes from the pouch and place them facedown on the cloth exactly where she pointed. Once I had pulled five and they were lined up as if at the four points of the compass and one in the middle, I was instructed to place my pouch to the side.

At first it was confusing with them both speaking at me, but, within a moment or two, I learned to concentrate on the woman's gentler — by comparison — voice, while ignoring goth girl's more hawkish gaze and tone. I was picking up on a word repeated over and over, "Jinky."

"Is your name Jinky?" I asked goth girl.

"Yes." Her gaze narrowed.

It took everything in me not to react. Jinky? *Seriously?* Somehow, her unfortunate — at least to me — name explained everything; I relaxed — a little.

"Mine's Kat."

She didn't respond. *All righty, then.*

The first rune I was instructed to lift was the very center one. I turned it over, revealing a kind of slanty upside-down capital *F.*

"In a five-rune spread," Jinky said, "this rune represents your current situation."

Currently, I thought to myself, *some part of my money will soon belong to these two.* I expected to be told something cliché, like an inheritance or a handsome stranger coming my way. Gypsy mom yakked some more.

"It's *Fehu,* except reversed or upside down." Jinky bit her lip. "This signifies a loss."

Which is definitely in keeping with my it's-all-a-sham-for-which-I'll-pay theory.

Next, I was instructed to turn over the rune to the left or due west of *Fehu.* It looked like two upright parallel lines attached by a small *x* that connected them from their tops to their centers.

"This rune signifies your past. You have drawn *Mannaz,* the symbol for man."

Hmmm. I'd have expected the "man" to be in my future, but whatever.

The third rune I lifted was above or due north of *Fehu.* It looked like a backward seven, but with the top slanting down at a more severe angle. As I turned this one over, the two exchanged a volley of rapid-fire conversation. Gypsy girl was all lit up, excited even, and seemed to be talking her mom into something; trying, anyway. Twice, she pointed at my tasseled cap. Gypsy mom prevailed, or so it seemed.

"As your help rune you have drawn *Lagaz,* the water symbol. This is a powerful symbol and besides water can also represent psychic gifts and intuitive knowledge." Though she spoke the word "powerful," her voice was once again detached and monotone. "The help rune indicates the thing that you can use during this situation, in your case loss."

Wasn't I supposed to be having my fortune read? And doesn't fortune mean luck? The good kind? I sure hoped they'd get to that part soon.

The fourth rune I revealed was the stone below or due south of *Fehu*. It looked like a straight line that stood upright: a number one with no hook and no base. Again, there was a lot of discussion going back and forth between the woman and her daughter. This time it seemed an angry exchange. For such a simple-looking symbol, it really didn't seem worth all the fuss. Besides, it wasn't like I was buying into their act. If they were any good at their proclaimed psychic abilities, they should have been pulling my doubts out like a giant magnet. Their exchange concluded with gypsy mom shaking her finger at her daughter.

"As your obstacle you have drawn *Isa,* the ice symbol," a pissed-off Jinky said.

That got my attention. I was in Iceland, after all. And, for the record, was Jack Frost's girlfriend. Plus, for all the heated chatter that had passed between them, it was far too short of a translation. Something had definitely been edited.

"What does that mean?" I asked.

"*Isa,* like all the runes, has many interpretations. It can mean a standstill or delay to events. It indicates an elemental substance, a source of mystery. It can also indicate reversed love."

I did not like the sound of that one. Especially given the doubts I was having about Jack. For sanity's sake, I figured I'd go with its elemental meaning, water below thirty-two degrees Fahrenheit. And chalk their arguments up to fiery personalities.

Finally, I flipped over the remaining stone. The one to the right or due east of *Fehu.* It looked like a capital *R.*

"As your result stone," Jinky said, "you have chosen *Raidho,* the rune of journeys."

Well, duh—I was on vacation. And if I had kept track of the five stones correctly, my fortune read as follows: My present is a loss, my past is a man, my much-debated help will be water, my highly disputed obstacle will be ice, and the result will be a journey. And how much would that all cost me?

"Are you not here for such a journey?" Jinky asked. It was the first time she had addressed me, not simply translated what her mom had said.

As if sensing a slight to her authority, the mother interrupted her daughter with a long, spit-punctuated lecture.

"I'm on spring break, if that's what you mean?" I said. Man, these two were an odd pair. I sure wouldn't want to sit down to one of their family dinners, an occasion at which I'd watch my back and my neighbor's knife. "With my *afi*. Here he comes now." I had never been so happy to see Afi's hunched shoulders and wiry white hair.

With those lightning-quick reflexes of hers, Jinky scooped up the runes and the cloth. By the time Afi was at my elbow, I was once again looking down at the table of jewelry.

"See anything you like?" Afi asked.

I felt a small tug at my sleeve and turned to see Jinky slip my velvet pouch into the pocket of my parka.

"They have some nice things," I said, ad-libbing, though I hardly knew why.

The woman held up a necklace and dangled it in front of Afi, speaking in Icelandic.

I gasped. It looked remarkably like the necklace Brigid had worn: the one that Jack had shattered. Though this jagged crystalline pendant hung from a strap of leather; Brigid's had been on a silver chain.

"She thinks this one would suit you," Afi said.

"I . . . I've seen one like it before."

Afi spoke again to the woman and then fished around in his pocket, producing a money clip. Before I could think of anything to say, he peeled three two-thousand krona bills from the fold and handed them to her. Six-thousand krona was, according to my rough calculations, about fifty dollars. I was in such a fog of surprise, I was hardly able to mumble an appropriate good-bye to the two peddlers. As we turned to leave, Jinky said, "Safe travels."

Though it was an entirely appropriate comment, it sent shivers down my spine. Partly because it had been delivered with a sneer, and partly because it seemed she wanted to say more.

Afi and I stepped away from their booth. I, for one, was glad to go. "Thank you, Afi. You really didn't need to buy it."

"The woman said it was a good-luck piece, and that it would be a nice souvenir of your trip."

I looped it behind my neck, twisted the metal screw fastener, and zipped my jacket up tight. Sliding my hands into my pockets, I jiggled the pouch of runes, not knowing what to think. Were they con artists? Afi *was* out fifty bucks. And just what was up with that rune reading? Because of a guy, I was to expect a loss resulting in a journey where water would help and ice would be an obstacle. And the necklace? So like Brigid's. I hadn't seen anything like it on the table when I'd first examined their pieces. And now I was to consider it a good-luck souvenir.

"The contests are about to begin," Afi said. "First is the tug-of-war."

Perfect, because that was exactly what was going on in my head: plain old common sense versus the weird and wacked. And dang it if the freaks weren't gaining ground.

246

CHAPTER THIRTY-SEVEN

The games took place in an open field adjacent to the small Viking tent village. A roaring bonfire separated the areas between the camp and the field. In the chill and weak light of the early-spring day, the fire's heat and glow was like honey dribbled on toast. And all the more welcome following the creepy-crawly tingle the rune reading had left me with. We found Baldur and Vigdis warming themselves by the crackling blaze.

"There you two are," Vigdis said. "Come, the games are starting."

We gathered around an impossibly long and thick swath of rope with two ginormous loops on each end.

The rope was stretched over one seriously nasty-looking mud pit. A foghorn sounded, and soon two teams of men entered the clearing from opposite ends of the field. The first team looked like ancient Vikings, with crude garments made of shearling wool, horned helmets, and even the odd chain-mail tunic. The second team wore capes and hoods fashioned out of—what I hoped was imitation—sealskins. No mistaking what this game represented. The original townspeople of Hafmeyjafjörður versus the selkie folk. The two largest men stepped into the looped ends of the rope, and the rest of their teams positioned themselves in front of them. Again, the foghorn sounded, and soon the men were grunting like wild boars while the crowd cheered and whistled. It was hard-fought, but, in the end, the seals were wallowing in the muck. The crowd went wild with excitement. It was clear just which side the average Johann was rooting for. I noticed that Afi, Baldur, and Vigdis—in the minority with their silver tassels—frowned at the outcome. I followed my small *selurmanna* group toward the next event.

We watched a net-mending contest, relay races on large, handled hop-balls made to look like buoys, and a crazy beachfront finale that was a sort of triathlon. Part one was a sprint to the water, part two a frenzied stripping of layered clothing, and part three a swim to the end of the wooden pier and back. I couldn't believe that so many people would brave those frigid waters, never mind bare such a sorry display of underwear. And when wet and drooping, more is definitely better.

It was after five. Darkness was pressing down. With a pinch, it squeezed the air from my chest. Torches and old-fashioned street lamps lit the scene, but, still, with the twilight came an eerie vibe. As much as the entire day was celebrated as a recreation of legends and stories, here, down at the water, I felt the oddest sensation. Air-ferried energies seemed to whisper in my ear, like a swell of ancient winds brushing over me. The crowds started to disperse from the waterfront, but I was rooted to the spot. I felt a presence and thought I heard the strange music again. I spun, scanning the beach. Down along the rocks, far from the gathering, I spied something splashing.

"Wait. There's still someone in the water," I said, pointing.

Baldur and Vigdis followed my finger with their eyes, but blinked back at me in confusion. "Where?" Vigdis asked.

"He was there a minute ago," I said. "Or maybe it was even a woman. It was hard to tell. Afi, did you see someone, or hear anything?"

Afi's eyes focused on the exact spot where I was pointing, seemingly even dipping his ear closer, but then he shook his head and said, "No, everyone's out. See? All the clothes are picked up."

So they were. On the beach, all the various pieces of

clothing had been reclaimed. Had someone or something been there, it wasn't one of the festival-goers. Afi and I exchanged looks. For the briefest of moments, I wanted to challenge him. Ask him again. I gazed out upon the rocks once more. Nothing. I distractedly fingered the necklace Afi bought me.

"I see you wear the Snow Queen necklace," Vigdis said.

"The what?"

"The Snow Queen necklace. They're very popular here. From the children's story the *Snædrottningin,* 'The Snow Queen.' Is reproduction of the mirror fragments that the queen uses to freeze hearts."

"I don't remember a mirror in the story," I said, my heart squeezing in and out like an accordion. I heard the whiny music and wouldn't have been surprised had a monkey with a collection cup jumped on my shoulder.

"If I remember correctly," Vigdis said, "it's the prologue. A story about a wicked troll who makes an evil mirror. While flying up to the heavens with it, in order to play tricks on the angels, it shatters and falls to earth, freezing the hearts of all those pierced by its fragments."

I found it bizarre that we were discussing *The Snow Queen.* Had Afi or I mentioned the musical to Vigdis? Even if we had, it certainly hadn't come up during the rune reading. When constantly tripping you up, coincidences — like long, scratchy skirts — became a nuisance.

"Who's hungry?" Baldur asked.

I, for one, was and welcomed the distraction. It had been a long time since Vigdis's rhubarb-filled pancakes, and something warm and hearty sounded good, provided the adjectives *blood, fermented,* or *sour-pickled* weren't part of the description.

Baldur pulled four tickets out of his pocket. "Dinner and dance is at the festival hall, just a short walk away. Shall we?"

I followed my companions, passing the warmth of the bonfire reluctantly. At least "festival hall" indicated something with walls and a ceiling, which meant, if nothing else, a break from the wind. I had always known Afi bragged to be of rugged stock, but an outdoor event with snow still on the ground? And swimming in an icy fjord? No, thank you. Tables, chairs, plates, and forks were all the incentive I required.

From the outside, the hall was a low, squat building. Inside, it was a cavernous space with a vaulted ceiling and thick walls with narrow transom windows. One half of the enclosed area had long, simple wooden tables pushed together and lined up one after another. This would be no private dining experience; more like a boarding-school hall: Hogwarts on the Fjord. The other half of the room was used for buffet tables, a stage, and a dance floor. Baldur handed over our dinner tickets, and we got in line. Rustic earthen bowls and huge platters were overflowing with food. A seafood feast seemed, to me, bad karma for an event celebrating fish people. I, personally, loaded up on the carbs and veggies: flat breads and dark ryes, mashed potatoes, boiled cabbage, pickled beets, the yogurt-like skyr, rice pudding, and a whole array of cakes and cookies.

We sat close to the dance floor at the end of one of the long plank tables. Afi, Baldur, and Vigdis slipped into a conversation in Icelandic, and it was actually soothing to hear the hum of voices but not have to concentrate on the words, the way instrumental music frees you from the influence of lyrics. Vigdis and Baldur, seemingly, disagreed about something; Afi, I think, sided with Vigdis. I watched Afi with his relatives. He looked happier than I'd seen him in a long time. Back home, he was lonely and missed Amma, I knew, but I could tell that it was more than that. Funny that I had even used the word "home," because that's just how he seemed here surrounded by these Icelanders — at home.

I scooped the last bite of a piece of chocolate cake into my mouth just as the band took the stage. The trio — a fiddle, flute, and bass guitar — wasted no time. After a short greeting to the crowd, they started up. It was definitely folk music, a lively, hand-clapping, toe-tapping-style throwback. Nothing that would get cred at the Grammys, but, still, it buzzed the place to life. Vigdis and Baldur were the first two to hit the dance floor. They were so cute together, if two pushing-seventy gray-hairs could be called cute. Afi watched that first number clapping to the music and with a big smile creasing his lined cheeks.

"Watch closely," he said to me. "We'll give it a go next song."

Uh-oh. This type of dancing had rules and steps and a very specific order to things. The men twirled the women in unison; there were kicks, and stutter steps, and bowing, and circles formed. It was nothing like shaking my booty with Tina and Penny at last fall's Homecoming dance.

"I don't know, Afi. It looks complicated."

The first song ended, and Afi pulled me to my feet. "People are complicated; this is just dancing."

For an old guy, Afi could move. I did my best. Kicked when the others kicked, ducked under a bridge of arms when I seemed to be next in line, and even got the hang of the twirls he snapped me back and forth from, but I was always a half step behind the whole darn lot of them, though almost every one of them had a good fifty years on me. I stumbled my way through two songs, then begged off. Afi quickly found himself a new partner, who, I had to admit, was very light on her feet despite her size and age.

At first, I watched from the table. Then I made my way to the drink station, pointing and ending up with some sort of cider. For a while, I watched the dancers from the back of the room. Someone tapped me on the shoulder.

"You still have your silver tassel, I see." It was the guy from the café earlier that day. The one who'd first mentioned the *selurmanna* to me.

I touched my cap. "For whatever it's worth, looks like my *afi* can trace his roots back to one of the seven sisters."

The guy lifted his eyebrows. "Impressive."

"Not really. I'd say the census keepers around here are the ones to be admired. Are we talking close to a thousand years of town records? Now, that's impressive."

"Anyway, it looks good on you. Legend says the sisters were all beautiful."

My heart dropped, landing with a splat on my kidneys, and all I could think of was Jack. There was nothing between me and this guy, so I was all the more confused by my physical reaction. And it was physical; I wouldn't have been surprised had a bruise bubbled to the surface of my chest. What had just happened? It had felt like some kind of . . . of what? The word that came crazily to mind was *loss*. But that was the word the old rune reader had used. Was I just projecting her words onto an emotion I couldn't identify? Was I feeling guilty that this guy was flirting with me? Was he flirting with me? He was still hanging around, eyeing me weirdly. But guilt I would recognize, right? This was different. A lurch to my gut as if something had happened. And if not to me, then to someone I loved.

"If you'll excuse me," I said, not even bothering to invent any more of an excuse than that.

I looked out to the dance floor. Afi, Baldur, and Vigdis were still high-stepping it. I grabbed my coat from the rack at the back of the room and plunged into the cold, dark night. A few people were gathered around the exit; I hurried past them, needing quiet and space to think. Lost in thought and disoriented by the darkness, I walked aimlessly, thinking about Jack. Was I imagining the coldness to our good-bye? Was I, so new at the whole relationship thing, inventing dramas? So what if he was too busy to get hold of me. He was, after all, at some arctic field camp. And devoting himself to the opportunity. Was I being juvenile? Acting like the schoolgirl that — for the record — I was? And just what was that drop I felt in my gut back there? I knew I hadn't invented that. Not even I could manufacture a reshuffling of organs.

Outside, the air had turned brittle. After the warmth of the hall, my lungs rattled at the contrast. My feet slapped at the pavement until I ended up on a promenade overlooking a different section of the beach than where the polar plunge had taken place earlier. It was remote, with only a few lampposts illuminating a pedestrian path up above the water. The nearly-full moon hung like a paper lantern over the inky sea. Was I north of the festival? Or south? A gust of approaching voices scattered my brain fog; a huddle of dark shapes advanced.

I'd lived in LA long enough to have a healthy stranger-danger radar. I had to make a decision quick. Continuing down the path would put me farther away from the hall and civilization — such as it was — though it would, at least, put distance between me and the others. Standing my ground, or an about-face, would force an encounter, an option with definite risks. The water was a dead end, nor did a scramble up the dark and sloped berm separating this path from whatever was directly above it seem wise.

The pack, ten or so in number, drew closer. My weak-kneed limbs had taken the liberty of going with a let's-see-what-they-want option. As the group pressed down on me, I could hear both male and female voices; they weren't speaking English.

When only ten or so feet separated me from these dark forms, one — a girl — spoke to the others and then halved the distance between us. I had no idea what she said, but her voice had a hard edge, and I would have guessed something along the lines of "I got this one."

Just as she was almost upon me, I was shocked to discover —

"Jinky?"

"Are you lost?" she asked. Her voice hadn't softened any with the realization that we were acquaintances; it wasn't a good sign.

"No. Just walking."

Another girl had joined Jinky away from the pack. She circled as if inspecting me, like I was some kind of used car. I didn't like it—or her. Had she tried to kick the tires, she'd have had a fight on her hands; I was getting pissed.

"You should be dancing with the *selurmanna,* no?" Jinky asked.

At the mention of the seal people, the still-circling car buyer reached from behind me and fingered my silver tassel. I spun around, giving myself points for knocking her hand away, but gave up a few for losing my footing in the process. Jinky, to my surprise, steadied me.

"Watch out," she said, removing her hand from my waist.

I didn't like her touching me, or the way she and her friends then laughed as if it were some kind of joke. Moreover, "Watch out" was something you said to someone before they fell, not after. Plus, judging by the way her eyes had narrowed and her voice had grown husky, I got the sense it was a warning—not a show of concern.

"Will do," I said, mirroring her icy stare.

So what the hell had I done to her? Afi had even bought their stupid necklace. I fingered it, remembering what her mother had said. Good luck—on whose authority?

With the festival hall as my determined safe house, I headed back in that direction, a course that required me to pass the others in Jinky's gang. As I approached them, they spread out, forcing me off the path, but no one pursued me. I passed and managed a quick look at their ranks. They were your basic leather-clad, pierced, and tatted punks. If you ask me, you *can* judge a book by its cover; these were tough reads with dark elements.

I walked fast, seeking the full bore of a streetlamp and the comfort of a crowd. When I reached the parking lot of the hall, I slowed my pace and punched my fists into the pockets of my parka. Empty pockets, *what the*—? I pulled the leather purse that came with my outfit out from under my coat, knowing it would be a pointless search. The pouch of runes wasn't there, either. I turned back to the dark stretch separating me from Jinky and her pack of thieves. Did I dare go back and confront her? Were they long gone by now, laughing at the easy American mark? Had she been after the runes specifically, or were they all her lightning-quick hands had found? This theft, on top of the weirdness that had overcome me earlier, left me breathing in shredded rasps. With a bad feeling, I entered the festival hall. I'm not sure what I expected—some sort of incident to have taken place in my absence, as if marking the elapsed time as significant.

"Ah, there you are," Afi said. "I was starting to worry about you." He smacked an itty-bitty glass down on the table. Not *too* worried, judging by the two empties in front of him.

"I went for a walk," I said, pulling my jacket tighter.

A spasm wracked my body, and even my teeth started to chatter.

"You've caught yourself some sort of chill," Vigdis said, rising from her chair and placing an arm around my shoulder. "Time to go. This poor girl is as white as a ghost."

Ghost, I thought to myself as we made our way toward the exit. *Like I don't already have enough to contend with. They can get in line behind the Storks, Ravens, hovering souls, wicked trolls, and gypsy rune readers. How much more wacked could it get, anyway?*

CHAPTER THIRTY-EIGHT

The entire drive back to Vigdis and Baldur's, my mind was casting about like one of those fly-fishing reels — but catching nothing. My shivers continued. Even I didn't know if I was sick, tired, or freaking out.

Somehow, I knew that Jinky's theft of the runes was deliberate; she got what she came for. Her witchy "Watch out" still had me spooked. And that drop in my gut, it had been some kind of visceral reaction, but to what? Creepy that it came so quickly on the heels of the odd rune reading. And she had mentioned a "loss" and "reversed love." I stared out the car window with worst-case scenarios rushing at me faster than the roadside mile markers.

We pulled up to Vigdis and Baldur's away-from-it-all home, and I was suddenly overcome with foreboding of what awaited inside. I didn't know what it was, but it was something. My antennae-like hackles were sure of it.

Vigdis, my backseat companion, put a hand on my knee. "Are you all right?"

"Yes." But for how long I didn't know.

We trudged silently from the car to the house, its location feeling all the more remote and as removed from reality as it was from civilization. Once in their tidy front room and removing coats, Vigdis said, "A phone message," and pointed to a flashing red light atop a paper-strewn corner desk.

Before I could brace myself, Vigdis took two pur-poseful steps and pushed a button. My mother's voice filled the room.

"Dad, Kat, I hate to bother you while you're on vacation." She didn't sound right, even allowing for her delicate condition. "But something's happened. I wouldn't feel right not telling you."

Oh, God, was it the baby?

"Stanley phoned earlier," my mom continued. "It seems Jack has gone . . . missing . . . as has Brigid. They were on a routine outing, but somehow they got sepa-rated from the others."

My lips were shut, my molars clamped, but somehow screams were careening through my ear canals.

"I wouldn't have called you"—I could hear in the way my mom's voice quivered, in the gulf from one word to the next, that she was searching for a way to soften her words—"except it's been over twenty-four hours and . . . well, just call me when you get this. I'll tell you what I know. Sorry, honey. Reverse the charges. It doesn't matter what time."

"Is Jack the . . . ?" Baldur whispered.

"The boyfriend," Afi finished for him.

I sensed six eyes raking over me with concern.

"I need to call my mom," I said.

"I'll dial," Afi said, reaching over me.

Whether the call was direct, or routed through an international operator, or the result of tin cans stretched kitchen-to-kitchen, I hardly knew. Nothing mattered until the phone was passed to me and I heard the sound of my mom's voice.

"Mom, what's going on?"

"Oh, Kat, I wish I had more information."

"Tell me everything you know."

The report, repeated three times, was that yesterday—Monday—at noon, two dogsled teams had departed from camp for a remote field station in order to collect ice samples. Jack and Brigid had been on one sled, and two scientists based at the station had been on the other. A storm had blown up. The scientists had made it back to the base camp; Jack and Brigid had not.

"The good news," my mom said, "is that Brigid, though

she may have become disoriented with the whiteout conditions, is familiar with the area."

"So there's still hope?" I asked. "They're still out there looking?"

"Of course. There's even a military patrol that's been called in to assist with the search and rescue."

"What aren't you telling me?" There was something. She had skipped a sentence. It was like a bad dub job when an R movie got cleaned up for TV.

"The dogs. They should know their way home. They're trained to return. It's partly why they're the preferred mode of transportation; their sensory tracking system is better than GPS. Usually."

"What else?" I asked.

I heard my mom draw in a long breath. "Brigid, before leaving on what everyone assumed was just routine data collection, packed up. She loaded the sled with all her things."

"What?" My brain heard the words, but I was still processing the information.

"It's such a mystery to everyone. From their location, there'd be nowhere to go. They had headed due north, where the terrain only gets more remote and more rugged. It's completely baffling."

I was quiet for a long time; too long—my mom sensed my mood.

"Kat," she said, "don't lose hope. They're still searching for them. Just because it's odd doesn't mean there won't be a good explanation later, when they're found."

"OK," I said with a catch in my voice. "What can I do?"

"There's nothing any of us can do. Those who are in a position to help are doing it. The rest of us just have to wait, and have faith."

The faith part would be hard, but I'd try. The wait part, that felt wrong already.

"You promise to call me the minute you have any more news?"

"Of course, honey," my mom said.

Before hanging up, I asked my mom how she was feeling. She said fine, but I could hear how tired and weak she sounded. If there were developments with her condition, she wouldn't tell me—not now, anyway.

Aware of the others looking at me and of the way silence had elbowed its way into the room, I walked to the couch and plopped down. Adrift in thought, I nervously fingered my new necklace, rolling it between my thumb and forefinger. With each back-and-forth pivot, the stone revealed a different facet, as if changing from a shard of glass to a ragged puzzle piece to a mirror fragment. I thought about Stanley's research attracting Brigid's attention. Her interest in Jack. His inclusion, as a high-school student, on the research team. His growing distraction and coldness to me, which started the very night of her arrival. Now both of them were missing. If I could deliver souls and Jack could manipulate the weather, what else was possible? Hulda had told me of the other realms, one of which was Niflheim: the land of snow and ice. As far as conclusions went, the one I was jumping to was nuts. The kind of crazy that came with a white jacket. Still, I remembered what the rune reader had said. I had a journey ahead of me. But where, exactly? And how? And what would I tell Afi and my mom? These questions battered me like a twisted ram's horn.

"I need to be alone for a little while," I said, already standing and moving toward the hallway. "I'm tired and need to lie down."

I wasn't tired, and the last thing I could think about at a time like this was sleep. But I did need peace and quiet to plan. Though I had no idea where I was going, how I'd get there, or what on earth awaited me. All I knew was that I had to find Jack. I'd go to any length — to the end of the earth, if necessary.

CHAPTER THIRTY-NINE

My hands moved items from various points in the guest room — my toiletries bag from atop the dresser, a sweatshirt from the hook on the back of the door, sweaters and jeans folded on the desk chair — but my mind wasn't there. It was miles down the road. My heart, unfortunately, had remained to plague me. The pain I felt was crushing; a wrecking ball couldn't have done more damage. Jack. All the misgivings I had had after his departure rushed over me: a river of regret, what-ifs, and what-nows. Jack. I needed him; he needed me; we needed each other. It was a fact as elemental as the chart hanging on the wall in Mr. Fuller's chemistry classroom. I felt so sad and alone. There was no one to whom I could divulge the depth of our connection, except Jack himself. And had I ever really? I'd felt too young, too inexperienced. I just hoped it wasn't too late. Jack. He had to be OK, because without him I wouldn't be.

My plan was to head to the airport first thing in the morning. At least three times I flipped open my laptop, hoping to check flights to Greenland, information regarding the topography of Northern Greenland, and download maps of the area. No Internet. Dang. Not being connected left me with a sense of frustration, like finding your keys dangling from the locked car's ignition.

In the end, I alternately paced back and forth and wrote out everything I could remember about anything that seemed remotely connected: Ofelia's warning, the selkie legends, the rune reading, and what Vigdis had said about *The Snow Queen*'s prologue. By one in the morning, my travel journal was crammed with random notations and my legs ached. Exhausted, I slipped into a long white nightgown, lay down on the bed, and finally succumbed to the tears I'd held back for a long time.

I huddled in a ball for hours, drifting in and out of troubled dreams. At some point, in the very darkest hollow of that night, I again heard the strange music. It was soft, but not melodic, more of a rhythmic series of long, sad wails. Then the tempo picked up: an urgent, commanding beat. I sat up with a start. Padding across the cold floorboards to the small closet, I pushed my toes into the pillowy fleece of my UGGs, pulled my parka over my nightgown, and crept silently into the kitchen. I found the flashlight and slipped out the back door. My eyes lifted to the moonlit sky and my ears followed the mysterious music as I picked my way along the rough path that descended toward the fjord. This time I headed in the other direction. The shoreline was even rockier here. Huge boulders jutted out into the water and created a kind of seawall. Like a drumroll, I could hear waves crashing over the black rocks. The rush of the water piqued my curiosity; something in its swell and spill was unusual. I ventured closer to the water's edge. A series of flat, shelflike boulders jutted into the fjord. I stepped onto one, then onto the next, and finally upon the third. The huge rocks were like made-for-giants pavers, but leading where? As if in reply, something splashed in the water. Despite the dark night, cold air, and slick surface, I crept to the very edge of the final stone and peered into the rippling waters below. Red hair. I swore I saw, by the light of the moon, red hair shimmering like a Garnier shampoo ad. It swirled in a billowy cloud. I dropped to my knees, scooping at the frigid waters with my hands. The fistful of golden seaweed I brought to the surface was confusing and disappointing. Just as I resigned myself to the notion that, for once, logic prevailed, I heard a rustle behind me, and a dark shape approached, advancing over the rock jetty.

Still in a crouch, I froze, terror icing me to the spot.

The figure continued forward, and I knew I was in a vulnerable position: trapped on the edge of a dark rock on a remote stretch of beach with an icy fjord behind me. As the shadow grew near, its size came into perspective. A child? No. A girl. Long ebony hair. Mahogany eyes. Jinky. *WTF?*

"A little cold for swimming, isn't it?" Jinky, now within six feet of me, asked, though it sounded more like an accusation than a question.

I stood and scouted left to right, readying, but for what I didn't know. "I wasn't. I thought I saw something is all. Anyway, what are you doing here? How did you find me?"

"It's a small town. And trust me, there are other places I'd rather be, but I'm the type who sees things through." She removed something from her pocket—my pouch of runes—and jiggled the bag. The stones tinkled within. "These are yours. I've come to—"

"You stole them," I interrupted, surprising even myself with the accusation.

"I borrowed them," Jinky said.

"What's the difference?"

"Their safe return."

Well, damn. That was true enough.

"You could have asked."

"I took the easier route," Jinky said, her lips curling in a self-congratulatory smile. "For the record, I wish I'd left well enough alone, but I didn't, so we can sit here and discuss the rocks themselves, or you can hear what I saw in them."

In them?

"What do you mean?" I asked.

"When I touched them, back at the festival, I had a vision. Though it was brief, it stuck with me. I knew I had to hold them again, but I didn't dare in front of my mother."

"Why?"

"Let's just say my mother is a businesswoman, not necessarily a rune reader. And no more a gypsy than she is the queen of Denmark."

"So the reading was fake?"

"No, because I wasn't translating. She doesn't speak English; I could have been reciting Shakespeare for all she knew."

Jinky hardly looked the type to quote Shakespeare. Anyway, I didn't think sonnets would be much help right now. Jack was missing, and she had seen something in the runes.

"So, then, you're a true reader? What did you call it?"

"An *erilaz*. And yes. But the ability comes from my father's side of the family. My grandmother is Sami, one of the nomadic peoples."

"You mean, like, from Lapland?" So maybe I

remembered a thing or two from that world cultures class, besides the international fashion capitals.

"They prefer Sami," Jinky said with a sneer as if I had offended her, her grandmother, and a long line of ancestors.

"I'm sorry. Look, someone important to me is missing. I only just learned about it tonight. Earlier, your reading meant nothing to me, but now —"

"A loss," Jinky said.

"Yes."

"So my reading was accurate. This is not good. Not good at all."

I didn't like the sound of that. She didn't even know Jack, so her reaction had to be based on something else.

"Is there something more I should know?" I asked.

"When I held the stones the second time, I felt —"

"What?"

"*Fehu,* the loss symbol, was so strong it throbbed in my hand. And I sensed —" She hesitated.

"Just tell me."

"A great loss, maybe even catastrophic. Crazy as that sounds."

I hadn't expected that. And was not much liking the word *crazy* these days.

"Listen," Jinky said. "This is beyond my abilities. With your family connection to the *selurmanna,* with the power of your runes and the intensity of the reading . . . only my grandmother can help us."

Great. A bigger gun was being called in. And if Jack missing and the threat of a "great loss" already put me beyond the average *erilaz*'s capabilities, what would she think about the whole Stork thing? My secrecy vows precluded me from telling her, but how much would that up the ante?

Jinky pulled a cell phone from her pocket, punched in a series of keys, yakked in Icelandic, and snapped the phone shut. "I can take you to my grandmother. Let's go."

"What — now? I can't just go. I need to tell my *afi,* or at least leave a note."

"There's no time," Jinky said.

"But I'm not even dressed." I gestured with open arms to my flimsy white nightie flapping from beneath my parka.

"You're fine," Jinky said, starting back toward shore. "Anyway, wait till you see my grandmother."

CHAPTER FORTY

Jinky turned and jogged over the breakers. I had no choice but to follow as she scrambled up the path. Jinky hardly looked like an athlete, but the girl could run. As much as I wanted to blame my by-comparison slow-mo on my UGGs, she was wearing heavy black boots. Engineered for hugging a muffler, or stompin' a mosh pit, but not for a footrace. At the top of the trail to Vigdis and Baldur's place, she turned in the other direction, cutting across a field and heading for the road. I clomped after her for Jack, and Jack alone.

Soon, thankfully, Jinky slowed. From under a pile of branches, she uncovered a motorcycle, which explained the boots, but hardly the fishnets, or the dog collar. She stood it upright and with a practiced move swung over the seat and down onto the kick start. It roared to life, and I understood then why she'd kept it down the road from the house.

"Get on," she shouted above the engine.

"What about helmets?" I asked.

Jinky glared at me. "Now," she shouted, revving the engine as a warning.

With a shake of my head, I climbed on behind her, wrapping my arms around her waist and hoping that her road skills were better than her people skills.

They weren't. As I should have guessed, she drove the same way she dressed: with abandon and no regard for rules. I had only been on a motorcycle once, and that was technically a dirt bike. If Jinky was older than me, it wasn't by much, yet she drove like a stuntman — woman, rather — head down and leaning into curves. My job, I figured, was to hang on for dear life and scream any-time we were airborne, which was more than once. I was so scared, I forgot to feel cold. We were headed toward the sea away from Hafmeyjafjörður and along the fjord on the main access road. I don't think we saw another vehicle; it was the middle of the night, but this was prob-ably a lonely patch of road at high noon. Coming to a tiny village, Jinky slowed and turned right and down a small street. We were approaching a marina with ten or so fishing boats anchored for the night. She parked the motorcycle alongside a beat-up truck and cut the engine.

"My cousin will take us the rest of the way," she said, swinging down from the bike.

I followed suit, looking around for the "cousin," or any sign of life.

Jinky took off down a rickety old dock, her hands shrugged deep into the pockets of her leather jacket. Again, I had no choice but to follow. At the far end of the dark pier, the hum of a motor sounded.

"The rest of the way is by boat?" I asked, struggling to keep up. Not that I wasn't thankful to have survived the first leg of our trip, but no one had warned me of a harbor cruise.

"Yep."

"Where are we going? Not to Lapland, I hope."

"Not Lapland," Jinky said with a condescending tone. "Iceland. Just not the mainland."

Mainland? It was already an island.

"What does that mean?" But Jinky didn't answer me. She strolled ahead to what I could now make out was our destination. A guy was waving a lantern at us from the deck of an old fishing boat, circa *Moby-Dick*. Within moments, I followed Jinky aboard the trawler, no pleasure boat for sure. The deck was littered with nets and lines and gear, and I almost fell over a bucket of fish heads. *Old* fish heads, judging by the smell. Eeew. I didn't want a ride on that boat any more than I wanted to get on the motorcycle. And a look at our captain, even in the dark, didn't help. He was short, wiry, and bearded, with a stocking cap pulled down practically to his small, dark eyes. And he was smoking. Enough said.

"Katla, this is my cousin, Hinrik," Jinky said. It was the first time she'd used my name. Odd that she'd called me Katla. I was sure I'd introduced myself as Kat; I always did.

Hinrik grunted a hello to me and then fired off a round of Icelandic at Jinky. It needed no translation. He wasn't happy to be there, either. By my count, that made three of us.

Hinrik went silently about the business of getting the boat ready. I had a thousand questions for Jinky and was internally sorting them by urgency. For a moment's peace, I went to the bow of the boat, where the headlight lit a shaft of water.

Hinrik called something out. I watched as Jinky performed a series of first-mate tasks with a practiced hand. She untied the lines securing us to the dock, hopped onto the departing boat at the last possible moment, and stored the ropes into a tidy shipshape spool. So the girl could read ancient runes, handle a Harley, and knew her way around a poop deck — big whoop. She still had the fashion sense of a vampire and as much personality as a zombie.

276

After that, Jinky disappeared below deck; I was not about to join her no matter how many questions I had for this unlikely companion of mine. Without Dramamine or a sick bag, I was an eyes-on-the-horizon sailing type. For the rest of the trip, I clutched the underside of the hard, wooden bow bench with the wind whipping my face and shooting my hair all around me like kite tails. I was freezing and shivering so hard I could hear the marrow crystallizing in my bones.

A hundred years later, as the sun burst over the horizon like a giant smashed pumpkin, land came into view. Jinky and Hinrik set about their mooring duties, while I scouted the scene. And I thought Vigdis and Baldur lived in a remote location. This was *seriously* out there. I found myself looking at a spit of shorn rock smaller than Disney's Tom Sawyer Island. Hinrik pulled the boat alongside a warped and collapsing dock. I hopped off and onto the rickety square of planks. Jinky was right behind me, but to my surprise, Hinrik and his floating bucket of fish guts immediately began pulling away.

"Where's he going?" I asked.

"Fishing."

Well, duh, I supposed. But what about us?

"He's coming back, right?" I asked.

Jinky didn't reply. *Hello? It's a fair question.*

I was about to say as much when something in the water caught my eye. Black heads bobbed in the surf, their shiny eyes watching me. Seals. I pointed, intending to call Jinky's attention to our visitors, but she had already taken off. As usual, I ended up chasing after her. We hoofed it up a steep slope to . . . nowhere and nothing, by the looks of it. Soon, though, a tiny house came into view. It was roundish and made of stone, as if nothing more than a natural heave or knob of the island itself.

Something much more enticing had me bounding up the hill. In a clearing near the cottage roared a large fire. The boat ride had left me so cold I was still shaking. The promise of heat was a welcome relief. Drawing near, I noticed that the area containing the fire was ringed by a circle of very large stones. There was also a tiny structure, a domed tent of sorts, covered in animal skins. I was so cold and so glad to be off that boat that I skipped like some garland-bearing maypoler.

The moment, though, I crossed over the stone ring, I felt a familiar sensation. As if falling from a mountaintop, air whooshed past my ears like a 747, and then everything went black.

CHAPTER FORTY-ONE

I came to lying on the hard, cold ground with Jinky and some old woman standing over me.

They spoke in Icelandic, though I was so disoriented that they could just as easily have been talking backwards or sideways, for that matter. And my mind was keeling with the memory of another experience of a single step that had felt like a fall through the looking glass. That time I'd woken up to Wade. Needless to say, I was suspicious, and more than a little weirded out.

Jinky extended her hand, an encouraging sign, but I was still operating on a code-red threat level.

"My grandmother welcomes you to her stone circle and says she knows now, after such a graceful landing, that you are truly one of the special among us."

I rose to my feet without help, brushing dirt from the hem of my nightie. "She could have just asked," I said.

Jinky, I discovered, did have the facial muscles required to smile. Who knew?

"I have told her of your rune reading," Jinky said. "She tells me she had sensed a disturbance in the energies of this power place. She has prepared the spirit breath for you."

That didn't sound good. And if you asked me, the situation didn't look good, either. As forewarned, Jinky's grandmother was a sight to behold. She was about four foot ten, tops. Her arrow-straight silver hair hung loose over her shoulders. She wore a colorful striped knit cap, a large fringed and patterned woolen shawl knotted at her throat, a belted royal-blue knee-length woolen tunic, and knee-high bristled fur boots. The boots were to die for, as I suspected some local furry critter had. She definitely had the look of someone who threw around words like "spirit breath."

"The what?" I asked.

The old woman rattled off a long directive. Jinky nodded and said, "Don't be afraid. My grandmother only wants to help. As a shaman, she can guide you, but she warns you: once through, the journey is your own."

Which was no help at all. *Seriously. Once through? Through what?* Shaman-granny then approached me, lifting my right hand and facing it skyward. She ran her hand along my palm. I was reminded, eerily, of the way Jack's grandmother had done this very same thing. Especially, as she, too, ran her finger into the inlet between my thumb and pointer. She said something to Jinky, who nodded her head and stepped away.

"Did you read something in my palm?" I asked the old lady. She looked at me blankly and dropped my hand. And then she also walked away.

Huh? Jack's grandmother had mentioned the "power of three," when she had done her palm-reading. A little translation might have been nice.

Instead, Jinky and her grandmother started doing—of all things—yard work. With shovels, they removed large hot rocks from the center of the fire, carried them to the small tentlike dome, and dropped them inside. This continued until there must have been a good-size pile of rocks in the tent. All the while I was warming myself by the fire; heat, glorious heat, I couldn't get enough of it. Minutes later, they dropped their shovels. From her pocket, Jinky's grandmother pulled a small bundle of dried branches, which she lit by dipping into the fire. She and Jinky walked over to the entrance of the low tent and started—*huh?*—removing their clothes. Jinky went down to her panties and a black tank over a black bra. She at least had a figure one wouldn't mind exposing. Shaman-granny, on the other hand, didn't. I was relieved when she stopped at a bone-colored slip, but, still, it was a little TMI for my tastes. They both turned and looked at me.

"What?"

"To enter the *savusauna,* you must remove your layers." Jinky looked at me impatiently.

I wasn't budging from my spot by the fire. I looked down. Under my parka there were only my nightgown and underwear. Besides, I was good where I was, *thanks, anyway.*

"You're insulting my grandmother," Jinky said. "Take your coat and boots off. Now."

Still smarting from her tone, I dropped my belongings onto the pile with theirs. I then crouched and followed them into the diminutive animal-skin tent. It was too low to stand in, so the three of us crawled to positions around the mound of stones set into a shallow hole in the center of the space. Jinky, the last one in, lowered a flap of stretched hides, plunging us into a warm and airless enclosure. As far as I could tell, the hot rocks were the only form of heat, but, man, they were kicking out some serious BTUs. Following Jinky's lead, I sat cross-legged facing the stones. Shaman-granny began to speak. She held out the smoking bundle of twigs and waved it around her head and over her shoulders. The sickly-sweet smoke soon filled the space, and I coughed into my fist. Jinky shot me a look.

What? I wasn't allowed to breathe?

The smoking bundle was passed to Jinky, who swept

it back and forth across her chest and even around her head, as her grandmother had. "We pass the smudge wand," Jinky said, "to cleanse the space and to purify our bodies and minds."

She passed me the wand. I copied their movements, not wanting to get in any more trouble. I had to wonder, though—"cleanse" and "purify"? The smoke was getting in my eyes; they were starting to water.

Shaman-granny took the bundle from me and placed it at her feet. Next she pulled a bucket to her side and spooned a ladleful of water onto the rocks. The water sizzled, venting a steamy mist into the small space. It got even hotter.

The old woman spoke in a chanting rhythm; both she and Jinky lowered their heads. I did, too. Man, that Jinky had me nervous as a chicken near a bowl of batter and a hot frying pan. More water was poured onto the rocks, emitting a hiss like a hot skillet. "We give thanks," Jinky translated, "to the womb of Mother Earth for this safe space, to the grandfather rocks for their wisdom, to the animals for their skins, and to the plants for their medicines."

Medicines, my foot. If anything, I was feeling worse. More water was poured onto the rocks; it got hotter still. I understood now why we had stripped down.

Shaman-granny talked some more, it was hard to follow. First off, I didn't understand a word. Furthermore, it was getting so foggy in the tent I really couldn't see straight. And lastly, it was so dang hot I was getting sleepy.

"The spirit breath surrounds you," Jinky said. "The first cycle of your vision quest will be a return to the past, to the source of loss. By way of travel, you will employ an ancestral gift. Are you ready?"

Hardly. My eyelids were so heavy they could have anchored Hinrik's boat. Had I even wanted to reply, I wouldn't have been able to. Though my legs could still feel the scratchy square of mat underneath them, I felt myself soaring away.

Flying. It felt great. And how had I — bird girl — never experienced this before? I felt the air roll over my feathers. Feathers! They were a dappled brown, and my wingspan was huge. *Score.* Once I stopped admiring myself, I took in the view: a bird's-eye perspective. I couldn't believe how crisp and scoped everything was, even though all I saw was an endless terrain of snow-covered hills and ridges. My chest filled with a puff of cold air as something below caught my eye. I dipped into a dive, thrilling at the rush of speed. Soon, a team of barking dogs pulling a sled came into view. All at once, the novelty of the experience fell away and I was left clutching only fear. I flew closer, recognizing the forms of Brigid and Jack on the sled.

Jack. From above he looked small. I dove even lower, now kiting above the yapping dogs, who did not welcome my surveillance. Contrary to my storybook images, this was no fancy carriage-style sledge. It was really no more than a rickety wooden platform atop two long and curved toboggan-style runners. A simple bench and backrest afforded a crude seat, upon which Jack was huddled. Behind that, Brigid stood upon the footboards with her hands on the driving handlebar. Their gear was tied in tarp-covered bundles in front of Jack, who, by the way he was cowering and cupping his left hand over his right, I'd have guessed was cold, but that couldn't be. And if not cold, then he had to be shaking from fear. It wasn't like him. Panic and a protective instinct tore through me. I had to do something, but what? I remembered that Jinky had described this cycle of the vision quest as "a return to the past, to the source of loss." Was it too late? Was what I was viewing a done deal, a *fait accompli*?

The dogs continued to act up. If this was the past, how did they sense my presence? In irritation, Brigid slowed the sled.

"What is wrong with you worthless creatures?" she screamed at the dogs. This was not the same Brigid I had known during her stay in Norse Falls. This one had a hard glint in her eyes and an imperious cadence to her voice. The dogs continued to fuss, two now snapping at the air. Brigid brought the sled to a stop. I dropped onto the perch of a low cliff overlooking them.

Brigid stepped off the back of the sled and strode through the snow to where the dogs were leashed in a fan-shaped formation of long nylon traces. Even in my current no-clothes-required state, I couldn't help but admire her travel garb: fluffy dove-gray fur pants tucked into knee-high suede boots laced tight to her calves. With a gloved hand, she yanked the collar of the loudest of the two yelpers, causing him to whimper and lower his head submissively. Brushing her hands, one over the other, she sauntered back to the sleigh. When close, she slowed and lingered, watching Jack in his withdrawn state.

"Dear Jack, are you still so very glum?" Though she tempered her voice, there was still a sharpness to it. She removed a glove and brushed his cheek with her hand. He recoiled as if struck, but then his body slumped forward in a very un-Jack-like display of defeat. I understood then that it wasn't cold or fear that had him shaking — it was pure hatred. "Still angry, are we? I'm sorry that you don't agree with my methods, but it couldn't be helped, really. You'd never have come willingly. I need you, though. Besides, what is there to complain about?" She gestured to the snowy landscape with open arms. "Just look at the beauty surrounding us. How could you, of all people, not be happy? And to think, soon all the world will be just as breathtaking." Jack turned away from her. She shook her head and stepped back onto the footboards. "Shame, your lack of enthusiasm. Anyway, soon you won't waste energy on anything as ridiculous as emotion."

I could see the way he shrank at the sound of her voice. I could also see a cloudiness in his eyes. I wanted to do something to help him somehow, to come between them. I jumped from my perch only to find myself being wrenched forward, through the air, through time itself.

CHAPTER FORTY-TWO

I came to on the earthen floor of the sweat lodge. I was shaking uncontrollably as much from the thrust of the travel as from the sense of helplessness and hopelessness.

Jack had seemed so angry, yet oddly resigned to his fate. Though he withered under her touch, he didn't fight to escape. As if he knew, somehow, that it was pointless. And judging by what I'd overheard, Brigid wanted it all, not just my world—which was Jack—but *the* world, too.

I sat up, lifting my heavy-as-barbells shoulders. Brigid had Jack. Did she intend to use him to deep-freeze us all? Regardless, Brigid had Jack. I'd do whatever it took to stop her—and to free him.

Jinky and her grandmother were still with me in the low tent. How long had I been gone? And how could they stand it? It was so cloyingly hot. The steam from the water poured over the hot rocks, and the smoke from the smudge wand still had the place banked in a fog that could rival both London and San Francisco — combined. Despite the creepy sensation of them both watching me, waiting for me to say something, I needed a minute to recover. All I could think about was Jack. If that was the past, where was he now? And what had Brigid meant when she said he won't be wasting his energy on emotions much longer?

Finally, Jinky's grandmother spoke, pulling me from my sulk. When Jinky handed me a cup of water, I noticed something bordering on respect in her dark eyes. The drink was cold and delicious and almost as rejuvenating as Jinky's small nod of approval. The old Sami woman's conversational tone changed, and she began chanting in an odd, choppy rhythm. She also added more water to the rocks, again shrouding us in a cloud of steam.

When the old woman finally stopped talking, Jinky translated, "My grandmother says that the spirit breath is now ready to take you on the second cycle. During this cycle you will find guidance."

Round two? I hardly knew if I was up to it. My breathing was labored, and it was so very, very hot. And with the crazy steam funneling all around me, I couldn't see. I felt sick to my stomach and so tired I couldn't even lift my arms, never mind fly again. All the while, Jinky's grandmother was reciting a phrase over and over. But guidance sounded good. I'd take some of that. Though I hardly had the energy to blink, never mind visualize. The air in the tent grew so heavy I could have pulled it up to my chin like a blanket, which reminded me of how very sleepy I was.

I came to feeling a glorious ribbon of cool breeze tickling me. It felt so great to be out of that stifling heat. Still groggy, I sat up, struggling to process my surroundings, until I realized, with a start, that I was on Hinrik's boat. We were adrift, waves licking up the sides of the pitching wooden craft. A gray mist gathered in shifting patches, obscuring the gulls who screeched their presence. I stood and made my way to the stern, where Hinrik, with his back to me, cast a net out into the water.

"Where are we?" I asked. "Where's Jinky?"

He turned to face me, and I gasped. This wasn't Hinrik at all. Though he wore the same knit cap and navy jacket, the guy before me was much taller and broader.

In a sweeping gesture, he removed his hat, revealing a head of light brown curls. He was younger than I expected, my own age. And if not classically handsome, attractive in some inexplicable way. "Ah, there you are," he said, smiling.

Despite being in the middle of the sea with a complete stranger — on a vision quest, no less — a sense of comfort washed over me. "There you are" implied an expectation and the "ah" a kind of welcome. His voice, too, was soothing. Although accented, it was fluid and confident.

"Who are you? And where are we?"

"I am Marik, a messenger."

"A messenger? From who?"

"King Marbendlar and Queen Safira."

"Who?"

Marik stretched to an imposing height. The fog had settled, collecting eerily at his feet. "King Marbendlar and Queen Safira, regents of Vatnheim."

"Vatnheim — like Water World?" I asked.

He nodded.

I squeezed my eyes shut. I'd only just resigned myself to the concept of Brigid being some kind of Snow Queen. Now the Water King and Queen had sent a messenger. I opened my eyes, half expecting a line of otherwordly figureheads to have formed behind him.

"You say you have a message?"

"I do," Marik said. "And an offer to present. Even before the recent summoning of the Bifrost Bridge and the resultant wedge . . ."

Ho, boy.

". . . discord among the realms had been building."

Discord? Not a good start. And definitely not something you want to crack the seal on.

"Humans are"—Marik continued—"an impatient species. In their haste to develop, they have irreversibly altered not only their own world but the other realms, too."

I inched closer to Marik, daring even to brace my arms upon the railing. The way he said "humans" insinuated that he was not. I regarded him: two arms, two legs, all the parts of the face in the right place and in proportion, appealing even. It was then that I noticed a stirring in the water. Below us, the sea was teeming with fish. They pulsed back and forth as if a single organism.

"As Midgard warms, we all warm." The once-cheery quality of Marik's voice had gone flat and sad.

"I'm not sure I understand."

"Vatnheim has suffered for Midgard's excesses. We have seen our resources dwindle. We have seen the extinction of creatures and the rise of pestilence and disease."

The plunk of something breaking the surface again drew my attention to the water. A billowy cloud of orange mushroomed in and out, coming tantalizingly close to the surface, only to draw back down again. Marik followed my eyes to the strange movement, grinning. And as if the scene weren't dramatic enough, that eerie music came wafting over the wind.

I had so many questions, yet I found myself unable to speak.

Marik nodded as if aware of my temporary impediment and continued, "Our worries were many before your plight, which has further disrupted the order of the worlds."

Yowza. My plight discussed in the same sentence with world order. *Other*world order, at that.

"Queen Safira hopes that your recent prophecy of a cleft-tailed siren is a portent of the future. She and all her people hope for an heir to carry on the royal line, but even she suffers the consequences of the environmental plague."

Cleft-tailed? As in split-tailed? Oh, no. Just like the crown-bearing mermaid I'd made up—kind of borrowed, really, from the Starbucks logo—at my first bestowal when Hulda said she sensed a fourth presence, one representing the water element. Her words came to me: "A very powerful symbol. The mythological siren. Dating back as far as the goddess religions themselves." Except the guy standing before me was no myth.

"Queen Safira believes," Marik continued, "that the door between our worlds was opened for a reason. A wedge when applied at any of the power places weakens them all. To this end, we know the location of a portal to Niflheim, and, with our assistance, your safe passage can be arranged."

"Assistance," I said, my voice returning high and clear. "How? When?"

"A bargain must first be made," Marik said. "There is one, in particular, who is willing to help. The very skin off her back, should you need it. The bargain, however, being: when the time comes, Leira — to whom the waters are home — must be returned to the sea."

I remembered the minstrel's story of Leira the selkie. Ofelia's warning, also, flashed across my mind: "A pact once made may not be broken." And I thought of Jack. *Where is he? And how do I get to him?* Thinking about Jack, I was overcome with dread. In that moment, I'd have agreed to anything, risked everything.

"Do you accept?" Marik asked.

"I do."

"Then you will receive a gift."

"Thank you," I said.

"Take heed, it is a gift," he said, enunciating each word slowly.

Uh. OK. "Thank you, *a lot?*" I tried. Before Marik could reply, something smacked the surface of the water hard just beyond the spot where we stood. I leaned over the railing to get a better look when I felt myself falling forward.

CHAPTER FORTY-THREE

Again, I woke up sprawled on the ground of the sweat lodge and immediately felt the crush of hot air. I had no idea what these heat-induced flights of mind were, exactly, but I was getting sick of them. They were confusing, and exhausting, and downright weird. And it didn't help that I had an audience. Jinky and her grandmother, cool as cucumbers, sat watching me with their pretzel-legged yoga poses. Meanwhile, I was downward-facing-dog, and probably had the slobber to complete the look. The old woman said something to Jinky.

"You have a final cycle to complete."

Well, let's hope, because I was back here, not on my way to find Jack. I sat up and looked around, patting my

hands beside and behind me. I was searching, ridicu-
lously, for some kind of gift.

"Are you looking for something?" Jinky asked.

Yeah. Jack Frost. And maybe a wrapped present. But
neither were confessions I was about to make.

"No. I guess not."

Shaman-granny spoke; Jinky translated, "My grandmother reminds you that once you reach your destination, you already have everything you need to succeed."

Jinky's grandmother waited for Jinky to stop speaking and then tapped her heart with her fist. I appreciated
the vote of confidence, but, still, it would have been nice
to have a map and even the most basic of itineraries.

"A little guidance couldn't hurt," I said.

Jinky relayed my remark; her grandmother
responded, repeating one word several times: *poro*.

"Find poro," Jinky said. "Trust in those who don't
talk back, but depend on yourself only."

Okey-dokey. I made it a rule to steer clear of anyone
who gave me lip, anyway. But, whatever. I filed the advice
away.

Jinky's grandmother clapped her hands. No need
for translation. It was the universal get-going signal.
Shaman-granny poured more water on the rocks; it spat
out a fresh stream of dragon breath, making me wonder
if they hadn't brought in hot rocks from the fire while I
was — was where?

"Are you ready?" Jinky asked, handing me another cup of water.

I downed its ice-cold contents in two loud gulps. "As I'll ever be."

Again, the old Sami woman chanted, her tone taking on a pleading quality. I became dizzy. Swirling lights tickled my skin, and that strange music danced before my eyes until I had to close them in confusion.

I woke on a deserted strip of beach. Water curled onto the pebbled shore; behind me were one or two large boulders, but beyond that, nothing but scrub. I stood, trying to tamp down the something's-wrong sensation in my gut, when a gray and shiny lump caught my eye. Upon closer inspection, it turned out to be a small roll of material. I lifted it and shook it out. Surprisingly, it was almost weightless and unfurled to a much larger garment than I'd have guessed. Though cut in an odd bulging shape, it appeared to be nothing more than a hooded cape. The material itself was rubbery, but the interior was of a silver low-nap fur, soft to the touch but twinkling to the eye. Overall, it was amazing and way too killer not to test out.

As I was draping it over my shoulders, I heard a laugh. From behind one of the boulders, I caught sight of a mop of flaming red hair. I was about to walk over and investigate, except that walking no longer seemed a viable option. *Holy crap.* The cape was wrapping itself around me, adhering to me, like, well, skin. *Eeeew.* I spun with no more success than your average tail-chasing pooch. The thing continued to envelop me. Once it had finished shrink-wrapping me, and I thought the worst had to be over, I breathed. Big mistake. As my chest filled with that precious gulp of oxygen, I started to expand like Willy Wonka's Violet, the inflatable blueberry girl. Needless to say, I ended up floundering on the beach like some belly-up roly-poly bug. Except it wasn't the insect family I'd joined; it was, rather, the aquatic vertebrate family. I was a seal. And my fate was—uh-huh—sealed. The word *fate,* even as a pun, made me think of Jack. Jack. There was no time to lose.

I rolled into the water with all the grace of a fat lady struggling into her Spanx. It took me many minutes to adjust to my newly acquired girth and get the hang of the flippers. I had a newfound appreciation for the whole fish-out-of-water sensibility, even with the circumstances reversed. After some floundering, I noticed a small group of black heads bobbing in the water. The foursome nudged me with their snouts and gently pushed me farther and farther from shore. Escorts?

I had always been a decent swimmer, but this was unlike anything I'd ever experienced. For such stumpy little things, my fore and hind flippers were pretty darn nimble. And who knew that an expanded waistline could be a streamlining tool? I could tell that my companions were taking it easy on me at first, keeping to the surface and submerging for short and shallow dives. Gradually, they descended deeper and for longer periods of time. It was fascinating. I could feel my heart rate slow as if I were conserving energy. And despite the increasing depth of our dives, my vision became clearer and sounds crisper. Never a big fan of facial hair, particularly on women, I had to admit that my whiskers were handy little navigational instruments; in combination with an improved eyesight and echolike sense of hearing I used them to *feel* where I was going. Besides the is-this-really-happening sensation of living out some deep-sea episode of *The Magic School Bus,* I was getting the hang of the physiology of being a pinniped.

Other seals joined our group; we dove deeper and for much longer stretches of time. At first, I was anxious; memories of another body of water and another descent into the cold, dark abyss weighed heavily on me.

Soon I stopped guesstimating how long I'd gone without my lungs exploding, and I started to relax and marvel even at my new ability. And relaxing without breathing is no easy feat.

Urgently, we pressed onward, due north, according to my whiskers. We swam forever. Once, after having been submerged for what must have been more than an hour, I was surprised, upon breaking the surface, to see the low fireball of an orange sunrise. A new day and still no end in sight. Though I had no way of confirming it, I sensed Jack was still unaccounted for. I knew because the valve formerly known as my heart was all pump, no passion. It knew, somehow, to switch into some life-preserving, halved capacity. It needed its other half—it needed Jack.

Later, when the sun was high in the sky, we surfaced again. I intuited among my companions an emphasis on this particular up-for-air break. I had no idea where we were; water, turgid and cold, pressed us in from every side. Then all their kind black eyes seemed to turn on me at once, heads nodding in the surf until, one by one, they dipped under the waves.

Here goes, I thought, gulping air as if it were something you could stockpile, like canned peaches. I plunged down, following the others, surprised that, this time, our descent was straight down. *Dear Lord,* I had no idea the ocean floor was so far. Even in my fat suit, I could feel the pressure against my closed earflaps. Still downward we pushed.

I knew I'd reached a critical juncture when the seals all stopped and formed a sort of floating ring. The circle was evenly spaced with no segment missing. I knew the gesture was symbolic. I swam through their hoop and continued downward. I didn't turn back; I didn't need to. They'd gone as far as they could. I was on my own.

Darkness on land is temporary. Darkness underwater is eternal and plain old scare-the-bejesus-out-of-you frightening. A flashlight would have come in handy, as would have a backbone. Seriously, my resolve was as firm as the blubber keeping me warm. Just when I thought I couldn't take it anymore and figured I had veered off course, a blast of warm water hit my face. I approached slowly, locating the source of the spray with my snout and whiskers. Rolling with my voluminous belly and extending my foreflipper, I found myself tangled in what had to be the tentacles of some mutant octopus. I struggled until I realized it wasn't fighting back. What I was caught in seemed to be an intricate system of roots to some sort of — what? — submerged tree. That couldn't be, because that would mean the tree was growing upside down through the ocean floor. No longer thrashing around, I started to float downward until I again felt vents of hot water. Then, without warning, I dropped precipitously. The force of the suction was excruciating. I flailed against the vacuum; everything whooshed past me until I had to shut my eyes against the rocketing landscape. The last thing I remember was screaming in a pitch that no B-movie horror-flick actress had ever achieved. I had a future in Hollywood, if I had a future at all.

CHAPTER FORTY-FOUR

In a fog, I felt a soft wind on my face. My eyes flickered briefly onto a huge nostril, a white furry snout, and big black eyes, but my brain had difficulty processing the information, until . . . something licked me.

Eeew. I rolled over, ignoring the dream and pulling the covers over me. Covers? Shiny covers?

With a start, I jumped up. Jumped with *two legs*. Excellent news. No more sumo-suit. My blanket was the sealskin, now reverting to a capelike function. Weirdly, my feet were covered in booties of the same shiny material.

In a state of confusion, I scrambled backward through powdery snow, bumping into something hard and scaring the something-licking into a buck and retreat of several paces. I jumped to my feet, senses alert, but my mind still wasn't accepting the information as reliable. The something-hard turned out to be a giant tree of Sequoia proportions. Though it wasn't a redwood, it had a height that was dizzying and a base that one couldn't lap easily. Its furrowed bark was mahogany-brown; it had limblike buttresses from which the medieval architects might have been inspired; and its base had a hollow or cavity that you could drive a truck into. A few scattered leaves on the ground were the size of serving platters.

I pulled the cape tight across my chest and looked around. The tongued thing — a reindeer? — had meandered over to a patch of field where grassy tufts had broken through the snow. I wondered, hoping I was wrong, but there was only one way to find out. I walked toward the antlered beast.

"You wouldn't happen to be Poro, would you?"

It lifted its head and looked at me with doe-eyes. Some small flicker of understanding passed between us.

Great. As guidance, I got Bambi's arctic cousin. I took a better look at my sidekick. It was, at least, massive. Judging by the many-pointed rack, a male, I presumed. As confirmation, I stole my head around its backside; yep, a boy. I also took note of a kind of padded seat harnessed across his upper back with attached stirrups and reins. *I'm supposed to ride this thing?* I wasn't much of a cowgirl. An incident involving me and a horse very fittingly named

Bolt was probably still legend at the Shady Acres Ranch in Calabasas.

Raising my gaze to a vast seascape behind the tree, I was overwhelmed by an endless stretch of rolling waves. Bobbing in the pale silver waters were a few icebergs; waves nipped at their pitching forms. I shivered and turned away from the imposing vista. On the front side of the tree, as if the tree were its wellspring and the hollow its mouth, a path meandered over a snow-cloaked tundra and then disappeared into a stand of snow-flocked evergreens, behind which a jagged-peaked mountain loomed.

A serrated wind scratched across my cheek. *Dang,* it was cold. I pulled the hood over my ears and receded into the down of its lining. Whatever it was made of was crazy amazing, and could put GORE-TEX and Tyvek both out of business. And the booties, not the most styling of looks, but warm, wickedly warm. What had been gentle rolls around my ankles had unfurled to now extend coverage to mid-calf. My toes were warm and dry, despite standing in a foot of snow.

Now what?

Judging by the sun's proximity to the horizon, there were only a few hours left in the day. Though the tree's recessed cavity made a natural shelter, my instincts told me to press forward.

"So, Poro, are we going to do this thing?"

Without a sound, he lifted his head and looked at

me. Well, I had to admit, strong and silent was definitely my type. I thought of Jack and felt something twist in my belly. Digging my left toe into the stirrup, I swung my right leg over Poro's immense flank. He straightened his horned head, and I pulled on the reins, though his velvety antlers sure made tempting handlebars. So now that I had both a companion and a mode of transportation, all I needed was a destination. I didn't suppose that Poro came with either GPS or OnStar. The path, interestingly enough, appeared to have but one direction: through the stand of trees and continuing up the mountain. Pressing in from every other direction was nothing but ice-clogged waves.

All righty, then, forest and mountain it is.

I gave Poro a gentle nudge, and he set out along the path. I knew then why Hulda had called Niflheim the land of mist and ice. A gauzy fog hung like curtains in the air, and it was so cold that icicles clung to my lashes. If it weren't for the cape, I'm sure I would never have survived. Within an hour or so, we came out of the woods. To both sides of the path there was nothing but icy tundra. Not far ahead, I could see the road begin its spiral up the mountain. Suddenly, voices sounded from behind us. I went rigid with fear. Poro and I had no protection. Had we still been in the forest, we might have taken cover, but out here on this open stretch, we were completely exposed. I jumped off Poro's back, as if escape planning required two feet on the ground. Too late, anyway, as a cluster of dark heads was already in sight.

Holding Poro's reins, I watched their approach, wondering how I was going to defend myself. I stiffened as the first two passed. Then another grouping of three overtook us without as much as a glance in my direction. *Huh? Was I wearing some kind of invisibility cloak?* Even if I was rendered transparent, surely my massive reindeer companion wasn't. I raised my arm to examine the cape, and one man turned in my direction. *Uh-oh.* But he gave me the emptiest, most disinterested regard I'd ever encountered, and then looked away. It was as if I were nothing. I looked more closely at the men, and a few women, filing past; they were all vacant-eyed and impassive. It was weird. And unsettling. Made even more so by the fact that something in their coloring — dark hair and sky-blue eyes — reminded me of Jack. They wore simple, unadorned clothing: heavy boots, crude fur-lined blue tunics, thick blue leggings, and close-fitting hats with long, furry earflaps. Many carried tools strung across their backs: long, toothy saws or long-handled axes. Loggers? Miners?

Toward the back of the group, a man ambled along, gnawing on a thick loaf of bread. My stomach lurched. I honestly didn't know the last time I'd eaten. Without even thinking, I stepped forward.

"Excuse me, sir, would you have a bite of bread to

spare?" I couldn't believe it even as the words were exiting my mouth. My empty belly had obviously hijacked my brain. And I'd clearly seen *Oliver* one too many times.

He looked at me expressionless.

Of course, I thought. *Stupid me.* Why would they speak English in Niflheim? It's part of Norse legend, so maybe Norwegian or Icelandic, or possibly their own language. Niflish? Niflandic?

"*Brauð,*" I said, using the Icelandic, even trying to give that stupid Icelandic *d* its *th* inflection at the end.

Nothing.

"*Pain,*" I tried in French.

He dipped his head forward in confusion.

"Bread," I said, having run out of foreign words, but this time I spoke louder — because that always helps — and charaded my hands to my mouth and fake chewed.

The man looked between me and the crusty bread without any show of emotion. He then broke the loaf in two and thrust one half in my hand. Without a word, he plodded on down the trail. I devoured it in a matter of moments. Food had never tasted so sweet, despite the fact that there were definitely crunchy bits of unknown origin sticking to my teeth.

After the group had passed, I stood in the road, confused. For one, how had I gone so unnoticed? Not that I considered myself a traffic stopper, but completely unremarked upon? How many silver-cloaked, reindeer-riding girls did they pass on a daily basis? I was sure the answer was not many, so the question became: why hadn't they reacted? And where were they going?

Standing there, watching the path, I gazed up to the mountain beyond. I was struck by something I hadn't noticed before. The clouds atop the mountain swirled and swarmed around its lofty spire with an intensity you wouldn't see back on old Midgard. The clouds appeared to be alive, dive-bombing like a squadron of nighthawks.

I swung up onto Poro's back, and we headed for the mountain trail. I figured following the workers was as good a plan as any. As we rounded a switchback and with an unobstructed view of the trail ahead, a flash of blue tripped my already skittish internal alarms. I swore I saw one of the workers, but the next moment he was gone. *Huh?* Within moments, I spied another—the one who gave me the bread—in the same area. I halted Poro, not wanting to alert the stranger to our presence. I held my breath and watched from a safe distance as the worker hopped up onto an outcropping of rock. At first, it looked as if he might climb the face. He lifted one hand up onto a small protruding edge. His other hand pressed against the rock wall at waist level with a soft, almost embracing gesture. He then leaned his torso into the wall. And all at once he was gone. Vanished. Turned to rock.

I gasped, and Poro brayed. Pitching myself off Poro, I ran to the spot where the guy had just been. Running my hands all along the crevices of brown craggy stone, I looked for some sort of fissure or crease. There was none.

"Stay here," I said to Poro. I might not have bothered. My trusty sidekick was already backing away.

Figuring it was worth a try, I stepped up and did as the worker had done. I raised my right hand to the small ledge of rock and extended my left at waist level, slowly shifting my weight into the cold, rigid stone. I felt the cold seeping in through my hands and cheek. And then, all at once, I was sliding.

CHAPTER FORTY-FIVE

I found myself with my back to a wall, literally. It was cold and dank. Behind me a gray stone wall towered. Before me a village meandered, as if straight out of a Dickens novel. Drab buildings of two or three stories spread out in a warren of streets and alleys. The lanes were narrow and cobbled, and one thing was certain: this was not a joyous place, nor a prosperous one. A pale light leaked from under old-fashioned street lamps. I heard footsteps, saw figures approaching from my left, and instinctively darted into the first alley to my right. The second and third stories of the buildings protruded over the alley, creating a kind of balcony under which I crouched, hood down, shoulders hunched. I needn't have bothered; the two people shambled past with an eyes-down disinterest.

I cautiously returned to the street; it was eerily dark and vacant of voices. Having no immediate goal except to get my bearings, avoid notice, and find Jack, I pressed forward.

Within a few minutes, the entrance to a small court-yard appeared on my left. It was poorly lit and reeked of garbage, which, in the gloom, I could see overflowing from a large bin. I could also make out a clothesline of laundry strung from one window to another. I took a few hesitant steps into the area. Dark blue garments, similar to those worn by the loggers, hung from crude pegs. Though so far no one had acknowledged me, I didn't know what to expect ahead. The clothes were, at least, an opportunity to conform. In a corner, I removed my cape, slipped on the blue pants, tucked my long nightie into the waistband, and shrugged the loose blue tunic top over my shoulders. It was baggy, shapeless, and so void of style that no belt or boots could save it. *Whatever.* The goal was to blend. I twisted my cape into a knot, noting compactible as among its many attributes, and shoved it into the roomy front pocket of the dark blue pullover.

I became aware of an upward tilt to the road. And then, over the rooftops, I saw turrets and towers rising above the cramped streets. My throat clamped with a knot of determination. A castle meant a queen; Brigid, I assumed. Where there was Brigid, I hoped to find Jack. My feet pounded the rising pavers urgently.

Figuring the working end of the castle would be the easiest to sneak into, I found a back door. Luckily, security was lax. Made me wonder how often visitors found a wedge through to Niflheim and then managed to melt into the mountain. Not many had to be the answer, because I sure didn't go through customs.

I found myself in the kitchen, which was full of workers busy at various tasks. I kept my head down and fell in line with a crew of potato peelers. No one seemed to notice me or question my presence. On the sly, I cracked my teeth into a raw spud and stashed what remained into my pocket. I was that hungry. Growing bolder and going positively Pavlovian with the smells, I soon abandoned the peelers and followed another worker carrying a sack of nuts. She moved to a long worktable, where I watched her pull a small hammerlike instrument and a small, but sharp, knife from a shelf under the workstation. She first used the knife to score along the nut's seam and then cracked it open with a single strike of the hammer. It was labor intensive, but not a bit of the nuts' meat was crushed. I concentrated on her blank face, wondering how anyone could be so unaware of someone shadowing them. *Helloo? Anybody home?* I found twins to her knife-and-mallet set and began mirroring her movements. For every three nuts I shelled, I shoved one into my mouth and one into my pocket, especially the broken ones. Something told me there'd be hell to pay for a sloppy job.

An older woman, with gray hair and a face with more lines than the DMV, approached carrying a wooden tray, a silver bowl, and a basket of dried fruits. She set the items down and turned away. I immediately dug my hand into the bowl of dried berries, intending to Hoover these, too, when she suddenly turned back and looked at me—*really* looked at me. I froze, waiting for her to sound the alarm. Instead, she dipped her head down and studied my shoes. *Crap. My shoes. My metallic, seal-skin booties.* There hadn't been any leather work boots in the courtyard, and I wasn't about to walk through the cold streets barefoot, but now I saw just how much they exposed me.

She lifted her hawk-eyes to mine. These were no empty sockets. They were lively and spry and now taking in everything from the dirt under my fingernails to the bulge of stolen items in my pocket. *Double dang.* I held my breath and steeled myself for some sort of confrontation. When—nothing. Hawk-eyes turned and left.

I went to return the two tools to the small shelf, but instead slipped one of them into my pocket, the old be-prepared scout's oath coming to mind. Next, I filled the silver bowl with a mixture of fruits and nuts, placed it upon the serving tray, and lifted both from the worktop.

My coworker lifted her head briefly and then continued mechanically shelling nuts. The kitchen, I noticed then, was unsettlingly void of conversation. Though many workers toiled, the noises were inanimate: the hum of machines, clatter of bowls, and hiss of boiling pots. They took no notice of me, because they took no notice of one another. *Period.* There were exceptions, obviously, and I made a mental note to stay clear of the old eyeballing bootie-police. Coworkers, I decided, were like bullets, best when blank.

I followed a line of servers heading toward what I hoped was the dining room. The Snow Queen was about to be served.

CHAPTER FORTY-SIX

The line of servers trudged into the dining hall: *hall* being an inadequate word for such a ginormous space. Interestingly, though, the room was mostly empty. One long, claw-footed table ran down the center, but it must have been built for many more. A series of many-branched candelabras spanned the length of the table, but the candles were drippy and half-used, and the tablecloth was stained and frayed. There was a stone fireplace, a massive thing big enough to roast an ox on a spit, but nothing but a smattering of ashes lay under its iron grates. The room was cold and lofty; its vaulted ceiling was supported with rough-hewn beams. The walls were wainscoted with panels of the same ebony wood, above which hung ancient-looking tapestries. Though threadbare in spots, there was no mistaking their themes. Nordic gods and goddesses in Viking garb and helmets threw lightning bolts, sailed monster-teeming seas, fought giants, and slew block-long snakes. The largest and grandest of all the scenes depicted a mist-haloed woman atop a frozen cliff with a world of barren ice below her. In one hand she brandished an icicle; from the other she dropped a black cloud; from her pursed lips funneling winds roared; under her right foot she crunched a pale yellow sun. That particular image curled my spine.

Like the others, I set my offering on the table and stepped back, receding into a line of attendants. One after the other, we fell back against the wall. I shuffled to the end of the line, which was closest to the arched passageway leading into the kitchen. It offered not only an exit strategy but heavy drapes. I tucked my booties under their folds. From the other end of the room — through a taller, grander arched passageway — entered none other than Brigid, whom I'd have recognized anywhere. She strode into the hall with a regal air. Her long, flowing, pale-blue gown billowed around her ankles as if hemmed in puffs of smoke; the tapered cuffs clinked at her wrists as if trimmed with icicles; and the sheer gem-blue overlay of her gown shimmered in an intricate pattern as if a million lacy snowflakes had been strung together.

Seeing Brigid like this for the first time, knowing it was true — that she was some sort of out-of-this-world evil queen—made waves of nausea burble up my throat. And raw potato is not something you hope repeats. My mom had welcomed Brigid into our home. My dad, for Pete's sake, had kind of dated her. Stanley, too, had entrusted her with access to his research. And Jack had followed her around like a leashed puppy. How had she fooled everyone? With a swell of my chest, I remembered she hadn't fooled everyone. I had never liked her. But a fat load of good that did me now.

Brigid took a seat at the head of the table, making a great production out of settling her gown. She lifted a small glass bell and rang it with a wimpy side-to-side shake. I watched as a hunched figure shuffled into the room and dropped into the chair to Brigid's right.

"*Eiswein,*" Brigid said with a clap of her hands.

From our line of servers, a woman stepped forward. She hurried over to the table and lifted Brigid's goblet. Upending it, she carefully dipped it into a shallow bowl. Even from across the room, I could see it had a sparkly rim. The server did the same to the other glass and then poured from a silver carafe into first Brigid's and then her companion's crystal goblets. The *eiswein*—ice wine?— was clear, so it hardly looked like wine to me. And was that a salt rim? Sugar rim? After a single sip, Brigid twisted her glass against the light. "Snowflakes: no two the same, and one here on Niflheim is like one hundred million on Midgard."

A snow rim, I should have guessed. But the conversion formula? Even my mathematician mom would be impressed by that one.

Brigid looked at her guest, who remained impassive. She shrugged as if nothing could spoil her mood. "An excellent vintage. *Skål,*" she said, holding her glass out expectantly.

"*Skål,*" her guest replied in a half-dead voice, lifting his head for the first time and clinking his glass against Brigid's.

My heart took a brief out-of-body. I heard wind rushing through the open hole in my chest. *Jack.* Brigid's lifeless dinner guest was Jack. It took every muscle bundling together in restraint not to rush to him in aid and comfort. How could this listless creature be Jack?

"Congratulations on another day of progress, Jack," Brigid said, setting her wineglass on the table. "With your help — today's storms — we are closer than ever to our goal." She placed her hand on his forearm. "You're exhausted, I see, but know that your sacrifices are appreciated." She gave his arm a tap and removed her hand.

Storms? I remembered the strange activity I'd seen atop the mountain. *And sacrifices?* Not the kind of thing that ever worked out well for the offeree. Just ask the proverbial lamb.

Even from where I stood, I could hear the emptiness of her words. She was gloating, not thanking.

"Our work is not done, however," Brigid said. "And I know you can do even better. Your skill is still developing. Your best efforts are ahead of you. I'm sure of it."

Jack, with no acknowledgment, stared at his empty plate. I felt a lurch in my stomach. How could this shell of a being be Jack? I brought my hand to my mouth to stifle a gasp.

Brigid cast a glance toward our ranks. I went rigid with fear. Had she noticed my movement? Her gaze, thankfully, pinpointed the other end of our line.

"Soup," she said, again clapping her hands like the despot she was and triggering one of the servants to jump to attention.

I stole a look at my neighbor, who remained impassive. Was I the only one who wanted to cuff those clappy hands of hers? For now, I reminded myself that invisibility was key. A brown broth was ladled into Brigid's and Jack's bowls. They supped in silence. He ate with his left hand, awkwardly clanging the spoon against the bowl, while his right lay listless in his lap. Meanwhile, my stomach lurched in pain and confusion. How could he sit there and eat with her? How could he do her bidding?

As if in reply, Brigid resumed her conversation. "What a stroke of luck it's been discovering you, Jack. More than luck, I'd suggest. Predestined by the fates." With this she gestured toward the large tapestry of the ice-covered world. "And to think, so recently I'd thought all hope was lost." She interlaced her fingers and steepled them under her chin. "Soon, all the worlds will pay the consequences of their actions. Not only will we reverse Midgard's ignorant and destructive ways, but we will have the means to bring their lands and Vatnheim's waters under the beautiful cover of Niflheim's mantle." She gazed at Jack with a beatific shine to her eyes. "Permafrost at last. Won't that be lovely, Jack?"

Jack's spoon moved broth from his bowl to his mouth in a mechanical rhythm.

"You didn't answer me, Jack."

She tried to keep her tone light, as if it were all about pretty snow scenes, but her rigid posture conveyed otherwise.

"Yes," he said.

"And with conquest we will never again suffer decline because of another land's excesses."

Conquest. Them would be the consequences.

"Never again," Jack said in that spooky deadpan voice of his.

"And to think, there were forces upon Midgard that thought they were equal to me. It's quite laughable." Except Brigid didn't crack even the tiniest of smiles. I thought of my beloved Hulda and how old and frail and near-death she was.

"Laughable," Jack said, his eyes as empty as his words.

"And your distant cousins, Jack, the Jötunn—the Frost Giants—are poised to return. How I've hated to see our lands separated by seas for all these years. But the temperatures are dropping, and the ice is thickening by the hour. Soon, very soon, it will be solid enough for the *Jötunn* to return. With their help, the *snjóflóð* will be possible." She trawled her spoon across the surface of the bowl. "Then you understand how urgent your task is. We need to strike while the portals are still vulnerable."

Jötunn? *Frost Giants? That didn't sound good. How giant? And vulnerable portals?* "Vulnerable" had been the word Grim had used that awful night with Wade. I had no idea what a *snjóflóð* was, but it didn't take much to guess that none of this was good. Not good at all.

Suddenly, a roar filled the air, its reverberation shaking the stone floor, and some kind of huge, saber-toothed prehistoric creature lunged into the room. I whipped my head side to side, expecting some kind of panic to break out among my coworkers. Nothing. Nonetheless, this was not a welcome development. *Because a spellbound Jack, a power hungry, revenge-driven Snow Queen, and ice-crossing Frost Giants weren't enough to contend with.* The beast was a coal-black leopard or maybe a jaguar or panther. It wasn't like I had much experience with the feline family, despite being a Kat myself, but somehow this seemed a cat of its own class. An ice panther? A black tiger? Kingdom, phylum, genus, species—whatever. The point was it was a several-hundred-pound man-eater capable of reducing this line of ours by one with a single slash of its meaty paw. *Come to think of it, what were we lined up for anyway?*

I must have flinched or skunked some sort of fear pheromone into the air, because the cat stopped, locked eyes with me, and snarled.

"Grýla, come here," Brigid said, clapping her hands and not even bothering to look at which of her laborers the cat had snapped at.

OK, so that clappy thing of hers had its upside. And Grýla—where had I heard that name?

The cat wrested its gaze from me, languidly padded over to Brigid's chair, and dropped its sinewy rump to the floor in a well-trained sit. Brigid trailed her hand over its bigger-than-a-beach-ball head and stroked with her long tapered fingers.

"Good girl," she said. "Nice kitty."

Grýla arched her head in subordination, but I wasn't convinced of her being either "good" or "nice." That cat was black to its core. I could smell it from across the room. On cue, I sneezed. The cat popped to a stand.

Crap.

"Sit," Brigid said.

Grýla's angry eyes searched me out.

"Sit, I said." Brigid's tone had lost its here-kitty sweetness.

322

The beast paced back and forth in front of Brigid's chair and shook her big blimpy head from side to side, casting agitated glances in my direction, but she sat.

Clearly, something about me raised the cat's hackles, and as far as hackles went, hers were long and pointy and ready to pounce. I wasn't going to wait around for dessert, the course I feared I'd become. I slipped behind the drapery panel, inched my way toward the arched passageway, slipped around the corner, and streaked out of there like a next-up-on-the-chopping-block chicken.

Behind me, I heard an angry feline roar, dishes clatter to the stone floor, and an angry shout from Brigid. I burst panting and gasping into the kitchen and was met by none other than old Hawk-Eyes. With surprising force, she collared me and hoisted me off my feet.

Dang it all. Could I never catch a break? If it weren't wild beasts, then it was snoop-minded old bats. The Grims of the worlds — plural — were out to get me. I was sure of it.

Suspecting I'd be turned over to Brigid, I did what I could to fight and flail. Unfortunately, I was no match for the squat kitchen marm, and next thing I knew, I was airborne and falling down a long, dark chute.

CHAPTER FORTY-SEVEN

I screamed. Not that it did me any good. I barreled head-first and at breakneck speed, a velocity one never really ponders until it's one's own neck about to snap. Moments later, I found myself somersaulting across a pile of — ugh — garbage. I lifted my hands, and from between my fingers oozed a slimy brown goop. I eased my aching buttocks from something sharp and pointy. Dear God — bones of some poor creature. My toes were buried in a pulp of potato peels, cabbage leaves, and who knew what. *Eeew.* An otherwordly garbage heap. Definitely not cool. I gagged from the smell of offal, which *so* deserves its homonym link to awful.

I sat there bodily bruised and mentally smarting from the humiliation of the situation when, like a punch line, I was struck in the head by one flying work boot, and then another.

What the heck? I picked up the second of the boots with the intention of throwing it back at the fates themselves, when it hit me like . . . well, a kick in the head. The boots weren't half bad. Secondhand for sure, but still usable. Now why would someone throw away decent boots? Boots that I could use. Boots that looked about my size.

I stood, not easy atop a mound of shifting muck, stowed the boots under my arms, and picked my way out of the heap. I was outside the castle and deep in the bowels of whatever Niflheim's mountain troglodytes called their kingdom. I found a low stone wall and crouched down behind it. I felt exhausted. With my cape as a blanket, I curled up. I worried about my mom; what was she going through? And my dad and Afi—where were they? What kind of panic had my disappearance caused? Tears, at the very least, washed some of the dirt from my face. And the wracking spasms my convulsive sobbing induced probably generated a little body heat. Doubts haunted me. How would I ever get out of here? What was wrong with Jack? What exactly were Brigid's evil intentions? How much time did we have? *No idea, no idea, no idea, and not much* were the unfortunate replies to those tormenting questions. The resolution I made was to somehow rouse Jack, to cut through whatever it was that stood between us. But how? At that moment, I had nothing. No plan, no clue, no idea. As the saying goes: I didn't know jack about nothing. *I didn't know Jack.* That thought brought on fresh tears.

I woke to the distant sound of trickling water. I staggered through the dark catacombs of the crazy cavelike city, until I found the source: a collection pool or cistern. Though the water was cold enough to make popsicles out of penguins, it was crystal clear and fresh. I washed myself thoroughly, even my hair. From my pocket, I ate the remaining nuts and rinsed them down with the chilly, sweet-tasting water. I didn't feel like much of a champion, but it was better than nothing. With my compactible silver cape and booties stashed in the deep recess of my pocket and my worker boots laced tightly, I roamed until I came across upward-spiraling stone stairs. They gradually took me to street level, and I started pounding the pavement. Eventually, I gave up on trying to make sense of the interweaving fretwork of streets and just started following clumps of blue-clad workers. Though dread coursed through me, I steeled myself and tried to think things through. Brigid had congratulated Jack on his progress: the day's storms. I remembered, too, the way the mountaintop had churned with activity. My goal became clear; I had to get atop that peak.

As I noticed a large group assembled in a particularly

gloomy passageway, its girth shifted and shrank before me. *Bingo.* I joined their ranks and was the last in line to melt through the mountain. This time, without the same level of fear, I was able to process the whooshing in my ears and sliding sensation.

I found myself back on the frigid mountain pass. Already quaking with the cold, I quickly pulled on my cape. It made an immediate difference. The air was even more glacial than it had been the day before. Not a good sign. My breath hung before me like whiskers. From this vista, I had a clear view down to the valley. Looking out, I felt my spirits drop. What had been, upon my arrival, an arctic sea, was now log-jammed with pitching icebergs. What had Brigid said about the ice thickening by the hour? Solid enough, very soon, for the Frost Giants to return. And with the portal vulnerable. Had my arrival compromised it further? Time, I knew, was crucial. Remarkably, Poro was just a few yards away grazing tranquilly on whatever he had managed to find under the covering of snow. OK, so as trusty sidekicks went, he was a little tight-lipped for my taste, but his dedication—I had no complaints on that score. I scrambled over his broad back.

I soon discovered that Poro was no novice mountain climber. And never again would I wonder about the origins of Santa's flying reindeer. While technically Poro didn't fly, he jumped like some kind of rocket-heeled mountain goat. His size, warp speed, and agility were way more than I had bargained for. And we were going up; gravity should have been against us. It was all I could do to hold on and avoid looking down, which was saying something given my bird-girl comfort with heights.

From almost the minute we started ascending the mountain trail, the ground below us became packed with snow. It crunched and groaned under Poro's hooves like the creaking timbers of an old ship. Or a haunted house. And I was nervous enough without spooky thoughts. My heart was pounding in erratic, nonrhythmic beats. A rushing sound buzzed my ears. And my courage and conviction failed. Everything felt wrong. I was sure I was lost, late, and unequal to the task.

As if compounding my gloom, the weather grew worse. I took it as a sign: Jack was clearly in the house — or, better put, on the house. A freezing gale drove wet snow down my collar, and the cape billowed around me like a sail. I put my head down, drew in like a turtle, and let Poro find the way. The closer we got to the summit, the more the blizzard thrashed like something caged. Even Poro was unprepared for the onslaught; he brayed and stonewalled. I knew we were getting close when the flurries no longer pounded us from above. A driving horizontal onslaught meant the source of the storm was nearby.

My last push up the trail was like meeting a bullet train head-on. The icy wind whipped my hood back, pressing it against my hunched shoulders, and huffed the full skirt of my cape into a bell-shaped parachute. The snow flew so thick it choked out the air itself. I feared asphyxiation as much as hypothermia or being blown to Oz, and where in the Norse cosmology would Oz fit? Though my vision was obscured by the blinding flurries, I found myself on a snow-covered plateau. It was as if the mountaintop had been leveled off with a long, narrow frosting spatula by some giant cake maker. The all-encompassing whiteout was disorienting. There had to be a drop-off somewhere, and I was no longer sure of forward or back — or up or down, for that matter.

During a momentary lull in the storm, I left Poro near a small bush. He quickly started digging with his hoofs into the snow. The flurries started up again. Making slow progress, I trudged ahead on foot across what I sensed to be a huge expanse. The snow continued to shift underfoot. Over the howl of the winds, I could hear the squeak of compression. I trekked across this barren snow-capped field until I could finally make out a distant blue figure. It gave me a goal, and a shot of hope. Trying to pass myself off as a coworker, at least initially, I pulled off my cape and stored it in my pocket. As I trudged slowly forward, fear squeezed the air from my lungs. When I finally reached the lone figure — as if by a flip of a switch — the blizzard stopped, and I found myself standing upon this snowy ridgetop and staring at none other than Jack. *Jack. Jack!*

I hurried toward him, but already internal alarms

were blaring. Though I'd recognize his sapphire blue eyes, shaggy dark hair, and lean frame anywhere, something about him was unfamiliar. He stood with his hands lifted in the air as if conducting an orchestra. He'd obviously halted in his storm throwing because he'd seen me, but the look he cast my way was more chilling than the tempest I'd just witnessed.

There had to be some mistake. Jack would never look at me with such a hard glint. He didn't recognize me. He didn't expect me here, of all places. I ran to him, tears of relief spilling down my cheeks. I had found him. Against the odds and into a separate dimension, I had found him. I threw my arms around his neck, and it was like embracing a marble statue. He didn't even lower his arms; they remained thrown up to the sky as if holding it in place. His skin was ice-cold, and now, up close, I could see it had a bluish tint. He looked thinner, older, as if more than just a handful of days had passed since that fateful good-bye party. And the look he still jabbed at me could skewer a marshmallow the size of a parade float.

"Jack, it's me," I said, dropping my arms and stepping back.

"I know who you are." He lowered his arms from his Atlas-like, holding-up-the-heavens pose, but his shoulders were still thrown back defiantly. "What do you want, Kat?" He backpedaled away from me. *Ouch.*

I was stunned. I had suspected that Brigid's mindfog

would keep him from recognizing me. I had hoped that the warmth of my touch and heartfelt affection would rouse him. To know who I was and still stab me with such a hard, cold glare was a crippling blow.

"I want . . . you." Even as I said it, I could hear how pitiful I sounded. My voice wobbled and cracked. "I've come for you."

He laughed, though there was no joy or mirth in its sound. "Look, I don't know what you're doing here, and I really don't care, but do me a favor: stay away from me, far, far away from me."

I walked toward him. He held up his arm.

"I told you to stay away," he said.

I didn't. I took two more steps in his direction. Though I wanted to appear calm, I teetered on my twitching-with-fear legs.

I knew by the lines scoring his brow that I wasn't getting through to him. "I was in the neighborhood," I said, trying a new approach. "I thought maybe you could use some help."

"Help?" He laughed, but it was scoffing in nature.

"That's what friends do. They help each other."

I was trying to jog his memory. If he had a flashback, even just briefly, of our relationship, of what we shared, maybe I could reason with him.

"We're not friends," he said.

"Sure we are. Don't you remember?"

He looked at me with such hatred I flinched.

"We were never friends," he said in a voice I didn't recognize.

So, the friends angle hadn't worked; I tried another avenue.

"You say that because we were more than friends." I walked the remaining steps that separated us and placed a hand on his arm. It was icy cold and, again, I noticed its bluish tint. I saw, too, the lines in his face and bags under his eyes. "We could be more than friends again, if you'd like."

I didn't have much experience in the seduction department. I had hoped, with Jack at least, to tap an emotion or awaken a part of him that was frozen.

"Don't touch me," he said, swatting my hand away.

Ouch again. Not that I thought I was some kind of irresistible temptress. But Jack? He had once confessed to being drawn to me. I had held on to some sort of naive belief that I could get through to him — that I just needed to be close to him, to touch him, to look into his eyes. I was hurt — and more than a little angry.

"Go," he said. "I have to get back to work."

Figures. Even doing someone else's evil bidding, the guy had a work ethic. Set him to a chore — even triggering a modern ice age and wiping out most of life as we know it, for instance — and he was good at it. I remembered how Penny had once said he was good at everything he tried. Except . . . My mind scurried back to an image of Jack awkwardly cradling a lacrosse stick.

"I was watching you just now," I said. "Seems you don't quite have that flick of the wrist down, do you?"

Jack whipped around to face me. "What?"

"You're too stiff-armed. There's no fluidity, no form."

"You don't know what you're talking about," he said. *Suck much? Fail ever? Jeez,* the guy really couldn't handle criticism.

"True. I'm no expert, but if even I can see your mistake, doesn't that mean it's all the more glaring?"

He flexed his fingers in and out. "That's a load of bull."

"Maybe." I tried to sound casual, but in reality I'd never been so unstrung. "Except, Brigid's not all that happy with you, is she? She thinks you can do better, right?"

Doubts rolled across Jack's face. I saw them snowball like . . . *Hold everything!* Snowball, as in gather mass, speed, and destructive force. *OMG.* This mountaintop of snow was a big stockpile, a snow warehouse. Until it was needed, anyway. And *snjóflóð,* the way it was pronounced in Icelandic, obscured the last letter. It sounded like snow float, but if it was spelled with a *d*—the way *brauð* was—it didn't mean snow float; it meant snow *flood.* As in avalanche! And if one snowflake in Niflheim was like one hundred million on Midgard—*Dear God,* I had to stop this.

"When will it be enough, anyway?" I asked, starting to panic. "She seems like the type who'll never be satisfied. And if you don't have it right yet"—I opened my arms wide—"when will you?"

"She won't like that I've stopped."

"So?"

"So, she won't be happy."

"And?"

"And there will be hell to pay when she gets here."

Here? Crud. A consequence I hadn't considered. I looked up at the suddenly clear blue sky. No blowing snow, no gray clouds, and no hiding the current work stoppage.

"Maybe you should start back up again. At least a little. We wouldn't want to anger her." My mind was sputtering like a dud firecracker. So I had a pretty good idea of what she was up to; it didn't mean I had a plan. Or any desire to cross paths with her right here and right now.

Jack lifted his arms and flicked his wrist with some serious 'tude. Nothing.

Uh-oh.

"Try again," I said, panic burning my throat.

He did. Still nothing.

"Like this." I charaded the movement, because that's all he needed: a top-of-the-world show-off.

"That's not right," he said, attempting again, but spraying only a very small circle of rain over us.

Yep, I'd pissed him off, frustrating him further. He never had been able to control his abilities around me.

"Well, go back to what you were doing before," I said.

"It's not working." There were more clouds gathering in his flinty eyes than there were in the sky.

"I think we should go," I said.

"I'm not going anywhere with you."

Oh, for the love of . . . He was still under her spell. All I'd done is disarm and disable him; he sure didn't trust me yet. It was like dealing with a petulant, contrary child. It reminded me of Jacob, which gave me an idea.

"You're too slow, anyway," I said. "You couldn't keep up. You'd be a liability to me at this point."

"*You* couldn't keep up." And for all the urgency and craziness of the moment, I could actually visualize the four-year-old Jack goading his parents or a friend. I almost wanted to cry, he was so cute.

I ran. He followed me; I could hear him panting behind me. I sprinted until my legs cramped and ribbons of shooting pains snaked up and down my thighs. He was on my heels the whole way. Had this been a healthy Jack, during football season, I wouldn't have stood a chance in a footrace against him. In his weakened condition, he couldn't quite pass me. I soon spied Poro in the distance. He had cratered a fairly big hole around the scraggly bush. I stumbled into the depression made by his digging and had to brace myself against the bush. *What the*—?

This was no bush. I'd never seen a bush with a flat leaf four times the size of my hand. So if it wasn't a bush, and its foliage was so large, then it was a tree. The top of a tree, a tree buried under *a lot* of snow.

"Poro!" I screamed, startling the poor creature. "Let's go."

I grabbed Poro by the reins and clambered up over his back. It wasn't my most graceful move ever, but I'd never claimed to be no cowgirl. Jack was still behind me. I turned and snapped at him, "Don't even think about catching a ride." I could see a defiant glint in his eye. Coldhearted Jack was not going to let me tell him what to do—or let me leave him behind. With a rather nimble move, he jammed one foot into the stirrup and swung up behind me. *Gotta love that Y chromosome. What a handy little play toy.*

He reached around me and grabbed the reins. His family kept horses, after all. Having him behind me like that, his thighs clutching mine with every jarring bound of Poro's full-out canter and his face pressed against the back of my right ear, I was a tangle of emotions. A part of me remembered our long, lingering kisses and the way the mention of his name sent a barrage of neurons firing like pop rockets; that part wanted to turn and bury my face in his chest. Its counterpart, the now-is-not-the-time voice of reason, had me staring straight ahead—but still totally undone by Jack's labored breath in my ear. It was the best I had felt in days, even though he never once spoke to me or acknowledged me in any way.

Though the skies had cleared, it was bitter cold. I longed for my pocket-stashed cape. It hurt to breathe, as if with each frigid gasp of air I was freezing from the inside out. The plunging temperatures only meant that Brigid's plan was working.

For a long time, Poro ran full out. In my head, our destination was the skyscraper tree at the bottom of the mountain, which I had worked out was another power place. How many had I been to at this point? So many I could write a dang travel blog. Despite the subzero temp, an intensity fueled me. Adrenaline is one wicked-cool fifth gear that nature keeps in reserve. I thought we were home free after the spiraling mountain pass leveled out and I could see the outline of the stand of evergreens in front of us.

I gloated internally that we'd evaded Brigid's notice, that we actually stood a chance of getting out of the Snow Queen's frigid land of ice, when — from behind the first line of trees — Brigid stepped forward. And, unfortunately, she had company. Grýla, snapping and snarling, pulled at a thick leash Brigid held in her hand. I saw, too, an ornate sled, harnessed to a team of huge dogs, just inside the line of trees.

Shit. So much for a clean escape.

Jack pulled on the reins, and Poro reared at the sight of the huge, growling cat.

"Going somewhere?" Brigid called out in a voice so cold it hung in the air like icicles.

Jack scrambled down, and I followed suit, not wanting to desert him. Something about Brigid's presence compressed the air around us. Whereas Jack could throw storms, Brigid, it seemed, could vacuum the wind out of the atmosphere in an abyss-like gravitational pull. Even my heartbeat reversed; it went *boom-ba*.

"I wouldn't advise a departure," Brigid continued. Grýla strained at the leash, her huge forepaws lifting off the ground and swiping angrily at the air. "See? Grýla wants you to stay."

"Let us go!" I yelled across the span that separated us. "Haven't you abused Jack enough? Can't you see you're killing him?" I gestured to him, expecting him to cower or shrink from her. Instead, his eyes were wide and shining and fixated on Brigid.

Brigid threw up a laugh that traveled like smoke up and away, mocking as it receded with an echo trail. "My kingdom has been reduced to a mere vestige of its ancient grandeur, and you think I care about his life, or yours, for that matter."

Grýla roared, a snarly release of frustration and anticipation. Her gaze never wandered from me. No mistaking who she had in mind as the first course.

"Yes, yes, my pet," Brigid said, running her hand over the onyx cat's sleek fur. "She is my gift to you. The boy, however, is still mine. A day or two of work left in him, I hope."

Grýla, frenzied by the offering, raised up onto her hindquarters and took a practice swipe at some imaginary target—my head, for instance, and dropped back down to all fours. The impact shook the trees behind them, dusting snow over Grýla's charcoal fur and Brigid's dark hair. The confined snowfall reminded me, crazily, of my Christmas gift, the snow globe that had belonged to Jack's grandmother.

Brigid lowered her hand to the base of Grýla's collar and fiddled with the clasp. Not that I'd ever given it much thought, but as I stared it down, death by mauling seemed one really awful way to go. Grýla was easily over eight feet long and three hundred pounds. Her huge round head housed canines that looked like ice picks, and her muscles rippled under her sleek fur. And I was her gift. *What kind of sick, twisted mind makes a gift of . . . Gift? Wasn't that the word Marik had used for my—*

"Attack!" Brigid yelled.

It was a crazy, desperate measure, but it wasn't like I had other options. From my pocket, I yanked out and snapped open the cape. Throwing it across my shoulder, I planted my feet in a boxer's ready-set and held my arms out defensively. If the Snow Queen was real, why not the Yule Cat? Grýla, once released, arrowed through the snow, pushing off with long vaults of her lean muscles. She landed just a foot or two from me, and I threw my arm over my face and braced myself for the pounce. Nothing. I heard a growl and opened my eyes to the riled cat circling me and Jack.

I lowered my hands, surprised and emboldened by the success of my idea. "A gift from Queen Safira," I called out, straightening the cape over my shoulders.

Again, Brigid's shrill cackle pealed through the air. This was no joyous laughter; it was part shriek, part war cry. "You think you can outwit me?" she screamed, advancing toward us in a rage. "Jack is still mine. Mine to command. Mine to do with as I please. To prove it, I'll drain the life out of him and make you watch. Come, Jack." She clapped her hands.

Man, did I hate it when she clapped her hands. And I especially didn't like the way she said Jack was hers. He wasn't: he was mine. And if anyone was going to do any draining or proving, it was going to be me.

At her command, a slump-shouldered Jack trudged forward like some sort of scolded dog. A barrage of emotions hit me. I was scared out of my friggin' wits. I was also so enraged by Brigid that I had to hold myself back from going at her like some kind of feral animal. And, on top of all that, zombie Jack was really starting to piss me off. As he passed, I grabbed him with my left hand, trying to hold him back. I looked up and saw Brigid flourish her crystalline blue dress and I remembered Hulda pointing out an ice-blue fabric that was perfect for the Snow Queen costume. All at once I was struck by the lack of vibrant colors in this world. Enough blues, sure, to fill the ocean and the occasional spruce or evergreen, but—other than that—nothing but grays, blacks, browns, and the endless panorama of white. Where was the marigold orange from the dreams I'd had of my unborn sister? Where was the chartreuse my pregnant mom was unwittingly drawn to? Where was the robin's-breast, color-of-the-heart red of my *amma*'s dress that I wore to Homecoming? I was seized with a furious desire to enliven the anemic landscape. Fiery orange. Earthy chartreuse. Blood red. *Blood red!* I grasped the shelling knife from my pocket and, with a swift and wild movement, plunged it into Jack's thumb, slicing from the tip to clear across the base of his palm. Ruby-red blood poured out like paint, splattering my cape and the milk-white snow. Jack gave me a withering, shocked look and fell to his knees, clutching the gushing wound to his chest. The skies opened up with a bolt of lightning as if the gods themselves had been summoned. Grýla bounded away with a yowl. And Brigid screamed like it had been her I'd slashed.

CHAPTER FORTY-EIGHT

"Get up!" I pulled at Jack's good arm.

I knew we had a very small window of escape. Brigid had been momentarily disabled. She was in some kind of catatonic state, writhing with fury. Twisting like a snake, she mouthed a single word: "Ragnarök. Ragnarök. Ragnarök." Whether she was weakened by the blood itself or the mere burst of a vital red into her icy world, the moment she recovered, there would be hell to pay.

Jack struggled to his feet, holding his injured hand. A crimson patch of blood soaked the front of his blue tunic.

"Kat," he said, "are you OK?" Shock and hurt trebled his voice. He opened his palm, and I saw something small glint there before it slipped away onto the blood-soaked snow.

I looked into his eyes and almost collapsed in relief. Jack was back. *My Jack* was back. I'd just hacked his hand open like some kind of crazed slasher, yet *he* was asking if *I* was all right. God, I loved this guy.

"I'm fine. You'll be fine," I said, my voice rolling through waves of both joy and panic, "but we have to get out of here."

Jack's first few steps were faltering. His legs gave out, and he stumbled to his knees. He was now feeling the exhaustion of the frenetic pace at which Brigid had worked him. Surely the pain of a gashing wound was no help.

A boom, a distant rumble of thunder, bowled over the winds. Though I suspected that the flash of lightning had been a release of Jack's pent-up emotions, he seemed too weak to produce this reverberation. Whatever it was, I intended to outrun it, a flight over fight instinct kicking in.

I practically dragged Jack across the path and into the woods. When Poro bounded up to meet us, I cried tears of gratitude. As if genuflecting, Poro lowered his swayed back, and I assisted Jack and then scrambled aboard. Poro, the massive beast that he was, ran agilely through the wooded and snowy path. He hurdled fallen trees and scrambled up rocky, snow-covered inclines. All the while, Jack slumped over my back and I could hear him grunting in pain.

About halfway through the forest, I again heard a loud rumble. Was it the groan of timbers? A shifting of the ice field? It was all I could manage to ride Poro and account for Jack behind me. Whatever their source, the cannonade splintering through the forest canopy was just one more thing to escape.

The trees thinned out, and we charged onto the snowy tundra leading to the massive tree, my arrival point and — God willing — our escape hatch. What I saw, though, left me more distraught than relieved. What had once been a seascape of frigid, turgid waters was now rock-solid ice, an endless panorama of immovable stone. Hell had definitely frozen over. But this wasn't the worst of it. Arriving en masse over this newly formed passageway were dark shadows: hulking, shambling figures as tall as trees. The *Jötunn,* Frost Giants. Their towering forms charged across the ice, growing closer to the shore with every thundering boom of their march.

From behind us, I heard the careening screech of a sleigh. Brigid, seemingly fully recovered, lashed the dogs without mercy and skidded to a sideways, snow-throwing stop only a few feet from us. Her face was contorted with apoplexy, and her eyes sparked with rage.

So not good.

"You think you can outrun me?" Her shrill scream cracked through the air like her whip.

I flung myself from Poro's back. Jack, mustering strength, did the same. We pounded the short distance that still separated us from the tree.

I could see that the first line of the hideous Frost Giants had reached the shore. From behind us, Brigid roared to them, "*Snjoflóð,* release the *snjoflóð*! Begin the reign of Ragnarök!"

Just as we reached the tree, I heard an explosion and I was slammed, headfirst, against its hollow opening. It was the kind of quake that shifted tectonic plates, the kind of jolt that accompanied a sonic boom.

My head dizzy with pain, I pushed Jack ahead of me into the cavity of that massive tree. If nothing else, it would at least temporarily shelter us from the avalanche I feared had been set in motion. My vision twisted before me, and I struggled to hold on to consciousness. I funneled my fragmenting thoughts as best I could. One snowflake on Niflheim was equal to one hundred million on earth. If the wedge kept the power place open, there was no stopping this cataclysm. Our only hope, Midgard's only hope, lay in sealing the portal—hopefully, with us on the right side of it. *Hopefully.* Though I couldn't help but think that our chances were also in that one-hundred-million-to-one range.

Jack, still stanching the blood flowing from his hand, crouched on his knees amid the snowy shelter of the tree's cavity. I scrambled over to him.

"Jack, we have to stop the avalanche. We have to destroy this tree. Can you summon the winds to topple it? Or lightning to strike it?" He looked at me with a haggard, yet rallying, expression. "You can do it," I said, seizing him by the shoulders. "I know you can do it."

He tried to stand, but stumbled. I got under his arm to support him and felt a charge of current buzz up my arms. With the surge, Jack came to a full stand. I knew that I had to believe, that we both had to believe, we were equal to the avalanche, the Frost Giants, and even the Snow Queen. "We can do this," I shouted. "A team, remember?"

Then, Jack, his face purpling with pain, released a bellow of visceral origin. His entire body spasmed as if being yanked upward by some invisible chain. My head spun with a building pressure. I closed my eyes and called on my ancient powers and to all the magical forces of the universe, casting wishes across the realms and back through time itself.

The pain became unbearable, an internal siren of screams. My fingers, still grasping Jack, contorted in crippling agony. The roar of the advancing avalanche drowned out everything. Just when I wasn't sure we could hold on any longer, we were slammed down hard and everything went dark and dead quiet.

I had the vague sensation of wings encircling me from behind, grasping me under my arms, and then Jack and I were gliding effortlessly downward. I felt we were safe until a sudden tug wrested Jack from my hold and there was nothing but emptiness where he had been.

346

CHAPTER FORTY-NINE

The phone rang. It was loud and obnoxious. Judging by the darkness pinning my head down, it had to be the middle of the night. It was cold. Too cold. I burrowed deeper into the misty brume of sleep, a numbed delirium. It was nice: a moony kind of drowsy. The cold was my only complaint. If it had only been warm, I'd have settled in for a good, long, everlasting sleep.

"Kat, wake up." From beyond, a voice crackled like a weak radio signal.

Don't want to. Shush.

"Kat, can you hear me?"

Can't if I'm sleeping.

Something jimmied my shoulder.

"Kat, it's Afi, wake up. There's a phone call."

My eyes snapped open as memories flashed through my brain like a movie on fast-forward. A spasm of panic wracked me, and I rolled to my side.

"Kat, are you OK?" Afi asked. "The phone's for you."

"Who is it?"

"Stanley. From Greenland."

Afi held a cordless out to me.

"What time is it?" I asked. Dread pulled me upright with its bony clutches.

"Eight a.m."

"What day?"

"Wednesday. Kat, are you sure you're all right?" He wagged the phone in my face. "I think you should talk to Stanley."

If it was eight a.m. on Wednesday, the day after the festival, had it all been a dream?

My hand shook as I pulled the phone to my ear. "Stanley?"

"Kat. Oh, thank God, Kat. Jack's been found."

Some gurgle or burble escaped my throat. As reactions went, it was strange, but one of pure relief.

"Found. Where?"

"Out on some remote Greenland shore. Miles from anywhere. And close to death. Too close for anyone's comfort, but he's OK now."

"Who found him? What do they think happened to

him? What about Brigid?" Questions were forming in my mind faster than I could vocalize them.

"Some fishermen found him. There'd been some sort of attack. There was evidence of a fight. A polar bear most likely. Brigid is still missing, as are the dogs. Well, it doesn't look good. There was blood at the scene."

"A polar bear?"

"It's all so improbable," Stanley said, his confusion transmitting loud and clear, despite our bad connection. "Jack's still too shaken to recount the whole episode, but he and Brigid had become lost in the storm. The dogs, instead of bunking down, had pressed on. And the attack, it had been sudden and swift. Jack was even slashed by the bear, or so we think. He doesn't remember it all."

"Slashed?"

"A deep gash to his hand."

I choked, a big hack of suppressed air — and disbelief.

"Where is he now?"

"We're still in Daneborg. We have a flight out later today, through Copenhagen, and then on home."

Home. Minnesota. *Home.* Anywhere Jack was.

"I'm coming home, too," I said, locking eyes with Afi. "Next flight out."

"That's probably for the best, Kat. I just spoke to your mom. All this worry and commotion hasn't been good for her — or the baby."

"Did something happen?"

"She's been hospitalized with contractions. They're administering drugs to reverse the onset of labor. There's every hope it will work."

"She's in labor?"

Not good. Not good. Not good. This was a full seven weeks early.

The line cracked; our connection, like everything else, was failing.

"Don't worry. . . ." Stanley's voice trailed off.

I sat clutching the phone to my chest. From the doorway, Vigdis said, "I'll call the airline." I blinked back tears, some of relief for Jack, others of concern for my mom and sister.

Afi sat on the bed and patted my arm. "I heard enough to get the gist of things. We'll get you home. But you know that mother of yours is tough, as was your *amma*."

"I know," I said.

"Well, get dressed and get packed. We'll get the first available flight." He looked down at me, frowning. "What have you got on?"

I peeked down at my nightgown, frayed and covered in dirt.

Afi exited the room, shaking his head. "I'll never get that grunge look of yours."

Grunge. If only he knew. If I — myself — only knew.

CHAPTER FIFTY

I remember almost nothing of the flight—make that flights—home. I suspect I was in some post-traumatic stupor, compounded by the time change and Dramamine. It seemed like both an eternity and a matter of mere minutes before I was standing at the curb outside baggage claim and wrapped in the protective arms of my dad. He let go and shook Afi's hand.

"What's the news on Mom and Jack?" I asked.

"Jack is home with his parents, last I heard. Poor kid. What an ordeal to have to live through."

What had he lived through? What had *we* lived through? Such questions had consumed me the entire plane ride.

"And what about Mom?" I asked.

His hesitation wasn't encouraging.

"Tell me," I said.

"She had the baby. It's a girl."

I gasped. "But it's too soon!"

"They're both OK for now, but the little girl isn't out of the woods. Her lungs are underdeveloped."

"Can we go straight to the hospital?" I asked.

"Yes. Of course." He looked pale and gaunt, and it hit me that he'd also be saddened by the news out of Greenland. Brigid was presumed dead.

As much as it pained me, the words stalling on my lips, even, I said, "I'm sorry about Brigid. I know you two were . . . friends."

Dad's Adam's apple punched up and down. "Thanks, Kitty Kat. It's been a tough twenty-four hours."

"Where's Stanley?" I asked.

"He's with your mom."

The car ride was quiet; my dad tried to make conversation, but neither Afi nor I were capable of more than a word or two in reply. I was a swarm of worries, and Afi was beat from our travels. As much as being with his cousin in Iceland had cheered him up, the schlepping about, not to mention the five-hour time difference, was tough on him.

Once at the hospital, I practically sprinted into the lobby. I was surprised to meet Stanley there, I'd expected him to be at my mom's side.

I broke his hug quickly, expecting bad news behind his front-door vigil. "Is something wrong?" I asked.

"Your mom's fine. No change on the baby, either. I thought I'd catch you and let you know someone's waiting for you."

"Jack?"

Stanley nodded and motioned with his head to an outdoor patio off to the side of the main entrance. "He really wants to see you."

I took a step in that direction, then hesitated.

"Don't worry about your mom," Stanley said. "She knows he's waiting for you. Just come on up and see her when you're ready."

I watched my dad, Afi, and Stanley head toward the elevators, and then I drifted through the sliding-glass doors out into the twilight of a long, exhausting day. A hissing fountain was the hub to spoke-like flagstone paths lined with budding bushes and early-blooming daffodils and tulips, now closing with the gathering darkness. I spied Jack on a bench along one of the walkways. He stood, and I rushed to him, barely able to see my feet for the tears clouding my vision. I stumbled into his arms.

For those first few moments, I couldn't speak, and he didn't have to. The crush of his hug said more than any words could. I couldn't breathe. Didn't need to breathe. For now, this was everything I required.

353

"Can you believe . . ." I finally managed. "You remember, don't you?"

"Yes. I mean, I hardly know. I still go back and forth between believing it was all a dream and—"

"But after what we went through, you know it wasn't." I pulled away, searching his face for validation.

He pressed his eyes shut for a long beat, opening them with a dip of his head. "You came for me."

"Of course."

"Brigid was . . ."

"Evil," I said.

"I can't believe how easily duped I was," Jack said.

"It was the shard—her necklace. And, anyway, everyone was. I suspect her charm was just that, a charm of some kind."

"You didn't fall for it."

"Well, maybe I had a little green monster whispering in my ear."

"I like that monster," Jack said, kissing me behind my right ear. "I thank my lucky stars for that monster, in fact."

"Lucky stars," I said, laughing.

Jack took a deep breath. "I think we've both had more than our share of luck."

"And our share of close shaves."

"Speaking of shaves." Jack raised his thickly bandaged hand. "Was this really necessary?"

"The shard had to come out."

"It was at the tip of my thumb. Did you have to cut clear across my palm? And so deep?"

"The blood. I knew there had to be a lot of red." I took his bandaged hand, carefully turning it upward. "But for the record, I am sorry."

"Me, too. For everything you had to go through."

I hated to darken this light-filled moment, but I couldn't help saying, "She's still out there. And probably madder than ever."

He cupped the back of my neck and brought his forehead into mine. "But not now. Not here."

"I can't think about it right now, anyway. Not while my mom and newborn sister . . ."

"I know. I know. You go." He removed his hand, trailing it across my cheek. "I'll see you later. Wherever. Whenever."

I hurried back into the building with confidence in his words, in him.

I located my mom's hospital room. From the doorway, she looked so small and weak and there were so many lines and tubes connecting her to beeping machinery that I hung back, hesitating. She patted to a small patch of white on the bed next to her, and I crumpled into her open arms.

"Mom, are you all right?"

"I'll be fine."

"And the baby?"

"We have every hope." With this, she looked up at

Stanley, who was stationed on her other side in an arm-chair. She turned back to me. "It's her lungs we're most worried about. They're filled with fluid. She's on a ventilator, and will be for some time. And she's tiny, but they're already calling her a fighter."

That I didn't doubt. "And she's going to have a big cheering section," I said.

"It will help," my mom said. "I know it will."

At moments like these, I super-loved my mom's can-do attitude. The baby *would* have lots of help, which reminded me of two who were missing.

"Where did Dad and Afi go?"

"Down to the cafeteria. Afi needed to eat something. He was feeling a little weak."

"Have you named the baby yet?"

My mom nodded and finally smiled. "Oddly enough, I didn't have to. Your *amma* took care of that."

"What? How?" I asked. My grandmother had been dead for six years.

"The summer before her death, while I was visiting, she told me, out of the blue, that I'd have another baby, a girl, and I was to name her Leira."

My heart didn't just stop, it flipped, then bolted, and was now flailing at my feet like some hook-in-mouth fish. My voice, too, had jumped ship.

"Pretty," my dad said, appearing in the doorway. "And an anagram, too. For Ariel, like the mermaid."

Oh, my God. A shudder worked its way across my entire epidermis. Even my teeth got in on the rattling.

"Oh," my mom said, pulling her hand to her mouth. "I hadn't thought of that. How odd, especially given the . . ."

"What?" I asked.

"There are some irregularities. . . . Apparently, more common than anyone would guess. And easily corrected by surgery."

"What?" I repeated.

"Her fingers and toes," Stanley said, "are webbed. The doctors have assured us it's a simple fix."

I could feel the room tunneling away from me. Fragments of knowledge floated from behind me into the foreground. Webbed like a water creature. A water creature like the mermaid I'd invented, or conjured, during the bestowal of my sister's soul. Hulda had called it a powerful symbol. The selkie legends and our family's ancestry tracing back to the *selurmanna.* And my pact with the childless and desperate water queen, one I was even warned of, "Leira — to whom the waters are home — must be returned to the sea." *What had I done? Dear God, what had I done?*

"Can you change her name?" I asked, hearing, for myself, the manic quality to my voice.

"You don't like it?" my mom asked, hurt evident in her tone.

"It's just freaky, don't you think?" I ad-libbed. "The coincidence."

"No, I don't think," my mom said. "Besides, the birth certificate has been recorded. It's her name. All the more special given your *amma*'s premonition. She was always kind of special like that. I think it's a good omen, not 'freaky,' as you say."

Great. On top of promising my baby sister to the regent of the Water Kingdom, I'd upset my poor mom, who was connected to tubes and gizmos. I couldn't even think, I was so filled with panic and guilt. Now was not the time.

"I'm sorry," I said. "You're right. It's a beautiful name. And special because of the connection to Amma. I'm just a little frazzled with worry about you and the baby, and tired after the long journey, and everything with Jack . . . and Brigid." Again, I could barely say her name.

"We've all been through a lot," my mom said.

"Can I see her?" I asked, needing an excuse to get out of that room.

My mom and Stanley exchanged looks. "It's a little upsetting," my mom said. "She's so small and helpless."

"I don't mind."

"It'll be from a distance, through the glass windows."

"That's OK," I said.

My dad offered to accompany me, but I said I'd find it on my own. I sensed it was something I needed to do alone. A few minutes later, I stood with my arms bracing me against the pane glass window looking down on the tiniest, most fragile little thing I'd ever seen. And I thought my mom had been hardwired with cords and plugs. Leira looked like something out of a sci-fi movie, part bionic baby, part featherless bird, part alien, as much as I hated to even think it. As if aware of the scrutiny, Leira fussed, lifting her intubated arm. I could see the webbing of her fingers, though the skin was so pale it was almost translucent. I remembered the odd way that Jack's grandmother had once tested the grooves of my own hand and her cryptic remark, "The power of three." Jack and I, combined, tapped three powerful lineages: Storks, Winter People, and the *selurmanna*.

What have I done? What do I do now? I couldn't stop either question from curling end-to-end from my tongue. A throbbing tug of remorse had me questioning every-thing, every little thing that had led me up to this moment.

I rapped my head against the glass. One of the nurses attending to the preemies looked up; I held my hand up in apology. The poor little things needed their peace and quiet.

I whispered encouragements to my sister. And I swore to her, though I had no right to ever again enter into a pact. Nonetheless, I made her a promise. I'd fix it. Fix everything. Or die trying. That last bit, an addendum, was easier to tack on than I'd have ever imagined.

After an imaginary seal-the-deal crossing of my heart, it began. The summons for a same-day, nine p.m. Stork meeting. Because, yes, it was *always* something.

CHAPTER FIFTY-ONE

Ofelia, bearing a potted plant, turned up at the hospital just as we were sorting out rides. Her offer to drive me home made perfect sense, given that she had her things to pick up. She didn't drive me home, not directly, anyway. Instead, we went straight to Stork Council.

We weren't the first to arrive. Grim and a few others were already in their places. After all the seats—except one—had filled, and the clock lunged to straight-up nine, we looked at one another with varying degrees of confusion.

"Who called this meeting?" Grim asked.

No one spoke up.

"Don't you know?" Grim continued, turning to me with a frown. For once, I had protocol on my side. As usual, she had the fine art of browbeating on hers.

"Fru Birta," I said. "Call roll. Then we'll figure out what's going on."

Fru Hulda's name was called last, and twice, though it was evident her dais-raised chair was unoccupied. Just as Birta was about to close the book, I heard a familiar "Present."

We all turned to see Hulda standing in the doorway. She was thinner and more stooped than ever, but everything else—her tangled nest of gray hair, orange hat with floral trim, and drab gray apparel—was hallmark Hulda. *Hallelujah.*

And screw protocol. I rushed from my seat and tackled Hulda like a fourth-down, minutes-to-go, championship-on-the-line play. For the record, she was smiling when I let go, and I don't care what Grim says; Hulda always walked with a slight hobble.

"Fru Hulda, you're back!"

The entire room came alive. Others hurried to greet her with hugs, and there was a buzz of excited chatter and laughter coursing through the air. Even Grim, I noticed, rose to meet Hulda. Her welcome was a brisk handshake, but it may have been one of the few sightings of Grim's crooked smile.

Hulda took her place, First Chair, and motioned for everyone to be seated.

"Thank you, to all of my sister Storks, for such a warm welcome. And I thank you for your assistance and vigil during my long illness and absence." Hulda gestured to Ofelia. "And what a pleasure it is to receive a new member to our fold. *Velkominn, vinur.* Welcome, friend."

Ofelia bowed her head in acceptance of the greeting. My own shied in shame for ever having suspected her.

"As to the nature of my affliction," Hulda continued, "there was indeed an enemy in our midst. One whom I detected within the hour of her arrival, and who, through sorcery and coldheartedness, sought to neutralize my powers and cripple my resistance — by trying to kill me."

A gasp worked its way around the room. The way Hulda had enunciated "coldheartedness" had me, too, sucking in air.

"Though she came close, know that this crisis has passed."

"But, Fru Hulda, why do you not name this enemy?" Svana asked.

Hulda gave me a brief in-cahoots once-over. "If only I could. Alas, it all happened so fast. I have only suspicions."

This upset the room, possibly even more than her "by trying to kill me" proclamation. I was seriously confused. Hulda had called the enemy coldhearted. She had to know. And what was up with that look we shared? If the crisis had passed, then why no full disclosure? My heart beat with big, blouse-lifting pangs of dread.

"But how do we know for certain that we are all

safe?" Birta asked. "Dorit's whereabouts, for instance, are still unknown."

"Trust me when I say there are no immediate dangers," Hulda said. "In the meantime, I thank you for coming out this evening without even a soul to bestow. I shall take this occasion to inform you of my absence for the next few weeks. These recent events have necessitated a trip to the World Tribunal. I hope to return with more information to share." Several of the Storks interrupted with questions. Hulda raised her hand to silence them. "For now, I ask for your patience and for calm. Know that I am, as ever, in your service. Peace be."

The Storks filed out, lifting a cloud of nervous energy with their old-lady shoes. Even Grim had a little bounce in her step.

"Katla, you will stay," Hulda said. As usual, it wasn't a question.

When we were finally alone, Hulda said, "You have been traveling." Again, not a question. Hulda would suck at *Jeopardy.*

"I was in Iceland with my *afi.*"

"And . . ."

So what if game shows weren't her thing. If she wanted it, the woman had a future in interrogation.

"Fru Hulda, all those things you told me about the other realms . . ."

"Yes, child."

"What if?"

"Go on."

Where to start?

"Did you know my *afi* was a descendant of the *selurmanna,* from the selkie stories?"

"Of course."

"And that Jack Snjosson, while he was recently in Greenland on a bogus research trip, was lured away to Niflheim, by . . ."

Hulda had been the one, way back last September, to tell me of the Snow Queen's fondness for blue, and of my connection to red. So why was it so hard for me to say her name out loud?

"By Brigid Fonnkona, the Snow Queen," I finished.

"This I suspected. Go on."

"I went after Jack."

Hulda nodded encouragement.

"En route, I met a messenger of a King Marbendlar and a Queen Safira," I said, speaking faster. Even knowing that Hulda was like me — para-abnormal — it still didn't make recounting the events any easier. "He helped me get to Niflheim, where I figured out that Brigid planned on deep-freezing all the realms as revenge for global warming but also as a power grab. We got out, and I'm pretty sure that Jack did something to close the portals, because we're back and everything seems fine: no eternal winter; spring is in the air, right? So, I think that's pretty much everything, in a nutshell, anyway." I took a big gulp of air.

God, it felt great to spill. And so what if I had left out the part about using my sister's soul as a kind of tollbooth token? I was going to fix it. No need to dwell. Besides, I could see by the look on Hulda's face that I'd given her more than enough to think about. She was, after all, still weakened, and the immediate threat was passed. She'd said so herself. She left me with a "Peace be," which, disturbingly enough, she turned into a question.

CHAPTER FIFTY-TWO

For their first dance as a married couple, my mom and Stanley swayed to Louis Armstrong's "What a Wonderful World." Some kindhearted fairy must have dumped a whole gob of pixie dust on my mom, because, all day, she gleamed like gossamer. It didn't hurt that her dress was the bomb: layered crepe, ankle length, and the color of latte foam. Its pleated waistline shook loose to a billowy skirt that swished as surprisingly smooth Stanley twirled and dipped her. If there were elfin creatures about, one of them had definitely hexed Stanley with some kind of happiness charm. Good grief, the guy was gaga for my mom. It was the kind of sweet and goofy you just couldn't mock. His ruffled tux shirt, on the other hand. . . .

Watching them, I got lost in a kind of dreamy recap of the whirlwind two months since our return. Prom, my seventeenth birthday, finals, and Jack's graduation had been more than enough to keep me busy. Factoring in visits to the hospital and shifts at the store, it made for one dash-till-you-crash existence. Had it not been for Ofelia and her help, I'm not sure what we would have done. A light wind ruffled my tea-length, *peau de soie* silk dress. I loved it: a coral so candy it hurt your teeth. My mom had wanted something in the pastel family; she'd even mentioned blue. As the only other female in the wedding party, my threat to quit was taken seriously. Anyway, knowing how I was about clothes, she'd given up years ago. It was sleeveless and had a silky gathered ribbon that trimmed the scooped neck-line and continued all the way around to a backless plunge. Should the evening grow cold, I had a matching silk wrap, but so far the weather had behaved, as if also under some sort of hocus-pocus. A waft of jasmine perfumed the air, and the tinkle of champagne glasses and the soft hum of conversation played backup to Louis Armstrong.

I felt a tap on my shoulder and turned to find Afi. He looked dapper in his charcoal suit and yellow tie, but there was no hiding the way the jacket hung loose over his bony shoulders.

"May I have this dance?" he asked.

"It would be an honor," I replied, placing my hand in Afi's outstretched palm.

Seeing as my date, Jack, had mysteriously disappeared as soon as the DJ started up, I was appreciative of Afi's offer, though I worried about his stamina. Since our return from Iceland, it was more than the still-hospitalized Leira rushing us to Pinewood General. A few weeks ago, Afi had collapsed at the store. Despite a battery of tests, the cause was unclear. He claimed to be feeling better, but I didn't like the sharp ridge of his shoulder blades or the sink in his cheeks. For an old guy, a convalescing one at that, he could still cut the proverbial rug. We danced two songs, and I noticed Afi glancing over at Ofelia and her sister. When the tempo picked up, he begged off and headed in the direction of the two single women. I took it as a good sign; he still had a little warrior left in him. I decided to go looking for Jack.

After a quick search of the outside tables, I headed inside, where I ran into Julia, coming out of the restroom.

"Thank you for everything," I said. "It's been a great day."

"I'm so glad. Your mother deserved a special day after everything she's been through. How's the baby doing?"

I noticed she rubbed her own midsection as she said the word "baby." *Curious.* I was dying to know, but she wasn't showing yet, and it just wasn't the kind of thing that came up naturally.

"A little better," I said. "The doctors are optimistic that she'll be home sometime in July, just a few more weeks."

"The wait must be hard on your mom."

"It's tough; she even says so. But she's at the hospital for hours every day. Leira gets plenty of mommy time."

From a swinging door to the kitchen, a waiter bustled past with a tray of silver-capped room-service meals, leaving an oniony aroma in their wake.

Julia scrunched her nose. "Yuck. Onions."

"You don't like onions?"

"Not right now." Again, she touched her belly. "They call it morning sickness, but for me it's twenty-four-seven."

My eyes jumped up and down from her tummy to her smiling face. "Are you?"

"Yes. Not far along, but expecting."

"Congratulations." I hugged her. It was probably a little odd, but I didn't care. I'd worked hard to get that little stinker on board.

"I couldn't be happier," she said. "It just feels . . . right, somehow." She waved and hurried off, claiming work duties. I watched her go and preened with self-congratulations. *Yes, now.* Success and confirmation. Things were looking up. I'd actively brokered a soul to a human, a venture I knew was beyond the ability of my sister Storks. Leira was getting stronger every day; they hoped to take her off the ventilator soon. That had to be a good omen: that she was meant to be here—*here* on earth. And with this glorious weather, there could be no mistake. We'd somehow closed the portals.

I should have known better by now than to gloat, even internally; it was a karma-buster, a big fat heap of humility. Continuing my search for Jack, I rounded a corner of the lobby, where, on a bench, sat none other than Hulda. *Hulda?* She hadn't surfaced in the weeks since she'd left me with the questionable "Peace be."

"Fru Hulda, is that you?"

"Ah, Katla. Come, sit." She patted the cushioned bench.

"What are you doing here?" I asked, dropping down next to her. A *Great to see you* or *How was your trip* would have probably been more polite. In my defense, the woman had a way of knocking the p's and q's out of me. Half the time, I was happy not to lisp in her presence.

"Saturday night is liver-and-onions special in the restaurant. I'm a long-standing customer."

I didn't know why I bothered to ask. Of course Hulda would show up the night of my mom's wedding, just as I was thinking that I had things figured out and under control.

"So everything is OK, then? Your trip to the World Tribunal, just routine business?" I bit my lip; probably now had streaks of Guava Colada lipstick on my teeth.

"No. Not routine. Many troubling disasters in this world."

Uh-oh. At least she said "this world." Personally, I wasn't ready to revisit the others—in conversation or in person. Of course, I'd been a little freaked at the news of volcanoes erupting in Iceland, but these things are cyclical. And kind of like the slots in Vegas, right? You never know when one will hit. Anyway, disaster was a very broad term. How many times had my mom declared my room a disaster? Too often to count.

"Oh. More than usual? I mean, there's always something, right?"

"Katla, the World Tribunal is privy to more than what is reported on CNN."

Yikes. Hadn't thought of that.

"There's more?"

"Katla, did Brigid say anything unusual?"

Crap. Brigid had said a lot, but in an almost head-in-the-sand reaction to what had taken place, I'd conveniently buried most of it.

"Now that you mention it—"

"Tell me." Hulda clutched my forearm.

"*Snjoflóð.* She was trying to create a huge avalanche."

"What else?"

"There was this one word."

Hulda's eyes popped forward like a boxed jack. I swear I heard the music, and then the coil of the spring. "What word?"

"Ragnarök." I said it in a get-it-over-with-quickly

tactic, the same way I approached flu shots or the inges-
tion of nasty-tasting medicine.

Hulda gasped. Definitely not a good sign. The woman
delivered human souls and convened with a clandestine World Tribunal commissioned with the guarding of
ancient secrets, for God's sake. This was bad. Very bad.
Like out-spooking Stephen King.

"Katla, have you discussed this with anyone else?"

Why me? Why always me?

"Jack was there, but we haven't discussed it. He was
probably too weak at that point to remember it."

"Katla, listen closely, you must speak of this to no one."

Sounded good to me.

"I may, again, be gone for some weeks," Hulda continued. "I trust you will lead in my absence."

"Of course."

A familiar voice at the hotel's front doors lifted my
eyes to the revolving glass door. I saw Jack, and then
my dad, entering the lobby. The craziest part was that
as my dad exited the rotating cabin, I saw the flash of
Hulda's backside disappear into one of the opposite par-
titions. *What the—?* For old and infirm, she sure had
boogied out of there.

"Kitty Kat, whatcha doing out here?" my dad asked.

"Just wondered where you both disappeared to."

"We were on bellhop duty," Jack said, "loading the
wedding gifts into Stanley's car."

Naturally, Jack had been off do-gooding. And what had I been doing? Alarming an old woman who, one would think, was way past surprises. It was not lost on me that she still knew nothing about my pact with Queen Safira.

"Has the dancing started?" my dad asked.

"Yes."

"I better get in there," he said, rubbing his hands together. "There were one or two of your mom's colleagues who came stag." He headed in the direction of the reception.

It was a relief to know that my dad's attachment to Brigid had been shallow. But honestly, my mom's colleagues? He was, as my mom used to say, incorrigible. But fun, and sweet, and a great dad.

Jack held his hands out, and I offered up mine. He pulled me to a stand, wincing as I applied pressure to his palm.

"You're never going to forgive me, are you?" I asked.

"Nope."

"Even though I traveled to another realm to rescue you?"

"For that part, I'm eternally grateful." He dropped an arm over my shoulder. "But, seriously, you severed a tendon."

"I know. And in the process ruined your chances at a lacrosse scholarship."

He peered down at me with a squint. "I showed real promise."

"You were never going to get that little flick of the wrist." I demonstrated, quite poorly, the maneuver. He snatched my hand and pulled it around his waist.

"So they're dancing out there?" he asked. I sensed it was a subject-changing ploy.

"Yep."

"You know I don't dance."

"You don't fast dance," I corrected.

"Thanks for the reminder."

He held open the patio door for me. It happened to be a slow song. Jack pulled me toward the dance floor. We passed Tina and Matthew, who made such a cute couple. My mom had let me invite Penny and Tina so Jack and I would have kids our age to hang with. Speaking of Penny, she waltzed by with my dad. I noticed one of my mom's single colleagues, an attractive brunette, looking on. Penny had come solo, she and Pedro's breakup definitely permanent. It was nice of my dad, sweet guy that he was, to ask her to dance over the comely brunette. Maybe he wasn't as incorrigible as I'd thought.

It was a Sinatra song; somehow I knew it was a request of Stanley's: old-fashioned, a little doo-dah, but a good standby.

The twinkle lights in the surrounding greenery were

the perfect backdrop to the evening. Looking beyond their perimeter, I thought I saw . . . of course, fireflies: sparkler bugs, as Jacob had called them. *Thank you,* I dispatched over the breeze. I puddled into Jack's arms and let my worries spool away from me. We had, somehow, sealed the portals. We were stronger together.

As if tapping my thoughts, Jack leaned down and kissed me. No matter what the future held, what our combined destinies triggered, we had each other.

Halfway through the next song, it began — a summer rain, starting up with a light sprinkle.

It grew in intensity. Fat drops splashed my beautiful coral silk. The crowd threw up cries of alarm and excitement. Jack shrugged out of his suit coat and covered my hair and dress. We hurried, with the others, in pursuit of shelter. The stampede for the doors was both comical and exhilarating. Once behind the shelter of the plate-glass window, I looked over the now-soaked and abruptly evacuated patio. Drink glasses remained on tables. Centerpieces drooped. The DJ and a few helpers were tarping his equipment.

"I swear," Jack said, holding me at arm's length, "I had nothing to do with this."

Caped in the warmth of his jacket, I brought a fist to my mouth, trying at first to hide the rumble, and then letting go with an all-out, body-shaking laugh. Because you can't control everything. Because sometimes it just rains. And the best you can do is be on guard, be prepared, and have a good buddy system worked out. I collapsed into the cavity of his chest, his wet shirt muffling my giggles. Jack leaned his head against mine and joined in the laughter. Yep, I definitely had the buddy system figured out.

ACKNOWLEDGMENTS

To the following individuals I give thanks, owe much, and hereby declare that you're simply marvelous.

My husband, Bob, gave me the gift of time and encouragement to pursue my dream job. There is much I wouldn't be without him.

My sons, Ross and Mac, tolerate my distractedness, pitch in when needed, and make parenting easy. There is much I wouldn't experience without them.

My mother, Elaine Peck, dedicated her life to her three daughters. She taught us independence, confidence, curiosity, and how to have fun. I've spent countless happy hours with my sisters Jennifer and Valerie and the entire extended gang: Ted, Taylor, Lily, Katie, and Jack. It's an honor to snap Christmas crackers and wear paper crowns with you all.

I belong to a talented critique group. Chantal Corcoran, Dawn Mooradian, Kali VanBaale, Kimberly Stuart, and Murl Pace have contributed honest and fair commentaries; their fellowship is a joy; and they get bonus points for making me howl with laughter.

I am grateful to Candlewick Press and its many team members who contributed to this book. Kudos to Kate Cunningham who designed, make that nailed, the covers for both *Stork* and *Frost*. I am in debt to my editor, Jennifer Yoon, whose contribution is invaluable. Jennifer is smart, meticulous, and kind.

Finally, I thank the agency of Artists and Artisans. My agent, Jamie Brenner, is my tireless advocate, greatest champion, and a savvy editor in her own right. Without Jamie's enthusiasm and support, the Stork trilogy may never have taken flight.